A Sobering Moment

To Mary
Best Wishes
Bill May 10/2014

WILLIAM BOLLEY

authorHOUSE®

AuthorHouse™
1663 Liberty Drive, Suite 200
Bloomington, IN 47403
www.authorhouse.com
Phone: 1-800-839-8640

This book is a work of fiction. People, places, events, and situations are the product of the author's imagination. Any resemblance to actual persons, living or dead, or historical events, is purely coincidental.

© 2009 William Bolley. All rights reserved.

No part of this book may be reproduced, stored in a retrieval system, or transmitted by any means without the written permission of the author.

First published by AuthorHouse 5/20/2009

ISBN: 978-1-4389-7038-7 (sc)
ISBN: 978-1-4389-7039-4 (hc)

Printed in the United States of America
Bloomington, Indiana

This book is printed on acid-free paper.

To Kenny B. with great thanks.

Chapter One

GRASSHOPPERS

Mason Walls stood panting and shocked, pinned to the door. He was frozen in place by the power of his own reflection. The unwanted magnetic pull was forcing an acute examination of his face. He was repulsed but could not look away. The tired, sick image was shiny and slightly wavy in the smeared, greasy mirror, similar to a reflection in a pool of slightly disturbed water. His mind registered a worn, yet still pleasing face. No baldness battle was evident as the hair was full, thick and in need of attention. Tussled forward, it almost covered the old pale scar that began above the hairline and continued two inches straight down his forehead, threatening his right eye. The scar reminded him of a dangerous time. The chin was complete but not fat. The nose was slightly crooked and prominent, but not bulbous. The cheeks, shallow but not gaunt. The facial coloring was troubling, being pasty and emitting a pale yellow hue, exaggerated by the naked sixty-watt light bulb in the entrance of the small dirty one bedroom apartment. A lack of proper nutrition and weakness of the frozen winter sun were the culprits, along with far too much alcohol and too many cigarettes. The real concern was the eyes. Sunken and rheumy, the whites were an uneven pink, bordering on red, and framed by protruding, dark gray lower pouches losing the battle with gravity. But it was the pain and desperation exuding from his eyes that left him hypnotically transfixed. The hell he had faced all his life flooded forth riveting him to this one place, in this one moment.

He stared at the stranger for endless minutes, held by the devastated eyes. With all his will he finally pulled away from the lost and lonely windows of the soul and staggered to the couch. His body landed hard on the heavy old springs causing a sharp metal twang. Immediately he curled into a tight protective position, while his whole being begged for answers. The mirror had not lied, showing a face full of trouble. He needed to understand the reasons for such a disaster. How had a life with such promise become such a painful mess?

During these critical reflective times Mason would attempt to relive the past searching for moments that would give an insight into his desperate current condition. The purpose was to find situations or relive experiences that would explain the warped shape of his adult life. He would begin at the first memory and like a puzzle builder attempt to put the pieces of his life together, one at a time, in order for the entire image to give up all its obscure secrets and make sense.

Through this process he was able to uncover what he believed was the first concrete memory, from which all others flowed. He remembered the brightness of a warm sunny day as he walked down the back alley on the way to the home of family friends. It was his first exciting solo journey. The directions from his mother were clear. Go right to the house, no stopping. The dry gravel scraped under his running shoes as the dust formed briefly around his skinny legs. The constant prairie wind whistled down the alley, collecting dust, leaves, paper and even the occasional tumbleweed, shifting everything moveable, with no discernable purpose or design. The dust stung his eyes and he stopped for a moment to rub them. The object hit him on the forehead causing his hands to leave his eyes and clutch the hurt. They came away anticipating blood, yet there was none. He looked down to locate the offending object and there stuck on his shirt was a large, ugly, brown creature. Based on his memory he would later research the insect, discovering it was a Carolina grasshopper or road duster.

He stayed very still, frozen in time, not knowing what to do. Likewise, the offending creature was motionless. Finally the insect moved slightly causing natural instincts to take control. The indecisive moment was over as he swiped the bug off. It fell towards the ground, never reaching it, as the wind and the opening of wings propelled it forward and upward. He turned and watched its soaring flight down the alley until it disappeared in a gust of dust. Recovering from the initial shock of the encounter, anger at the attack took control. He stormed into the long brown grasses at the edge of the tire ruts, causing a cloud of hoppers to take flight. In an irrational reaction he stomped the grass seeking revenge. This was how his furious mother found him twenty minutes later and six houses down the lane.

The back alley would become a place of wonder and experience. It was ground zero for his memory. He walked the alley later that summer, exploring and searching for five-year-old adventures. The boundaries of the summer travels were clearly defined by his mother. As was the case in most situations her instructions were simple and direct, as too much verbiage would result in the inevitable loopholes to be exploited. This was a method she employed throughout her short time of influence.

The Walls family's first house was on the outskirts of a prairie city. This provided both the urban and rural experience. Every direction of the compass offered risk, both real and imagined. All paths needed to be investigated and probed. The thrill of seeing a new place kept him constantly on the move. It was a need that could never be satisfied until he hauled his tired body into bed, his mind whirling with images witnessed and experiences tasted. He would awaken recharged and invigorated, ready for more. Then he would be off again choosing the direction at random or through deliberate choice.

North was a long expanse of street, running straight with endless houses on both sides. This was a direction initially taken with adults in the car and later, at nine or ten, on the bus, with all the jerky starts and stops. The final stop was the downtown area where buildings towered above the ground, dwarfing small bodies.

There were bridges downtown that offered forbidding views of dark, swiftly moving water, black when seen at great heights. The nagging question was always present in a deep place wondering what it would be like to jump. The white concrete bridge was a favorite with its downward sloping pitch providing a swift descent. The uphill climb was seldom attempted unless it was in the form of a dare presented by a friend, acquaintance or young stranger. The gauntlet once thrown down was always accepted. The contest often ended with a lean over the thick concrete railing. Upon completion of the lean there was the self-satisfied sneer and the swift jaunty stride to disguise shaking legs. Along with fear was a certain respect and attachment to the white bridge.

Not so the black bridge. It was an ancient steel behemoth with looming rusting girders, holding the fear of old stories. One had two metal workers, during initial construction, falling to their death on a snowy, bitterly cold January morning. The heavier of the two fell from such a height the body crashed through the thick ice, disappearing in the flowing water only to be found many miles downstream in early summer. The lighter, younger man was impaled on the sharp branch of a felled tree reaching out over the river. Then there was the boy who, on a challenge, attempted to bumper shine across the bridge, only to realize too late that the snowy slippery streets were replaced by the traction of the bridge's bare metal. The booted feet lost footing while the small hand was trapped between the body of the car and shiny metal of the bumper. The boy was dragged screaming and bouncing until the small arm was pulled off, leaving the lad's body crumbled and bleeding. The driver, listening to loud music, did not know of the tragedy until she arrived home and went to retrieve groceries from the trunk. One stayed off the steel bridge after a mandatory, quick crossing.

South was endless prairie and patches of scrub bush scattered with poplar trees, in summer filled with tent caterpillars. The openness provided pathways to the shaded areas, offering cover for the bicycles, where a hidden fort could be built and secrets shared. One would smoke in the fort if the dumb courage could be mustered to steal a cigarette from a parent's package.

The prairie provided endless hours of gopher hunting with sharpened sticks and palm size throwing rocks. Sometimes the hunters were distracted by the lure of a nearby new housing construction site. This would result in boards being moved and ramps made for jumping bikes. All would be fine until the deep growl of a nosy neighbor resulted in an end to the fun. Then it would be back to the field in a mass confused dash for the safety of the fort, where the story of the chase would be relived with laughter and slaps on the back. Dirty and tired but at peace, the bike ride home was full of today's adventures and tomorrow's potential.

The west offered the wonders of the fair grounds, with its huge gates locked most of the year, except for the one week of magic each summer. During fair week the empty space filled, brimming with the noisy activities of rough, dirty, cigarette smoking men, loud, brightly dressed hawkers and large strong women specializing in the delivery of sensations that could only be found in this place at this time. The entire purpose was to welcome the embrace of a numbing and fierce assault on the five human senses.

While there were many parts of the fair, the midway was the ultimate goal. It offered the bellowing roar of activity, full of dust, movement, excitement and incredible noise, both human and mechanical. Initial memories were of boats with bells, tired ponies and cars with horns moving in a circle, forever chasing but never catching the one in front. Later it was the faster moving airplanes, space ships with ray guns and helicopters that moved upward by pulling back on a metal stick. Finally there were the big rides with outlandish names such as Calypso, Tilt-a-Whirl, Scrambler, Twister and the Wild Mouse. The transition to these roaring, speeding machines was difficult and inevitable, full of reluctance, fear, acceptance, release and finally a wobbly sense of triumph. Once accomplished, the desire for more mind-numbing movement became insatiable and was only sated by the exhaustion of funds or the lateness of the hour.

Further west was the old cemetery where one could connect with long forgotten lives. Large monuments with strange names and dates beginning with the number eighteen were scattered about as though from the toss of a large hand. Some were straight, some leaning, while others were lying on their sides in muddled defeat. The odd stone was very small with dates close together. It was known but not verbalized that a child was buried there. In many places the graves were overgrown with flowing grasses and weeds with long stems, broad leaves, and tiny, bright, stunted flowers.

The journey from the dead place would lead down to the riverbank for a relaxing pause as gazes focused on the ever-changing reflections brought by the mixing of sun and water. The river was wider here, but slower, which allowed for a certain serenity that was not found later as the watery snake twisted through the center of the city.

On one occasion, Mason and two friends made a decision to venture further upstream where a small abandoned shack was discovered. While the wooden walls were discolored and tilted, the shack itself was relatively sound, with the exception of the hole in the roof. The door hung by one hinge and was latched by lifting the bottom and pulling inward. The three boys found old rusty pots stacked in one corner along with a bent spoon and a fork with two tines. A single metal bed with twisted springs lay on its back, its legs pointed in the air like a dead horse. The soiled mattress, located under the hole in the roof, was torn and bent in half, the discolored soggy stuffing forming mounds on the floor.

Once the search was completed, imaginary games began in earnest. First, they were pirates planning how to move treasure down the river. Then cowboys ready for a fight to hold on to the fine cabin with its log walls and fancy brick fireplace. Finally as outnumbered soldiers in World War Two, ready to repel the Nazi hordes. This was often the game of choice as it brought the boys closer to their fathers who had fought in the war. While discussions with fathers were often brief, information was gleaned from many sources, including imaginations, taking a sketchy outline and creating a finished portrait of bravery and heroism. This day, the play became so intense that all failed to notice the increased swaying of the shack, until the wind became so strong it whistled through the cracks in the walls, creating a dust storm within and rattling the pots in the corner.

The fun was over as the scramble for outside began. The door, which was simple to operate when all were calm and the sun bright, was now difficult to move. The struggle was made more demanding by panic clouded movements as small hands worked against each other. Finally in a concerted effort the door was moved a few inches, caught by the wind and thrown against the outside wall. Exiting brought on an exhilaration of freedom that was short lived, as the wind screamed and attacked with fury. The sky had taken on a deep blue-black bruised color. Prairie children learn at an early age, the color meant danger.

All three mounted their bikes in a running motion, followed by furious peddling, as the escape route was sought. The wind shook the trees, rattling large ones like the shaking of a feather duster, while causing slender saplings to touch their toes. The tall grasses were whipped against chilled legs as the temperature dropped suddenly. Then the situation worsened as rain began to fall. Even with the roaring of the wind the approach of the falling water could not be disguised. The noise level of the rain grew as it crashed through the trees, advancing quickly, making contact inevitable. The collision occurred just as Mason reached the outer edge of the cemetery. He looked up in fascination as the lead rider, Joey Forrest, was engulfed in a wall of water. An explosive flash framed the disappearance. This was immediately followed by the loudest meanest sound he had ever heard. The crash of thunder caused the bike to bounce off the ground. At that moment the pounding rain consumed the second rider, Tug Johnson. Mason's burning legs strained, futilely hoping an increase in speed would result in a more favorable outcome as he entered the waterfall. The impact lifted the front tire off the ground and the pressure on his chest threatened to tip the bicycle backward. He fought to push the front end down by leaning his slim chest over the handlebars, bringing all his weight to bear. His legs continued to move at maximum speed as the bike began to regain balance. Lightning and thunder simultaneously fought for supremacy as both wheels returned to earth. The furious movements had resulted in the bike veering dangerously off the worn path. Water surrounded him as wind gusts drove the rain mercilessly sideways, ripping through the light shirt leaving the sensation that he was porous. He was breathing hard now from the exertion of energy. His legs turned to rubber as the storm began to win. Suddenly he realized that the path had disappeared. He swung to the left and with limited vision aimed the bike closer to the looming gravestones. Due to speed and the rushing water, he over-shot the goal and crashed the bike into the overgrowth on the other side of the path. He was correcting the misdirection as the front tire slammed into an object hidden in the grass. The tire dug in and twisted causing it to stop short, pitching him over the handlebars. He lost track of up and down, left and right, as his world cartwheeled. His left shoulder hit the ground with a cracking thud. A sliding sensation was evident until his head hit a solid object, stopping the motion.

Mason lay in the grass panting for breath as the lightning, thunder and rain intensified. He took stock of his body, instantly realizing his left arm no longer worked, although any attempted movement caused sharp dizzying pain to shoot through his shoulder and lodge in his head. His shirt was ripped on the left side of the chest and watery red was spreading on the soiled whiteness. A metal taste was evident in his mouth caused by blood running down his face from a forehead gash. The bike lay in a crumpled metal pile a few feet away. He crawled over and dragged it through the grass with one arm until both were tucked up against a large gravestone in the lee of the gusting wind and driving rain. The continuous lightning and thunder was a backdrop to his uncontrollable sobbing and moans of pain as the shock of the accident became overwhelming.

His tears began to lessen while the rain came down in sheets, pounding the grass flat. He pulled closer to the gravestone that still gave off a hint of absorbed warmth from the forgotten sun. The carving on the stone read Walter Glear. The man had been dead for many years. Strangely, in the daytime darkness of the storm the name gave him comfort and suddenly he felt somewhat protected. He huddled his broken little body against the rough hard surface and shivered, beginning to believe the rain would never stop. Mason imagined that the river would rise and finally take him and Walter to a different place.

The lightning continued, as the thunder began to lag behind. The crackling in the air was replaced by a heaviness as the rain began to slow and wind lessen. The temperature rose as the storm swung to the north and headed into the center of the city. The rumblings of constant thunder were no longer close and terrible, now sounding more like distant drums pounding out a random senseless beat. The rain lessened and then stopped. A bird's song seemed to signal all clear, as the woods began to live again.

Mason leaned against Walter, attempting to stand. His only thought was getting home. To that end he righted his bike and examined the damage. The front tire was bent and flat. The handlebars had been twisted from the impact, while the chain was hanging limply off the front gear sprocket. In addition, the left pedal had been knocked off the arm and was missing. Getting home was going to be difficult as both he and the bike were broken.

The sun emerged as the last edge of the storm clouds moved north. It was welcomed, melting the chill and awakening muscles. He set off leading the squeaking bike. The damaged front tire made the process difficult and laborious. Soon the hot sun that had given encouragement began to drain what little strength remained.

At the edge of the cemetery Mason took a moment to rest. Looking back he could see the steam rising off the large gravestone. He would always remember Walter, thinking of the graveyard many times during the dark times ahead.

The rest of the walk home was uneventful but brutal. The mud and water in the fair grounds made progress slow and ponderous. The flattened wheel sunk in the thick wet clay and put extra pressure on his working arm. Mason was at the point of leaving the bike when the sloppy earth gave way to the smoothness of the midway's pavement. After the muddy struggle, the flat surface made the bike feel weightless for a time and soon the exhibition grounds were a vague memory.

By the time he reached the traffic lights across from the power substation beside his house, sweat was stinging his eyes. Although the moisture clouded his vision the stars that raced across his world were crystal clear and plentiful. The only way to gain his breath was through forced panting, which resulted in a continuous ache to his chest.

A strange awareness suddenly occurred and the goal was realized. The released bike clattered onto the concrete blocks of his back patio. On weak legs he entered the porch allowing the spring at the top of the screen door to pull shut with a loudness that made him jump and brought him back to the present.

Hearing his name yelled from the living room caused him to straighten. "Mason, where have you been?" bellowed his mother, Alice, with a mixture of worry and anger. The footsteps grew louder as she came nearer. A combination of exhaustion, fear, pain and shock plus the stunned look on his mother's face caused him to grin awkwardly and faint.

The broken clavicle and the resulting sling were popular with friends and neighborhood children. The story of the graveyard adventure and the monumental walk home dragging the destroyed bike was requested and told repeatedly after a short period of convalescence. The local newspaper sent a reporter and photographer to his home to do an interview for a storm related story. The article and photograph previewed on the third page and was cut out by his mother.

In spite of the fact that his worst childhood injury occurred in the west, the most fearful direction was east. As in all cities there are different neighborhoods, usually with some form of rivalry. It can be based on cultural, ethnic, religious differences or even sporting teams. Mason's community's battle was due to economic disparity. In the 1950's the growing middle class was beginning to assert economic power in the commercial marketplace. This was especially evident in the housing market, where new suburbs were being created to meet the increased demand. These housing developments were often adjacent to more mature, established neighborhoods. In many cases the new and old highlighted each other's strengths and after a settling period, differences diminished and mutual supportive living was established. In other situations a suspicious dislike was fostered, often growing toxic. This was the case in his community.

Mason's father, Gus Walls, was a self-taught man who began at the bottom of the farm equipment manufacturing company and worked hard to move past others on the employment chain. The commitment to work was often at the expense of the family, which was a trait of his father's generation. Gus's advancement to the management level resulted in the family joining the budding middle class.

The decision to move from a small apartment bordering downtown had been difficult, due to financial concerns. Buying an older house had been the preference of Gus and Tough Joe Walls, Mason's paternal grandfather. The man had gained his nickname while helping establish unions in the 1930's. They had offered the "cheaper" argument and maintained that remodeling could be accomplished on a continual basis. While Joe was an accomplished carpenter, he was also a drinker who loved heavy dark ale called stout. Gus was neither motivated to do renovations or talented with tools of any kind. Alice Walls weighed these factors carefully then insisted that a new house be purchased. Tough Joe was disgusted that his son would be "hen pecked" into buying new and made this view known to all who would listen. Gus still feared Tough Joe due to the rages heaped upon him as a child. However, after all attempts to convince a very determined Alice failed, he agreed to her wishes realizing there was much to lose and nothing to gain by siding with his father.

The new home was purchased in a development that was adjacent to a small town. Due to a strange natural occurrence, the soil, normally rich prairie loam, was sandy and weak, thus the farming was poor. With no local industry the area was depressed financially, but emotionally the people accepted the limitations. The inhabitants were fiercely independent and committed to their town. Then came annexation, which the city fathers believed would improve the impoverished lot of the villagers. Of course, the well-meaning, delusional beliefs of the city administrators could not have been further from the wishes of the town's people who objected vehemently to any annexation. As in most cases where a larger section of society believes that progress is being impeded, the weaker voice is usually silenced. This indeed was the case as the community was annexed to a backdrop of swastika placards, numerous demonstrations, a fistfight on the steps of city hall, the confiscation of an unloaded .22 caliber rifle and two arrests. The result was a bitterness that was prevalent for many years.

After a period of time, the adults grudgingly began to be assimilated into the city. However, the children remained quite isolated, as they had no acceptance of any of the "rich kids" in the surrounding new development. As a result numerous conflicts occurred with children of all ages. It was a very clear adult directive on both sides not to wander, either inadvertently or wantonly, into the other's territory. Though totally aware of the danger, Mason had taken fate-tempting excursions, both singly and with friends. Afterwards he was usually left with a strange feeling of pity for the inhabitants who seemed to have so little.

Growing up in a prairie city surrounded Mason with many possibilities for adventure. In hindsight, he realized that thoroughly enjoying the freedom of constant new wanderings and experiences would not be allowed to continue. It was too pure, too simple, and too childlike. It was inevitable that the early thrill of living would have to be curtailed. Thus began school.

Although the beginning of school disrupted his exploring, there was a grudging acceptance that he must attend grade one. This made sense to him at the time, but much of the meaning was lost when he did not do well. It was difficult to maintain focus during times when the room was hot and the teacher droning. He was forced to practice printing and, later, writing until his right hand ached. Unfortunately it never seemed good enough, as the letters would start out neat and then turn into scribbles as his concentration wavered and he hurried to finish. His grade three teacher, an ancient, wrinkled blue-haired woman with thick glasses and quickness with the yardstick, told his parents that he would never amount to much. When his parents did not openly dispute the observation he took it to be true.

Detentions were common and of assistance as the stillness of the room and the lack of other students often resulted in a good quantity of completed and acceptable schoolwork. In general, Mason was a good-natured boy whose socially motivated clowning and silliness, along with the lack of academic understanding and production brought him to the attention of teachers, usually with negative consequences.

Although school was an arduous and demanding exercise, it produced certain perks. Sporting activities seemed to be acknowledged and encouraged so he played all with vigor and prowess. He signed up for all the sports at school, especially excelling at track and field. Long distance runs were favored.

Most addictive and intriguing of all the sports encountered and embraced was golf. His father introduced him to the game when he was six. He remembered marveling at the distance the white ball would travel when struck properly. Gus could hit the ball so high and straight. Instruction was given using two cut down old golf clubs with grips of black electrical tape. Slowly Mason began to understand and develop a technique for success. He realized that the harder the swing the greater the possibility for error. All aspects of the game were embraced including the intricate process of putting on sand greens. These early putting areas were made of sand mixed with heavy oil. The mixture allowed the ball to effectively roll and not bog down. Even with the difficulties of sand greens he loved to putt.

Although the love of golf was recognized at an early age, he seldom played at a real course, often relegated to hitting golf balls around the school grounds. His father provided the means of playing and only took him to golf courses when they went away together. At certain times Gus would be required to go on business trips into the surrounding countryside. Alice, often overwhelmed by Mason's busyness and good-natured but determined demeanor, would insist that he be company on the trip. This displeased his father. The hesitancy and the accompanied rejection were not unique to the business trip. It was a reoccurring theme in the relationship between Mason and his father. Nevertheless, mother would prevail and once the trip started his father would warm, telling childhood stories to an enthralled Mason. He would listen carefully and fight to control the annoying fidgeting, in the futile hope of winning his father's love.

It was on these trips that father and son would be together playing a game they both enjoyed. It was usually nine holes at the end of the day before going back to the hotel. Mason treasured those moments and in later years, when good feelings were almost impossible to find, it seemed that the golf course could stimulate the return of that feeling of love.

Mason would also never forget the early family times at his grandparents. Joe and Millie Walls lived in a musty old house surrounded by trees. There was a huge garden out the back and tart delicious crabapples in the front. Grandfather had a large woodworking shop at the back of the yard that smelled of fresh sawdust, fermenting beer and oiled tools. Mason was told to stay out but would sneak in through a side door and read the True Detective magazines stacked in a dusty corner. The headlines, screaming of mayhem, and the pictures of scantily clad women were thrilling, often making his loins ache. Grandfather would sometimes take him out to the shed and show Mason around. At these times Tough Joe was loud and happy, smelling sweet. Later Joe would get tired and Millie, through a cloud of cigarette smoke, would insist her husband have a nap. Grandmother would smoke more than usual during these times.

Mason loved to sit in the screened porch and listen to the adults talk, smoke, laugh and argue. All held strong beliefs that would result in unanimous agreement or endless debates, which became heated later in the evening. He would often doze off in one of the big chairs or in the arms of one of the debaters. The ride home would be lost in sleep or in an examination of the inner roof of the car as it was repeatedly illuminated and darkened by the endless running streetlights. These were happy times, with an excited expectation of what was to come.

There were other memories from the early years, both wonderful and sad. The images would come into the house through the fascinating new square box that brought the world to Mason's living room. The news was very important to his father, so Mason showed an uncomprehending interest in the serious television man and the pictures presented.

The most exciting event was the night the family watched the Beatles on the television. The four young men with strange haircuts wearing black suits, smiled, sang and changed the young girls in the television audience into screaming, crying, writhing creatures. In the poor dull light of the ornate pole lamp, Mason watched his sister, Violet, emulate the other girls until his father threatened to turn off the television.

Mason was fascinated by the images on the screen but also by the confused, concerned looks on the faces of his parents and Uncle Stan who came over for Sunday supper. It was as if the adults were witnessing something strange and scary for the first time. They appeared bewildered, while murmuring quiet, unsure comments as to the silliness of the scene they were witnessing. The comments were half-hearted and did not detract any of the power generated by the four men. Unaware of the performance's significance, Stan, a sergeant in the army visiting while on leave, pensively scratched his buzz cut and wondered how anyone could wear such long hair.

Mason could sense the importance of the remarkable event. There were not words to describe what had taken place. It was more a feeling that the world, as he knew it, would never be the same. This was verified on Monday morning with an immediate impact at school. The influence of the performance was reinforced in an avalanche of emotional discussions, focusing on clothes, hair, music and the reaction of the adults, as a generation made the four young men their own. The girls suddenly became aloof, having new imagined lovers who were like gods, beyond criticism or rebuke. Boys imitated the heroes forming bands, while discovering a real reason to go to music lessons. Dress and hairstyles morphed over night, along with language and values.

The performance was a signal bell announcing changes that would sweep the world. Mason followed the developments with an emerging understanding that occurred with growing age. In his own life, changes were also evident as he began grade seven with a small, cute girlfriend who was fun and constantly smiling.

Mason Walls had accomplished the first twelve years of life with a breathtaking energy. Arriving at the opening door of puberty he was ready for the adventure of the contest. Growing up had been an experience full of excitement, fun and at times danger. From a young age he had met the challenges with determination and commitment. Mason was cared for by his parents and had an extended family that was supportive. He was a part of a community and this gave him the roots of a strong self-concept. He knew the streets, the rules, the back alleys, the short cuts, the norms and the people.

In all ways this prairie city was his home.

Chapter Two
CHANGE

Some writers, scholars and philosophers tend to describe a life in the context of roads, journeys or experiences. When dealing with his memories, Mason seemed more comfortable classifying them into chapters or short stories that had a beginning, center and ending. In this way he could isolate the moments and see how they affected the theme of the individual segments of his past. Through the initial recollection he was able to piece the subsequent memories together gaining a sense of harmony. The different experiences involved interactions with his environment and others of all ages. With an adult's introspection he was able to find the excitement of the early times and believe that he had started life well.

Beginnings and endings often occur with the same incident. This was certainly the case with chapter one and two of Mason's development clearly signaling the close of his childhood and the initiation of adolescence. To say it was the loss of innocence was perhaps too tragic or grandiose but the impact remained. In later years his drunken thoughts would return to this one place and time, obsessing over circumstances and pondering a futile question. How would his life be different had he not opened the door?

Late October is a time of change on the prairies. Most noticeable to the eye is the color of the land that is altered from shades of green to yellows, oranges, reds and hundreds of tinted browns covering the widest of spectrums. To the body, the transformation is evident with temperature. The mornings begin cold, on a good day changing to a bright afternoon where the last warmth is wrung out of a quickly disappearing sun. Apparent at this time of year is also the quickness and sudden vengeance of the weather as its bipolar nature fluctuates between the sunny disposition of summer and cold death grip of winter.

Mason had experienced the cold of the morning noisily cracking thin ice on the way to school. By noon, when he came home for lunch, the ice had lost its battle with the sun and the warm breeze. He had returned to school full of food and goodwill as the sun heated his shoulders covered by a thin jacket. With closed eyes he imagined the sun of spring growing stronger and bringing on the exciting fantasy of a hot summer.

It was during the afternoon recess that the day turned. A verbal confrontation with a disliked rival began on the playground, spilling into the hallway after the bell rang. As usual the insistence on having the last word resulted in trouble. Unfortunately his final flurry of verbal blows was colorful and loudly uttered in the presence of a grade two teacher. Haplessly any opportunity to escape detention was crushed by the arrival of Mr. Schmidt, a grade eight teacher who ran the after hours activities for "disrespectful punks." He was very well known to "the German" and equally disliked. While his day began to slide into the muck, Schmidt's was elevated as witnessed by the broad yellow grin.

To make matters worse he was late to get to the detention room due to social tardiness. The German's grin seemed enormous as he outlined the additional time to be served. With exaggerated and almost gleeful gestures Schmidt began releasing one student after another until only Mason, his captor and a large white clock remained. Receiving absolute ignorance from Schmidt, Mason's focus became the sweeping second hand, as it was the only object moving in the room.

Just as the onset of dizziness began, Schmidt slammed a large book, rose and walked out of the room. Mason waited patiently, relieved that the negative presence was gone. Soon the door opened and one of the cleaners entered. Shaking off the startle, the cleaner shook his head and stated that the teacher had left the school. Still Mason sat until the man told him to leave.

Exiting through a side door Mason instantly felt an ominous feeling as if something was very wrong. The howling wind and icy stings of frozen rain pellets heralded the worrisome premonition. Any recollection of the sun's heat was sandblasted from his shoulders by frosty air that penetrated the light jacket as if it were tissue paper. The freezing rain made the sidewalk treacherous so he walked in the adjoining grass until shoes were soaked and feet numb. The wind lashed his back propelling him onward, as each step increased the sense of dread. By the time he reached home both his body and heart were frozen, as there was something very wrong.

Mason stood in the lee of a large evergreen tree for a long time. All attention focused on the back door. The idea of entering resulted in a real fear, soon to be triggered by an unknown event. He knew the negative impact of opening the door would be swift and powerful. Waiting in silence as the sleet turned to blowing snow, he attempted to rationalize the fear. When this did not work he chose to face it.

After the wet cold, the hot stale air hit hard causing his head to spin. He steadied himself, kicked off the wet shoes and proceeded into the kitchen. His mother and sister were in Violet's bedroom. The door was closed but Mason could hear muffled voices interspersed with sobs. His father was in the living room as Mason could hear the rattle of ice cubes.

Entering the room Gus looked up issuing a broad smile, normally only presented to attractive women or powerful men. "There he is," he beamed. "Studying late at school. Good for you." Mason recognized that his father was somewhat drunk due to the ruddy complexion and forced exaggerated good humor. This heightened his anxiety as the tension and painful energy in the air should not have resulted in elation.

"I have some great news for you," Gus stated, setting the glass and spreading his arms. "We're moving!"

"Where are we going?" Mason uttered, while his stomach flipped.

"About one hundred and fifty miles south. It's going to be great once everyone gets used to it," his father quipped with false optimism while leaving to mix another drink.

The impact of the words hit him hard. Mason knew what city was a hundred and fifty miles south. The two prairie cities were antagonists in all areas from sports to the procuring of government dollars. He knew the trouble classmates had given new kids from that city. All had reacted brutally and with believed justification. He remained motionless while his father attempted to solicit assistance in winning over Violet. Mason had expected an illness, death or some other disaster. But this news was worse than any he could imagine. Life was good, life was right. This was his home. He could not move away.

He slid into the kitchen where his father was gazing out the window. The only movement was the continual drinking motion. Quietly moving down the basement stairs the first suppressed cry escaped. With a covered mouth Mason staggered into the furnace room, sat against the wall and wailed so hard no sound escaped. After a long moment he gasped for air and his body, racked with grief, released sob after sob of pain. He heard the whiskey glass smash in the sink. He wept until he was weak and tired. He wept until he was dry of tears. He wept until he was defeated and numb. Nothing would change the decision or alter the outcome. A sense of hopelessness hovered and then entered his chest. He had never felt such a deep foreboding feeling. It was not just fear, it was stronger and much worse. The house was still as he silently climbed the stairs and slipped into bed. Perhaps dawn would bring back sanity and right his listing world.

The dull cold morning did nothing to improve the bleak outlook. The once lively home was tomblike as his sister took a vow of silence. Mason, too, spoke little, worried that any escaping words or sounds would either result in tears or infuriate his father whose moods had become foul. He felt sadness watching Alice prattle endlessly about the excitement of the new adventure. His mother had no understanding of what her children were to face and any attempt at forced comprehension was met with scepticism. After many tries he and his sister gave up, resigned to their painful fate.

For the next week Mason wandered through life, lost, experiencing no joy and sharing nothing with others. His friends finally learned the truth, offering a token of sympathy while systematically disconnecting. He was no longer included in activities with friends. Enemies avoided him as if satisfied that his future fate would be worse than anything they might put upon him in the present. The only attention he received was from Schmidt who brought salt and gladly rubbed it in his wound, sharing disturbing stories of the treatment that lay ahead.

The For Sale sign soon read Sold. The weather continued to be grey and cold, always threatening to unleash a storm that did not come. Endless partings, with family and friends occurred, which left him empty and disillusioned by the hollow commitments to "stay in touch". Gus Walls would be very busy with the new job, so no return trips were to occur before the following summer.

There were no more tears when the moving van pulled away from the curb that November morning. It had been one month to the day since receiving the "good news". A last walk down the back alley was the hardest. The lane was empty and desolate with Mason's only companion being the ever-present cold wind. The snowflakes began as the wind increased. In a moment masses of white were swirling the alley's length making it hard to see. The tempest of snow and wind had finally been loosed. It was fitting that the storm would herald the departure from home and the arrival in hell. Mason sighed deeply, tasting snow. He turned and stiffly walked back to his former house with deliberate movements like a condemned man resigned to meet a black hooded fate.

The Walls' new home was located on a long crescent in the centre of a twenty-year-old development. His parents had come earlier in the month and decided on a mature home rather than buying new. They believed putting the profits from the last home into the cheaper older house would reduce the mortgage. With mother cautiously hopeful, the family arrived and attempted to settle into their new old home.

At the first chance Mason escaped into the streets to scout. He was an experienced wanderer, quick to identify new surroundings. He proceeded cautiously through the area which offered little in the way of human contact. This was due to the strong wind chilling the already cold air. Fortunately he was warm in a new winter jacket.

The first contact in the community resulted when he rounded a bend in an alley. With its nose in a paper garbage bag the dog did not immediately notice Mason's presence. The beast was a large German shepherd. He thought of Schmidt and the predictions of pain and torment. The animal growled once, then attacked. It was on him quickly, catching his heavily coated arm near the shoulder with its large mouth. It tore the coat down to the elbow as Mason shook the head free while pounding on the dog's nose with his other hand. The dog reversed arms, catching the coat and tearing a hole above the wrist. Mason attempted to climb a fence but ascent was limited, as the dog had closed its mouth, encompassing his right hip. His screams were interrupted by a loud high-pitched yell that hurt his ears. The dog immediately let go and grovelled on the ground.

The lady was small, wiry and swarthy. Wearing a thin cotton housecoat that reached down to the knees of her thin legs, she screeched continuously at the dog in a foreign language. Her pink slippers hardly touched the ground as she shook her fist and pulled her wild grey hair. The dog winced with each phrase, ears flattened to its head, tail trapped between its legs. Mason stood sobbing. The woman, with exaggerated motions and loud strange words, ordered the dog through an open gate.

He could feel the rage as she approached him, failing in her angry attempt to offer comfort. She moved him this way and that, pulling on his arms to ensure they still worked. The major damage was to his new jacket. In addition to the arms, there were teeth tears in the pocket and lower area that covered his hip.

With the same motions and verbal commands used on the dog, she ordered him through the gate and across a yard strewn with garbage. She directed him to the side of the house, where the fenced dog lay cowering. The entire situation spiralled towards utter insanity as she motioned Mason inside the kennel. He could not understand the words, nor disobey the powerful orders issued by the strange wild-eyed little woman.

Slowly moving into the dog's home Mason could smell and taste his own fear. The dog leapt to its feet and began to growl, baring teeth and tensing for attack. He took one smaller step as every muscle tightened. Suddenly there was a flash of movement. The crazy lady flew by with speed that froze both he and the creature and in one blinding motion broke a hockey stick over the dog's back. Neither he nor the dog saw it coming. The dog howled and retreated, totally defeated, into the corner of the kennel anticipating another blow. The lady, calmer now, grunted, tossed the handle of the stick against the house and signalled Mason to leave. He staggered out of the enclosure and made his way to the alley, while pulling great gulps of air into his fear-constricted lungs. In the yard all was deathly quiet as a light rain began to fall.

On shaky legs he wandered aimlessly through the neighbourhood, down streets and up back alleys, overwhelmed by the experience. Mason cried quiet tears at first, soon stopping, drained of emotion, alone with the rain. The random route brought no comfort, but it did offer a certain acceptance that his life was over. Mason realized that although he had been worried about the move, he had not been worried enough.

He came out of the daze upon entering his street. A tortured giggle began upon seeing the street sign, which read Payne Crescent. The enjoyment of the chuckle was interrupted by the arrival of three bike riders. Two boys and one girl looked at him with an odd curiosity as they stopped their bikes. One of the boys wore a mean smile, the other showed no expression and the girl looked bored. He attempted to pull up the arm of his torn jacket, but it would not stay in place. His wet matted hair hung down in his red eyes.

"You the new kid down the block?" asked the boy with no expression.

"Ya, just moved in today," Mason said with a tight smile.

"Let's go," whined the girl.

"What grade you in?" was the next question.

"Seven."

"That's just great," commented the sneering boy with undisguised malice. "Another loser from up there." The boy laughed, but there was no humour in his tone. It appeared that Mason's parents had been sharing information with the new neighbours.

"Let's go, I got to get home," said the girl loudly. Increasing the volume increased the whininess, hurting his ears.

The one boy said, "see you Monday." He was immediately parroted by the ill-tempered sneering companion.

"Ya. See you Monday, loser. Nice jacket." Then they were gone, speeding down the street. As the laughter faded, Mason continued the solitary march home. It was with certainty that more trouble awaited due to the condition of the new coat.

Mason's father screamed at him for being everything from disrespectful to irresponsible, until quieted long enough to hear the story of the attack. Alice repaired the coat at the insistence of Gus who refused to replace it. Although accomplished at sewing there was little that could be done to hide the damage and while the coat remained functional it ended up looking like the stitched face of Frankenstein.

The school he attended was called Berle Sergeant Elementary. It was named after a teacher who had taught school for a hundred years, a hundred years ago. It was a low squat brick building shaped like a square C. Many of the students had been there since kindergarten. By Monday the entire class knew Mason's city of origin and the coat story.

He was immediately isolated. With direct and indirect verbal and physical actions the persecution began. At times it was blatant through the picking of a fight. At other times it was subtle as being picked last for a team. Slowly his personal pride was driven away. Mason began to believe the negative statements exaggerated by his classmates. The vehicle of his destruction was driven by the sneering kid whose mission became to make school life miserable. For reasons he never understood, the bastard wielded enormous power in the grade seven and eight classes.

The education process was a dismal failure as Mason's usual unfocused learning style was pushed and prodded to total distractibility. To this point he had accepted school as a difficult but necessary evil. Now he saw it only as evil. Attempts to encourage learning were met with blank stares and shrugged shoulders. Teachers began to see the lack of progress as his fault, which in many ways was true, as Mason did little to hide the lack of commitment. It took all his energy simply to get to school and remain for the entire day.

His mother attempted to support him by attending all the school meetings. Alice encouraged him each day, while helping with homework at night. Gus withdrew, often quoting Mason's grade three teacher or mumbling inaudible swears. A heated parental quarrel occurred when the school stated that it would be best if Mason were retained in grade seven. Gus believed it was a good idea and sermonized that failing would teach a valuable lesson. Alice vehemently supported moving Mason on to grade eight unleashing all her pent up worry for her children at her husband. She also brought her emotional guns to bear on the school and in the end Mason went on to grade eight. He never forgot the unlikely support.

The only thing Mason learned at school over the next two years was how to fight. When he thought back about this black time he remembered little kindness and no enjoyment, but he remembered the fights. He won none, as the odds were never fair. If he were losing others would jump in. If he were winning others most certainly would jump in. Perhaps this is why Alice protected him from the school and Gus, as she was powerless to protect him from the meanness of the students. At a certain point she quit asking about the cuts, black eyes and bruises. Her silence stopped his lies.

Mason only fought the sneering kid once at school, being at the point of unleashing serious damage when two other bullies grabbed his arms. While he struggled and cursed his nemesis kicked him between the legs twice. After that the sneering kid only directed the assaults making sure to stay a good distance away.

By February of his grade eight year he learned an important new technique for managing the torment. The official name was truancy, the slang expression skipping out. He would arrive at school with a bag lunch, go to the classroom, feign illness and leave. Alice believed him to be at school, while the school believed him to be at home. Neither wished to talk to the other, so no communication ensued. While the avoidance of school offered safety it did nothing to encourage his self-esteem, which continued to plummet and was soon almost non-existent.

In the future Mason would reflect on how a strong belief in one's self could be crushed and eliminated in such a short period of time. Certainly the move to an abusive city, in conjunction with the onset of puberty, had been fundamental in the demise of his once strong and beautiful self-confidence. Other elements included the loss of extended family connections and ongoing beatings which resulted in the constant erosion of personal strength, like a pebble that attempts to face the rushing water only to be constantly worn until all that remains is fine sand that cannot be held.

By the end of his grade eight year the transformation from the wonderment of life to a resigned grudging obligation of suffering had been completed. Mason slept a great deal and began to accept the depression that filled him with emptiness. His once lean, muscled body grew weak and flabby with inactivity. Alice tried to bring hope in the form of feigned excitement about entry into high school, as he had been passed on to grade nine by a principal that wanted no further interaction with the family. In secret, both knew the result would just lead to bigger fists and bigger failures.

His family had not been the same since the night by the fir tree. A rift, beginning with a vow of silence, had widened to a point where Violet seldom spoke to her parents. After raising a fist to his daughter, during an altercation about behaviour involving a cursing challenge, Gus withdrew. Violet's exchanges with his mother were short and sharp. She was now seventeen and seldom at home. Repeated attempts by Alice to seek a pacified compromise were met with either a stoic unforgiving silence or a loud vulgar attack culminating in the crunching slam of the outside door. It was clear that no forgiveness should be sought as none could be offered.

Mason spent little time with Violet, as her boiling anger and his lethargic depression were a deadly mix. She would curse the lack of energy and the resigned acceptance to the sad downfall of his life. He would remain silent, filling his empty shell with a seething hatred and designing ways to kill her. After these altercations she would not return home for days, allowing each time to ready for the next battle.

It was inevitable that a marriage could not last under these conditions. Out of necessity Mason's parents sought a separate life under the same roof. Gus, immersed in work, left early and arrived home late. He worked most weekends. Alice befriended a divorced woman who had older children and lived on the corner. She seemed to relate well to Diane and often came home giggling or sleepy. Mason would smell the sweetness of alcohol and an unfamiliar musty odour that was strange, but pleasant.

In the middle of the night, halfway through a tumultuous grade nine, Mason was awakened by the telephone. He stood in the bedroom doorway and watched his father's shoulders slump as the muffled emotional conversation began to rise and fall. He could make out little of the discussion, however, sensed that it was not good. When the telephone was cradled, Gus remained silent for a long time. "Everything all right?" Mason spoke first.

"No, not really. I need to go visit your grandparents," replied Gus with a worried expression. "You may as well come too. We'll leave in the morning."

The apprehension of the pending trip, along with the droning noise of high and low voices deep in discussion, resulted in little rest. All were red eyed and grumpy the next morning as overnight bags were packed and the mysterious journey began. His mother came out to the car wearing a nightgown, an overcoat and winter boots, her bare legs exposed to the raw winter wind. His parents stood looking at each other for many minutes while Mason watched, captivated from the front seat of the cold car. Then they embraced and held each other tightly.

With apparent reluctance Gus finally got into the car and wiped his moist eyes. "Damn cold wind always makes my eyes water," he stated with a cracked voice.

The miles were uneventful and quiet. For a brief twenty minute interval information was shared as to the reason for the emergency. His grandmother desperately needed help with grandfather. Tough

Joe had changed horribly. It had begun innocently with extended walks and pausing word searches in conversations. Activities would be planned based on long ago memories that grandmother recognized. At first both found the flights of fancy humorous, resulting in a feeling of nostalgia. There soon became an insistence and urgency in the planning as if someone would be disappointed if Joe did not do the impossible self-assigned task. Initially Millie could cajole Joe into giving up the enterprise, but he had become more insistent of late, finally accusing her of deliberately sabotaging his plans and dreams. The paranoia was a constant companion and had begun to grow daily. Everyone from the government to once trusted neighbours were involved in the conspiracy. Verbal tirades had evolved into rages where once prized possessions were destroyed. In recent months the aggressiveness towards her had increased dramatically, beginning with pushing and shoving culminating in physical attacks with fists and feet. The assaults had increased in ferocity over the last few weeks as ludicrous accusations had been levelled against grandmother, condemning her for perceived sexual transgressions. In addition, his grandfather had begun to complain about headaches and dizziness. Attempts to get medical intervention had resulted in a complete and total refusal. After an impassioned telephone plea from grandmother the family doctor came to the home only to have the door slammed in the physician's face as grandfather believed the man to be from the government intent on destroying the family home and constructing a parking garage for city garbage trucks.

Perhaps to dull the pain or in a delusional way make sense of the world, Tough Joe had begun self-medicating with alcohol. An attraction for stout had turned to an almost maniacal desire for Scotch whiskey. Joe would slip out in the morning and return mid-afternoon drunk, with a part bottle stuffed in a coat pocket. Grandmother would attempt to reason with her husband. This either resulted in uncontrolled verbal nonsense or the now strange man would sit very still watching her every movement with a small sad faraway smile fixed on the crazy face. After many such episodes she had surrendered and withdrew to a spare bedroom at the back of the house, lying quietly hoping her husband would not remember she existed. Some nights it worked, some nights it did not.

Last night had been the worst as grandfather had stormed into the bedroom wild in a belief that sexual favours had been given to secure the destruction of the house. All grandmother's pleas were ignored as lies. Tough Joe had attacked her with a belt, screaming that the whipping would drive out the evilness. She had fought back out of self-preservation not anger, hitting grandfather on the head with a thrown lamp. Bleeding from the forehead, the intensity of the attack had increased resulting in her being knocked to the floor, where a prolonged beating had occurred. Exhausted from the physical rage, his grandfather had staggered from the room. Quietly sobbing on the floor she had listened to the incoherent mutterings from the kitchen. After grandfather had passed out at the kitchen table she had struggled to her feet. Not knowing what to do, she called Gus and through bleeding and swelling lips had spoken quickly, until the unspeakable truth had been told. The unwanted story had now been shared with Mason. He was now part of the experience and would be a part of the outcome.

"What are you going to do?" Mason asked, breaking the thinking silence after many miles.

"I really don't know," was the dull reply. The comment came out weak, honestly lacking in any form of resolve. "We'll just have to see what happens."

That was all that was said as silence rode in the back seat and accompanied them for the rest of the trip. Each had more to say, but initial wedges of verbal inhibitions, formed early, had grown to walls of dense detachment over the last few years. The inherent connectedness between father and son had gone missing. It had begun slowly and without real notice. The events of the last few years had accelerated the process dramatically. The separation was now quite complete as any natural closeness had been hopelessly lost due to a careless lack of commitment to their relationship. Both were responsible and both felt the sadness, unfortunately neither knew how to begin the rebuilding. Both dreaded taking the first step, horribly fearing the risk of rejection that could not possibly be tolerated. So each withdrew and chose fear, letting the critical minutes and miles go by, escaping forever.

Mason would never forget the impact of seeing his grandmother. She was almost unrecognizable through the mask of physical trauma. Her right eye was completely shut, while the left was slightly closed, darkening and showing blood spots on the white sclera. Both cheeks were swollen and discoloured. The right side was worse having turned an angry dark blue colour. Her mouth was swollen and she continually wiped away fresh blood. No teeth had been dislodged as all had been removed years ago. However, her mouth was so swollen she could not put in the dentures she wore faithfully. This left the lower part of the bruised cheeks sunken and collapsed. She moved very slowly dragging her leg and forever clutching her right wrist. Her breath was shallow and forced. The entire appearance was one of horrible damage, both physical and emotional.

Great Uncle Auggie was sitting on a kitchen chair, with tear-wet cheeks. "I'm so glad you're here." He held out a frail spotted hand.

His father shook the hand weakly while staring at Millie. "We need to get you to a hospital and we should call the police." There was anger in the voice.

"NO!" grandmother weakly shouted as fresh tears exploded from her eyes. "We both need to go to the hospital, not to jail. Just help us get to the hospital and then all will be fine."

"Where is he?" Gus said in a flat voice.

"In the workshop. I tried to talk to him but he wouldn't say a word. He won't listen to us," Uncle Auggie said with a cracking voice. "He is just not right in the head."

"Drinking?" Gus asked. Both nodded.

"Everyone had better stay here."

"We're coming," replied Millie. "It isn't safe." Mason remained silent, not liking the way the situation was developing. The strange feeling of impending doom experienced that long ago snowy night had returned. It was stronger now and very scary. He believed a confrontation with his grandfather was a bad idea but, as was his place, said nothing.

They found Tough Joe in the main room of the shop, standing and facing the workbench moving bits of wood back and forth. No reaction occurred as the four entered. His grandfather was quietly humming a simple tune. "Dad. It's me, your son," Gus stated in a gentle voice. "I'm here to help."

There was a long uncomfortable pause before Joe spoke, "help with what?" Mason could see his father struggle and search for the exact words to say. The struggle lasted too long.

"Help with what?" Joe repeated, the words taking on a new meaning due to the menacing tone laced with malice.

"Help with what?" was repeated in a raised voice accented by a mocking parrot cadence.

"Just calm down, now," Gus replied, with a throat full of tension.

"I am very calm and know exactly what to do." The determination and finality of the softly spoken comment filled the air of the small shop with the electricity of fear.

All Mason's senses were alive as his glance swept the room, absorbing the tense shoulders of Tough Joe, his father's clenched fists and grim face, grandmother's silent outpouring of bloody tears and Uncle Auggie's swaying shrinking body.

It was Millie's whispered *please* that changed the entire atmosphere of the room. Gus glanced sideways and was gently smiling as Tough Joe turned quickly, swinging the four-pound ball peen hammer with a force and quickness inspired by madness. Feeling a movement, his father innocently turned back to face the onrush of air created by the weapon. The flat surface of the hammer landed flush on Gus's now turned forehead. With the sickening loudness of a heavy door being angrily slammed in a small room the weapon shattered and collapsed the forehead bone driving the fragments into his father's brain. The collision caused the skin to split as blood flew in all directions. Mason stood helpless as his father's feet left the ground. The body remained suspended in the air forever and then crashed to the cement floor. For the briefest of moments all was deathly quiet and then each person reacted.

"Try to build a fucking garage now." Tough Joe victoriously roared, as the eyes poured forth insanity. The strange man charged through the open door, still grasping the bloody hammer.

Grabbing at the air Millie began to scream. In the future, when thinking of her, the first remembrance would be the sorrowful shrieks heard that day echoing off the walls of the dark shop, declaring excruciating pain and inconsolable loss. Sometimes late at night when full of hurt and alcohol Mason would irrationally believe she was still screaming.

Uncle Auggie had fallen backward against a stack of paint cans and empty boxes, gasping for air and clutching madly at a useless left arm. His uncle's jaw was moving rapidly, with no sound escaping.

His father lay motionless on the ground and then, as if racked by a massive electrical charge, the whole body began to vibrate wildly, bouncing off the floor. Mason knelt and tried to hold the head still, but the movements were so erratic and unnatural he soon stood and mutely waited for the motion to cease. There was one final contorted spasm, a bark of released air and then, the body lay still.

Later Mason would be praised for going to the house, calmly using the telephone to call the operator and get assistance. At the time, it was the need to be removed from the carnage and escape the endless screaming that had driven him to action. Unable to return to the shop he sat patiently on the back steps waiting for the future to take him away.

He made the front page of the paper that day. A local freelance reporter heard the dispatcher's call on the two way radio set to the police band. Being very close to the address of the domestic dispute made it easy to arrive before the police. Mason watched as the man peered over the short metal gate, between a break in the thick hedge, startle, turned pale and left. The man returned with a camera. A number of pictures were taken. The ringing in Mason's ears and an extreme physical tiredness had stopped all movement. He was covered in blood from the blow, the attempt at helping his father and the fierce shaking that had splattered red around the shop.

The reporter soon left. Mason later cut the picture from an old newspaper examining it many times over the years. The grainy photograph showed an unrecognizable person. Each viewing resulted in compassion for the strange young man. The picture somehow allowed him to exhibit genuine sympathy for himself, as the world seems to offer none.

According to official reports Gus Walls was declared dead at the scene, due to massive damage to the prefrontal cortex of the brain. The cause of death was due to a single blow from a blunt instrument. It was ruled a homicide.

Uncle Auggie suffered a heart attack and was taken to the hospital by ambulance. He stabilized well and was soon up walking in the hallways of the hospital. A subsequent massive attack occurred on one of his walks with a young nurse, blowing out the bottom of the heart.

Millie continued to scream until the paramedics administered a strong sedative. Once the medication became effective, she stopped screaming and never spoke again. The results of the initial medical examination showed that she had a broken wrist, two broken ribs and a fractured tibia. The cheekbone around her eye was shattered. She was taken to live with a distant sister, where she died four months later.

The authorities issued an all points bulletin. Joe Walls was deemed armed and dangerous. For three days fear lived within the population of the city as no information about the old man's whereabouts surfaced. Then on the fourth day some teenagers, fishing the open water by the dam, saw a person huddled in a copse of willow trees.

The police responded with a quick and massive intervention, surrounding the area. Unfortunately, Tough Joe had seen the boys and had moved further downstream, scaling the bank and heading onto a drive that ran adjacent to the river. A young officer cruising the street had almost collided with the incoherent half frozen man. Still clutching the hammer, blows had dented the hood and scattered the front window of the patrol car. Upon exiting the car the young patrolman had been struck with a backhanded swing of the ball peen. Lying on the ground, with a broken jaw, the policeman had emptied the service revolver into Joe Walls advancing chest.

An autopsy was done, not for the cause of death but for the cause of the insanity. A tumour, the size of a small lemon, had been found in the left lateral ventricle area of the brain. As the tumour had grown so had the aggressiveness until Mason's grandfather had been replaced by a madman believing in a plot to destroy all he was.

In the end, four people Mason had known and loved all his life were gone. His family, whose existence had been on the verge of collapse prior to the disastrous trip, was now swept away forever. For his mother, the loss of her husband and the circumstances of the death was a load too oppressive to carry. After a quick and lonely funeral she stopped leaving the house, except to make the daily walk to Diane's home where she could have help forgetting.

Violet came home long enough to attend the funeral and get drunk. At first she attempted to sustain her anger, but soon realized that neither Mason nor her mother had the desire or strength to quarrel. When the anger could not be released the emotion came out as wailing grief. Mason numbly held her during the explosion of feelings saying comforting words he did not believe in an effort to ease her guilt. Later, while she vomited, on her hands and knees in the snowy backyard, he held her hair and rubbed her back. Incoherent and stinking, he tucked her into bed. In the morning she was gone. He did not see her for many, many years. Two years later he would receive a rambling letter explaining nothing. He kept the letter as a reminder that he had a sister.

Life with his mother settled into a weird existence. The weight of the failure Alice had experienced as a wife, and especially as a mother, caused a withdrawal from exhibiting any further parental obligation. Soon after his sister left, Alice initiated a convoluted conversation where she spoke and he mostly listened. At times he could not understand the meaning of the strands of words strung together in a desperate attempt to say what should never be said. He eventually interrupted the verbal outpouring, asking questions as the two struggled to expose the real meaning of the talk. The clearest way to clarify the discussion was that his mother was firing herself as his mother. It was dressed up with reflective comments and praise of his maturity, but in the end Mason left the conversation feeling utterly lonely, while Alice left relieved and empty. In practice the new living situation began immediately. No longer was he asked to account for any of his actions. There were no rules to follow, nor consequences for any behaviour. He was forced to learn to cook through trial and error. In most ways they became silent roommates sharing a quiet tomb.

Mason continued to go to school, knowing but not believing that the experience was important. Due to the extended and sensational media coverage he was treated differently. The sneering kid and his minions were no longer a problem. When a chance meeting occurred he could tell they were very uncomfortable, usually taking evasive actions to avoid any contact.

Due to lessened expectations by teachers and an acceptance that every F meant he would have to redo the material, Mason's grades improved. He would study in his basement bedroom late into the night working hard on all subjects hoping his mother would come downstairs and notice. She never came down and never noticed the improvements.

They lived off a pension set up by his father's life insurance policy. There was no extra cash available after paying for food, utilities and Alice's recreational needs, so it was necessary for Mason to find employment. The first job was bagging groceries at a local store. He had a talent for hard work and liked the job when it was busy. He worked from five until eleven o'clock from Monday to Friday. Each night he would walk home, study until three, sleep until seven then go to school. On the weekends he would hide in the basement doing schoolwork. Sometimes he would cover himself with pillows and cry for all he had lost and all he knew he would lose in the future.

Each payday a portion of his check would be left on the kitchen counter. Later the money would be gone with never an acknowledgment. The rest was saved in a jar behind a loose board in the wall shielded by the bed. In this way time went on, the days offering little purpose other than fulfilling a daily structure. Questioning the reason for this existence was a waste of time and more importantly a waste of energy, which was too valuable to squander.

Two unrelated events happened during the same month following his seventeenth birthday. Both would change his life.

The first was an innocent and surprising invitation to a large house party by a new student in his Friday remedial science class. He brushed it off, but John persisted, arriving on the Saturday evening and insisting Mason attend. The party was huge loud and crazy. A cute blond girl met them at the door handing out coffee mugs full of a pink frothy liquid. The music pounded from an expensive stereo located in the living room.

"Have a drink?" she yelled.

"What is it?" he questioned.

"Who cares?" she replied and was gone.

John smiled and emptied the mug. "Go ahead, drink it."

"I don't drink."

"You do tonight," said John directing the mug to his lips.

As he drank, John pushed the bottom of the mug offering only one option. The blond girl returned nodding with approval. She took the mugs and offered full ones from a tray. He felt the burning sensation as the powerful punch slid down his throat.

"What the hell is this?" he gasped.

"High test. It's called "drop your pants and run." It's got Everclear in it," stated the girl.

They were soon swept further into the house where drinking and bizarre behaviour was demanded. As the warmth of the punch spread Mason began to feel at ease and confident. This was a feeling not experienced in a very long time. He suddenly was a social animal moving from group to group, sharing stories and good cheer. Everything was funny. He laughed long and hard loving every moment. For the first time in so very long he cared nothing about what people thought of him, his family or his shitty life.

He lost John, then lost his inhibitions and finally his balance. The first two mattered little, but the last was more important when running out the backdoor after the police arrived. Missing the first step Mason landed hard on his right knee but felt no pain. Staggering across the backyard he passed through the gate and lurched down the alley. He heard sirens coming from all directions. Slipping between a garage and a fence he fell, rolled on his side and lay panting, attempting to stop the spinning of the dark dizzy world. Cars raced down the alley. Shouts and cursing echoed for a time then grew dim and finally stopped. Waking to the light of predawn, he attempted to stretch and found cramps had formed from the cold.

Mason arrived home feeling old and weak and climbed into bed. When his eyes finally opened it was again dark. With a coated tongue and a pounding head he reviewed the previous night, realizing on some emotional level he was strangely at ease. Somehow the liquor had made his real existence disappear long enough to offer a false peace. In a hung over state a personal direction was set that would be a companion for many, many hard years. Alcohol allowed him to escape from himself. At the time this brought an overwhelming sense of relief, bordering on euphoria. Suddenly he had a friend he could rely on.

The second event occurred in the middle of a Tuesday night. He was seldom disturbed by the return of his mother from Diane's house. She was usually quiet and took care not to wake him. On this night she could not control the noise level as she could not control her companion. The man had a deep voice and a high-pitched laugh, which Mason hated instantly. The slurred words were difficult to understand so he crept up the stairs and listened at the closed basement door. The sound of a heavy falling body caused him to open the door and ask if everything was all right.

Alice reacted with anger, barking that she was fine and he should go to bed. The deep voice echoed his mother's comments and then the shrill laughter began.

Mason closed the door and went back to bed. Sleep would not return and was soon made impossible by the distant rhythmic sounds of violation. He was reaching for his Louisville slugger baseball bat when he heard faint female cries of encouragement. The sounds had a paralysing effect on his body. The only movement was the tears rolling down his cheeks.

Mason and his mother had separated years before but neither had moved on. His mother's actions on that night proclaimed that she was now free of him and on her own. Her actions were interpreted as the most callous abandonment imaginable. As she proclaimed her pleasure, he began to formulate a plan. He would not be discarded or join some new grotesque family initiated by his mother's lust. She had chosen her direction, leaving him no alternative but to choose his.

Nothing happened for six days and then the same late night coupling occurred. The repeat performance reinforced Mason's resolve to act. He would leave this place as quickly as possible. School would be a casualty. Surprisingly he experienced some remorse as a great deal of hard work had resulted in academic success. Unfortunately the gains could not possibly continue due to his mother's infidelity.

The hidden money yielded a total of seven hundred and forty-nine dollars. This was a healthy amount and would translate into many miles on the open road. A beard was necessary, as shaving became a luxury. It started thinly but soon began to fill in, adding age, which was a welcomed side effect. Clothes were sorted with the focus on strength and durability. Others were purchased cheaply at the Salvation Army Thrift store. At a local army surplus, a heavy coat, strong hiking boots, a thick canvas backpack, waterproof gloves and a long heavy hunting knife were bought. A large hippy hat, with a wide brim, was purchased in a *Head* shop downtown. He stuck a colourful bird feather, found by the side of the road, into the band. Through John a connection was made with the school forger who sold him a fake ID stating he was twenty-two years old.

He began to pick up every shift possible attempting to reach the total of one thousand dollars before it was time to leave. Unfortunately that would not be possible. As the planning for departure accelerated so did his mother's behaviour. Her sexual activities became nightly. He could always hear the high-pitched laugh, but now there were other men's voices and, on one occasion, a woman's loud cries.

Perhaps the hardest preparation was the letter to his mother. It had been written and destroyed repeatedly. Attempts to find the words proved difficult. On quiet nights before she arrived home, imagining her peacefully sleeping alone in bed, the letter was full of forgiveness and understanding. When written in the middle of the night the tone was of condemnation and hateful name-calling. In the morning, tired and exhausted the focus became an embarrassing empty prose containing self-observations that simply made him sad. All were burnt by the open basement window.

Two nights before leaving an unexpected event occurred. After a drinking session in John's garage he had walked home. The night was cold and misty. Turning a corner a figure was framed in the streetlights. Mason knew the walk. Staying in the shadows he followed at a close but safe distance. The chance came as the figure lurched across a small park. He quickly skirted the field and waited behind a fence on the far side. When the figure was close Mason stepped out of the shadows and faced the drunk, unprepared sneering kid. He unleashed the outrage that had been accumulated from all the beatings and all the cruelty. The blows were not wild or thrown in haste. They were precise sharp pounding jabs thrown with the full force of the body. The results were serious damage. As the boy staggered backwards the arms came up for protection, leaving the body and genitals exposed. The attack shifted. All the fighting techniques learned from the countless beatings were used. No pain was felt in the two dislocated knuckles as the attack continued on the ground. Finally, in the dark recess of anger he realized that if the beating continued the boy would die. He stopped suddenly, leaving the sneering boy crumpled and moaning on the ground.

"How does it feel?" Mason whispered to the boy's bloody head. "If you mention me I will kill you. I have the blood of a murderer in my veins."

Mason waited all the next day for the police to arrive, but they did not come. He was glad the boy had listened because he had been serious, as there was nothing to lose.

The leaving may have lingered except for the arrival late one night of a group of men and one other woman. All were drunk, with the noise level louder than normal. He dressed quickly, collected his money, slid the baseball bat into the backpack, picked up the sealed stamped letter from the dresser and for some strange reason left the small lamp by the bed burning. Quietly going up the stairs, he opened the door and stood on the landing listening. His mother's voice could clearly be heard as well as the varied voices of men who directed the women with loud precise sexual orders. For a moment his hand stretched back to touch the handle of the bat, hesitated and then reached for the doorknob.

Mason walked out to the front of the house where two cars were parked. Sliding the knife out of the scabbard he calmly and slowly put the tip through the sidewalls of all eight tires. The loud escaping air provided a satisfying sound that seemed to dull the sexual voices echoing in his head. He walked to the corner, opened the mailbox and deposited the letter. In the end, after repeated attempts at describing how he felt, all that came out were three short sentences.

"I have left. I am never coming back. HOW COULD YOU?"

Mason did not sign his name, as that would have been too painful.

Chapter Three
MOVIN'

The travelling which began with the mailing of the letter, proved to last a long, long time. Vast landscapes and natural panoramas were encountered, at times exposing breathtaking beauty. When reliving some of the memories there was a nagging feeling of disappointment as if the views were seen but not experienced. Many times the awareness of the world's existence would be lost in pointless confusing internal debates about what might have been.

For twelve years no place was home, but Mason was never homeless. The ability to find and maintain employment was a distinct advantage when it was time for food and shelter. Hard work was neither difficult to find or avoided. In addition, he was a quick learner as the understanding of and working with tools came easily.

Much of the self-exploration during this time proved disappointing, usually reinforcing old negative messages, with little personal growth noted. In contrast there was an extensive expansion in his employment education. Some jobs lasted a day while the longest went on for fourteen months. He worked inside and out, liking the outside jobs the best but staying at an inside one the longest.

School crossing guard, driving a gravel truck, planting flowers, carpenter's helper, roofer, painter, building swimming pools, working in a book store, cutting grass, selling cars, grave digger and delivering mail were all jobs he enjoyed. Cooking French fries in a fast food restaurant, selling shoes, delivering furniture, security guard, plumber's assistant, night janitor, selling vacuum cleaners, pumping out septic tanks and being the local dog catcher were hated jobs. The one job that lasted the longest was physically demanding and at times incredibly disgusting. But there was a uniqueness, which somehow caused him to feel special in doing tasks that others could hardly comprehend and certainly would never attempt.

Mason met a thin, older man in a bar soon after arriving in a small city. The man was short, wiry, sporting a two-day beard and possessing a crushing handshake. They drank the evening away speaking of many things. Near the end of the night, drunk, Victor spoke of his job explaining the process of slaughtering animals. At first Mason was sickened by the vivid descriptions of each step. However, he soon became fascinated, asking questions and probing further wanting to understand how animals were turned into packages of meat. By the end of night, as Victor was physically placed into an idle taxi, he realized that adding the profession of butcher to his resume was necessary.

Applying the next day, Mason copied Victor's long Polish name off the crusty bar napkin as a reference. Returning every morning he was able to strike up a cordial relationship with the personnel secretary. She was a middle age woman who seemed to enjoy flattery and attention. He willingly provided both and was soon hired.

Although the job was hard and repulsive the money was good. A strong militant union was in place, resulting in excellent pay and decent working conditions. At the time he was comfortable with most aspects of the job using the large paychecks to settle into a small second floor apartment in a quiet building.

Mason's friendship with Victor grew as both had common interests, enjoying smoking, drinking and the ladies. Victor was attracted to large women with big bodies. He enjoyed small girls with heavy breasts. It was with unspoken acknowledgement that while together each was a single man making independent decisions when desired. It was not uncommon to leave the table for a few minutes, return and find Victor gone. On other occasions they would close the bar together or, each having a lady in tow, share a cab to one or separate locations.

Mason began to feel comfortable with the city and the job. He set up a bank account, bought a stereo, purchased an old truck from a fellow butcher for four hundred dollars and then met Sara. She was training to be a nurse and was out one evening celebrating the engagement of a friend. Victor focused on the oldest in the group, who turned out to be a married nursing instructor. Having little success and being very drunk Victor soon left. Staying later, Mason soon became very interested in a short brunette with a shapely figure. There was a quality about Sara that immediately caught his attention. Soon he was seated with the ladies, telling stories, flirting with all and laughing at the inevitable sexually suggestive comments, while secretly watching the brunette's movements and mannerisms with growing excitement.

During the final band set he was able to dance with the ladies from the table in a large circle, manoeuvring towards Sara for the final song. As usual the last dance was melodic and tender, speaking of cherished love. Most nights this was a time to take stock of the chances for sexual gratification, but this night he experienced a strange feeling when taking her in his arms. He first noticed the way she fit against him. Not in a grinding physical way but with warm comfort somehow resulting in a sensation of reassurance, like the distant light of home on a dark cloudy night. Resting her head on his shoulder she surrendered her body to his lead. This was different than the usual last dance which was often a pull and tug affair due to intoxication or a desire to exert control. She seemed to trust his dancing abilities even when he did not. At first worrying about failure he stumbled, growing more nervous with each mistake. Yet she stayed faithful never taking charge while simply willing him to relax and dance. Finally entering the music and accepting her faith he committed to the motion. The result was miraculous as the two melded together, gliding in small loops intensely aware of each other, yet lost in the dream of the moment. Oblivious to others and the surroundings they moved about the floor only stopping when the sporadic clapping signalled the end of a life instant that he would never forget.

Mason had no expectation regarding the possibility of sexual activity as they left the bar. Sara sat against the window humming quietly. There was no recognition of the tune, however, the lack of melody was soothing. The sound was sweet reminding him of cherries. Savouring the moment he said nothing, blocking out the noisy engine sound and losing himself in Sara's simple purring. Arriving at her residence she paused, looked directly into his eyes, kissed him softly and said good night. With a pounding heart and a light head he began to pull away from the curb. She remained standing on the sidewalk, as if wanting the night to continue. "I'll be back at the bar next Thursday. Another engagement." She smiled and left.

He spent the next week trying to understand the feelings and thoughts running through his body and mind. Sleeping was difficult, as his active brain seemed to have found a new focus. He relived the evening searching her every movement, gesture and word looking for confirmation that she was interested. Just when he was sure she was, doubt would roll in like a barrel moving down a steep hill, creating havoc and causing anxiety. By the following Thursday he was a mess and almost did not go to the bar. Uncontrollably, the fear of never seeing her again drove him forward. He arrived full of apprehension and nervous energy.

She was there, beautiful and waiting. They sat close, anxiously speaking safe words. The small talk soon turned to discussions of future goals. Mason suddenly realized that he had none. No plans or direction, no desires or yearnings past the everyday survival needs that were currently fulfilled due to a full-time job. He began to feel inadequate as she spoke of an education, a career, a home, a relationship and the resultant children. With gleaming eyes she spoke of the beauty and joy such a life would deliver. At first he was overwhelmed, attempting and failing to view the images and join her future. His thoughts of family brought on strong emotions of loss and utter disappointment. He fought for emotional control as the attempt to enter her world resulted in a return to the desolation of the past. As the struggle continued he was interrupted by her easy giggle.

"You're so serious," she stated as the giggle turned to a hardy laugh. "Your face looks like you've been eating lemons."

At first he did not know how to react. Then he began to see the humour and laughed along with her. As he relaxed the negative energy escaped leaving him staring at her pleasant glowing face. From there the evening proceeded, flowing from one conversation to another. She talked while Mason listened, absorbing the information in an attempt to understand this fascinating woman. At times he told safe funny stories, which made her laugh. Time and the importance of the world became lost as love began to blossom.

The physical closeness with the innocent touching became natural and desired. Both began to willingly fold into the relationship with no thought of future or consequences. It was so easy and felt so wonderful he allowed good feelings to flow. The angry disappointment driven by loss was buried, hidden from her. Questions about his past were redirected or laughed off as unimportant. He was determined that she would not see the hurt or be subjected to his pain.

Although both wanted to leave they stayed until the bar was empty. Only then did it seem appropriate to take the risk of what the night might offer. With a sandy mouth he suggested a nightcap and music at his apartment. She nodded anxiously, avoiding eye contact. There was no sweet humming tonight only the thick air of nervous anticipation. Words were withheld due to the fear of a misperceived comment or an ill-conceived statement that might change promise to rejection. Fortunately the tense drive soon ended. The turning off of the ignition created true silence. No sound was made, as constricted breathing was the only noise inside the cab. His hands seemed glued to the steering wheel, while her's were locked together in her lap. Suddenly both moved at the same moment. Exiting the truck they entered the apartment on unsteady legs.

The effort up the flight of stairs was accomplished in a daze, with their physical motions wooden and tight. The lovemaking began awkwardly with him not wanting to make any mistakes and the lack of experience making her cautious. Tentative movements resulted in a lack of commitment to the process culminating in frustration. Each began to worry about the other, becoming concerned that the entire relationship was in jeopardy. Clad only in bra and panties she excused herself and went to the bathroom. With heart racing Mason lay on the bed not knowing what to do, feeling it may be better for her to leave and forget the whole botched experience. He decided to put on some quiet music and then returned to the bedroom. She was waiting. They embraced near the end of the bed and began a slow dance. The moment was reminiscent of the first meeting and soon they were moving sensually in a tight circle. All the fear and indecision began to melt as they floated and caressed.

The pleasuring lasted all night. It was gentle and giving, rough and taking, playful and teasing, slow and grinding, resulting in the zenith of repeated orgasm. She wanted to learn all he knew and please him in every way desired. He took her to heights of ecstasy she had never imagined during her few previous dull sexual experiences. Both were exhausted when the birds began to waken. Lacking strength for further lovemaking they lay in twisted sheets silently gazing out the bare bedroom window watching the lightening sky. Not wanting the night to end, each felt a regretful resignation as they shyly rose from the tossed bed and with averted eyes searched for the scattered clothing.

Later Mason drove to the plant and avoided human contact, worried that mundane conversations would destroy the wonderful dreamland he had entered. Surrendering to work his thoughts soared in all directions, with the images always returning to Sara. They were raw and graphic portraits resulting in numerous erections that were barely hidden behind the rubber apron. By the end of the shift he could hardly walk due to the throbbing ache in his loins. He rushed to the bar hoping she would be there. She was waiting with glazed eyes and moist lips. They stumbled to his truck as she groped in his pants. She rubbed against his body and sought his hardness as he drove recklessly. By the time the door of his apartment slammed they were all over each other, licking, biting, grabbing, clutching. There was no shyness now only intense passion with the sole purpose of pleasuring and being pleasured.

During the first four months they left his apartment only to work or go to school. On weekends, provisions would be hoarded with the two days racing by with the urgency of the next impending orgasm. They would discard clothes immediately upon entering the apartment, as garments were a hindrance to pleasure. The blinds were never drawn, as there were none. As a result, at times the community shared in the carnal displays. The sound of car horns would indicate approval of the exhibition. The loudness of the lovemaking would roust the neighbours who would pound on the walls with fists or on the ceiling with broom handles. They were never deterred, wanting the world to know and share in their sexual prowess.

On certain nights, when Sara was asleep, Mason would analyze the situation in the dark. Her gentle snore would relax his thoughts, causing a willingness to think about the future. When they were together, with the total focus on physical love, all was very well. Yet he knew from past discussions and current hints that she needed the relationship to become more. He listened with a growing sense of alarm at descriptions of the perceived future she so desperately desired. Early in the relationship the comments were accepted as there was little thought that he would be involved in her dreams. When the desire to be together increased to a burning need, fear on many levels began to appear. All were driven by the strong belief that any commitment to a permanent courtship culminating in a marriage would end badly. Even identifying the possibility of such a future resulted in a sickening knot of fear forming deep in his core. She sensed his reluctance to speak of a future together, carefully choosing her words in an attempt to gain his acceptance. He loved her more for not pushing a commitment agenda but he realized that her patience was fraying. Soon Sara began to set up double dates with friends or request his attendance at community events. He found the pressure to perform as a couple difficult and awkward. Powerful resentments began to boil within. The unresolved pain was again active awakened from the dormancy brought on by the intense sexual activity. He felt it percolating inside like an uneasy stomach just before retching.

The intake of liquor that had slowed in the safe confines of the apartment began to increase when out in public. He embarrassed her on two occasions with slurred words, staggered steps and surly behaviour. Unable to take any responsibility he blamed the quality of her friends or the lameness of the activity. She began to watch the drinking closely, lecturing on how alcohol changed him. They began to disagree about many matters. Little mannerisms that had been cute and endearing soon became annoying. At times they would retreat back to intense sexual intimacy in a fruitless attempt to rekindle the relationship. This would be successful for a short period of time, but the incompatibility was soon surfacing with growing strength.

The final nail was driven deep when Sara's parents arrived for an unscheduled visit. Her father was ex-military, a retired major, rigid and demanding with a piercing stare. The man was all business when dealing with everyone, including her mother, who would cower under the military scrutiny. The Major doted over Sara, giggling and sharing private jokes or comments only they understood. Mason disliked the man immediately. The pompous, authoritarian attitude went totally against his character. The Major instantly decided that the longhaired butcher was so far below his daughter on the social scale that the sooner the liaison ended the better for all. Mason was treated with aloof tolerance with neither parent attempting to hide their disdain for the relationship. At the first meeting Sara appeared to superficially stick up for him, pointing out positive qualities or mollifying the Major with flattery. He was sickened by the performance, but welcomed the support.

The Major decided on a dinner date in an expensive restaurant for the following evening. Mason had no dress up clothes and was forced to borrow a suit from one of Victor's nephews. The jacket was too tight across the chest and the pants too short in the legs. He felt ridiculous in the ill-fitting suit and mismatched tie.

After spending the day apart, Sara's attitude changed noticeably at supper. It proved difficult for her to mask the disgust over his choice of clothing. The severe contrast was magnified as she wore a beautiful new dress purchased that afternoon by her parents. With her hair freshly coiffured she looked like a princess, while he resembled what he was, an uncomfortable, ill-attired suitor outnumbered and outclassed. Any support was gone as Sara and her parents talked of mutual acquaintances and remembered cherished family events. Mason began to feel miserable and unwanted.

The Major was quite comfortable and magnanimous controlling the flow of conversation and liquor. Drinks were ordered, making them doubles for the men. Due to feelings of nervous estrangement Mason drank the first one quickly. With a knowing smile the Major ordered a quick replacement for the empty glass. With diligence the man ensured the flow of alcohol never faltered.

After the initial neglect, the Major suddenly graciously included Mason in the conversation. With the liquor beginning to take hold he became chatty. The Major encouraged his verbal outpourings and he began to relax. The more he drank the more sharing occurred. Mason cared little for solid content as the alcohol began to give the false courage to continue on this unsafe path. Sara realized what her father was doing and attempted to stop the process through not so subtle hints and gestures that would have been effective if his liquor induced sense of invincibility had not been so pronounced.

It was over strong aperitifs that the attack began, with the Major seeking opinions on issues of a personal and public nature. Mason's booze-soaked brain was slow to respond, resulting in laboured comments lacking in substance. The Major baited him by disagreeing and seeking clarification. When the slurred replies were deemed inappropriate the Major launched into a complex analysis and then sought a rebuttal. Sara got involved making quiet yet sharp verbal jabs about Mason's opinions or current condition. Her frozen comments became more critical. Reeling, and with the hope of a positive conclusion to the evening in serious danger, Mason retreated to bar methods of dealing with antagonism. His choice of words became coarser and louder. With drunken difficulty Mason finally understood what was happening. The alcohol and Sara's father were now in full control. Attempts to block the quiet, increasingly hostile and personal comments proved hopeless, as the Major, having smelled blood, was relentless. Mason knew serious damage was being done to an already weakened relationship and struggled to focus on how to stop the final destruction. He glanced at Sara, with pleading eyes seeking assistance. It was very evident that she was not prepared to side against her father. Sitting quietly, her face was a mixture of compassion, anger and sadness. There was compassion for Mason's helplessness, anger that he was drunk and unable to protect himself, and sadness that her first serious relationship was clearly over.

While it was apparent that the Major had won the war, the mocking continued to the point where the situation turned cruel. Even his wife, usually compliant to every mood and command, attempted to change the focus and calm her husband. The Major would have none of it. Defeating the enemy was no longer enough. Crushing Mason's spirit became the goal. With his mind whirling from rejection and alcohol, Mason tried to ignore the Major, directing all his attention on Sara. He leaned in close and began to speak softly, asking then begging her to leave. She remained silent, as her cheeks began to flush and her eyes filled with tears. When begging proved ineffective, Mason became agitated. He began to demand answers as to why she would treat him so poorly. She turned away from the questions as the water began to flow down her cheeks landing on the new dress. Seeing the hurt brought on instant guilt. He reached over to hold her hand and felt a stinging pain in his left shoulder. The Major had silently moved around behind clamping down on the trapezius muscle between the neck and shoulder. Due to military training the Major felt comfortable in managing the drunken ex-suitor and was lifting Mason out of the chair when the dam of anger control burst, releasing a massive rush of energy. Mason had been in many fights before and reacted instinctively, dropping the restrained shoulder, stepping back with his left foot, pushing the right side to full height and swinging his right fist in a tight controlled arch, catching the overconfident and unsuspecting Major flush on the mouth.

He heard the pleasing sound of popping teeth, as the pressure on the shoulder was released. The blow forced the Major backwards onto an adjacent table, causing cutlery to fly and glassware to shatter. A woman screamed and her companion howled in protest. With deluded thinking Mason believed defeating the Major would result in winning Sara's love. While many punches were thrown only two more blows landed, one to the midsection of the now frightened and panting man and the other a glancing shot to the cheek. Further damage was avoided by Mason's state of drunkenness and the intervention of numerous appalled customers.

One of the patrons was an off duty police officer, who immediately jumped to the stricken man's aid. Six male university students, celebrating the end of exams, willingly assisted the officer in holding Mason down while the maitre d' called the police. When the officers arrived he was screaming mad. In handcuffs he was taken out of the restaurant. He remembered yelling Sara's name and looking back to see her crying, while holding a white napkin over her father's profusely bleeding mouth.

Being drunk, struggling and having just beaten up a much older man did not endear him to the arresting officers. Once outside and away from witnesses the nightsticks were liberally applied to his upper legs, buttocks and arms. Alcohol and adrenaline provided protection from the pain, but the treatment was severe enough to cause him a moment of submission. The officers having made their point slammed him into the backseat of the police car.

The next battle occurred at the local jail. Alcohol and anger made cooperating impossible. As a result the jail guards continued the attacks. When Mason would not submit a powerful water hose was used. He fought the water with a wasted fury that soon left him gagging and exhausted. From the floor he was taken to a very small isolation room that had a metal bed and cinder block walls. Struggling, he was thrown on the bed landing face first. His upper lip became warm and he knew blood was flowing. The screaming and cursing soon turned to uncontrolled crying ending only when his voice was hoarse and his throat raw. He finally lay exhausted on the cold steel, curling into the fetal position, occasionally sobbing at his place in the world. Unable to cope with the inflicted trauma, his body and mind soon shut down in protest.

Waking to the darkness, he was unsure of his location or circumstance. His head pounded, eyes hurt and his mouth tasted of metal. Straightened legs brought the assault of pain and the resulting nausea as his stomach flipped, spilling the remains of last night's supper onto the floor. The next sharp pain was emotional as the alcohol haze dimmed and the memory of the previous night's debacle took hold. Remembering Sara's anguish flooded him with searing remorse. He replayed the scenes, tumbling through the fuzzy images in search of reason or explanation. None could be found. In the end he chose only to blame himself. This was a destructive pattern that was well established and acceptable in a self-punishing way. Soon, totally overwhelmed by this inevitable but unwanted process, escape was found through sleep.

Movement awoke him the second time. In the blackness it seemed that the entire room was bouncing. The fog cleared reluctantly and he realized that it was his body shaking. The cold concrete floor and walls offered no warmth for his near nakedness. The underwear and shirt were still damp from the forced soaking. Evaporation continued to rob his body of the little warmth it was managing to produce. Rolling into a tight ball the iron bed vibrated with the ridiculous motion as his teeth threatened to shatter from the severe force of the rattling.

Mason remained this way for a long time as guilt-ridden thoughts began to shift from the past to the future. No longer were the tragic events of the previous night the sole worry. Consequences for behaviour became a very real concern as he pieced together his offences. It was conceded that the Major, having ultimately been physically defeated in front of wife and daughter, would have absolutely no trace of forgiveness and would pursue the full punitive force of the justice system. In addition, there were the altercations with the police and later the jail guards. Resisting arrest, with the possibility of assaulting a police officer, would seriously compound the fragile situation. His menacing yelling and screaming would result in an uttering threats charge. Include destruction of private property, as the restaurant would demand full compensation for damage to property and reputation. A public drunkenness charge would be justified and certain. Another spasm of retching resulted from the realization that he was in huge trouble. The dry heaves continued until he was physically wasted. He soon slipped into a dreamlike state, where a consciousness dance occurred between sleep and reality. The opening of the heavy metal door interrupted the restless, maddening sleep. Three burly guards entered the small room filling it with bodies. Mason lay very still unsure as to the purpose of the visit. All stood tensely watching until the eldest of the group spoke.

"You're not going to give us any trouble, are you boy?" The question was stated in a calm even voice. With the bright light from the hallway hurting his blood shot eyes Mason shook his head.

"Good. Now, on your feet. Time to get cleaned up."

The lukewarm shower was glorious, washing away the dried blood and warming Mason's aching being. Movements were slow and deliberate as his body was tight from the severe beating. The blows to his legs and arms were causing the skin to turn multi-shades of angry colours. His lips and nose were swollen with his left eye blackening. Physically, emotionally and spiritually he was beaten. The guards provided a shirt and pants made from a heavy scratchy cloth, which helped his body find warmth. He was given a bowl of heavy vegetable soup and a piece of thick stale white bread. It was delicious, soothing his rumbling stomach. He was moved to a larger cell that had a bed attached to each wall and a metal toilet in the nearest corner. On the bed were a thin mattress, a pair of worn sheets and a coarse wool blanket. He was ordered to make the bed and left alone. No human contact was desired as he climbed into the hastily made bed.

For five days Mason remained in the cell. The only contact with the guards occurred when they delivered meals or roommates. They displayed a heightened alertness and were very watchful during the visits, asking after his health and questioning if everything was all right. This caused him to become suspicious, as he could not understand the reason for the concern.

The only other communication was the quiet conversations he practiced when alone. He carried on a two-way discussion with Sara, stating his feelings and responding to her anticipated replies. The arguments justifying his behaviour were well made, articulate and delivered with humility. An apology to Sara was composed, full of real tears and voice stealing emotion. Paragraphs of regrets were also constructed for her mother and eventually for her father. The later two where more designed for appeasement, with the hopeful possibility of swaying the judge to leniency when it was time for final sentencing. As is usual in the case of self-induced emotional injury the mind begins to accept the events through the application of layered rationalizations, not unlike the healing of a sliced hand where the wound is closed by the growth of new skin. The events of Mason's last night with Sara resulted in the extensive accumulation of scar tissue, as many layers of emotional skin were necessary to subdue the pain and contain the injury. By the time the fourth day arrived his body and mind had recovered sufficiently enough to face the outcome of the trial and most likely further incarceration. In addition, the abstention from alcohol caused a positive impact on his outlook of the future, whatever that might be. Although now clearheaded, Mason noticed physical symptoms of alcohol withdrawal, as he had been drinking heavily and daily since seventeen. He began experiencing uncontrollable tremors in his hands and periodic cold sweats that left his face pale and forehead moist. His thoughts began to focus on getting out of jail so he could return to the confines of a friendly bar and drink to forget this whole mess.

On the morning of the fifth day he was taken from the cell and delivered to a small room with a heavy table and two flimsy chairs. There was natural light filtering through a narrow thick frosted glass window the colour of heavy lake ice. No outside shapes were discernable through the barrier. The natural light, while welcomed, was painful on his sensitive eyes. Mason was directed to an uncomfortable chair and sat alone for many minutes.

Just as his patience was being tested the door opened and a small cheap-suited man, smelling of hair grease and inexpensive cologne, rushed into the room. Before he could ask any questions the man began to talk quickly. Having not carried on a conversation in many days Mason struggled to keep up. The man was Victor's cousin, Marvin, a lawyer who would be representing him at the hearing. The story of the restaurant incident and the subsequent incarceration had just reached Victor the previous night. Upon hearing the guards had not offered an opportunity for a telephone call, the man began to write in a small ringed notebook. At the insistence of the lawyer Mason relived the entire experience, including every remembered detail. Furious notes were taken. Clarification was sought at certain times. Great interest was shown in the reaction of the police and guards. Mason was asked to remove the shirt and pull down the pants. The lawyer gasped upon seeing the numerous now jet black bruises, removed a small camera from his worn brief case and began taking pictures from different angles. The interview ended after the lawyer was satisfied all the information was contained in the important book. The little man was now smiling and seemed quite pleased with the content of the interview. The hearing would be tomorrow morning. Street clothes would be provided and Mason was cautioned to say nothing unless directed to do so. When his only question was how much extra time would be spent in jail, Victor's cousin barked out a loud laugh, slapped him on the back and stated not to worry. It was inevitable that the comment, designed to cause relief, resulted in a heightened sense of anxiety. The afternoon was spent back in the cell silently contemplating and analyzing the lengthy meeting. After diligently reliving the interaction Mason finally, with trepidation and reluctance, decided he must trust the legal stranger. Once he released control of his freedom to Marvin a strange peace occurred. That night his sleep was undisturbed, with no negative thoughts of what consequences the trial might bring.

The next morning, dressed in street clothes, Mason was placed in handcuffs and leg irons by three guards who stormed into the cell sullen and wary. He was taken by van with four others to the local courthouse. It was a large stone building with ornate pillars and heavy wooden doors containing old glass. There was chiselled writing, both English and Latin, on the stone front extending to the peak of the imposing structure. Large cement coats of arms were visible, containing strange symbols, beasts and intertwining plants. A great diversity of people were coming and going through the front doors. Some appeared to be there for a purpose while others wandered slowly back and forth or drifted up the stairs apparently in no hurry to answer for their actions.

While the outside of the courthouse appeared noble, strict, and purposeful exuding organized efficiency, the inside was barely controlled chaos. Men and women with briefcases and exploding files rushed along the crowded hallways, while others less fortunate soberly shuffled along, heads down gazing at the floor. Loud conversations were occurring in all directions. The language was coarse, full of anger and resentment. Others huddled, whispering quietly, with an unconcealed urgency. The areas around the sand-filled ashtrays were crowded, as dirty men and women shared the limited space with impeccably attired lawyers and their beautiful assistants. None seemed to care about the others' appearance, simply desiring one last jolt of nicotine before fates were decided. It was obvious with the speed of the pulls on the cigarettes and the deepness of the inhaling that the unclean had much more to lose. The strong smell of assorted body odours, perfumes, colognes and smoke, filled the air with a dense thick mixture that seemed to stick like toxic glue.

Surprisingly, Mason and the other prisoners were led through the front doors, down the busy major corridor and into a small courtroom at the end of the long hall, where all were ordered to sit in a small prisoner's box containing solid wooden benches bolted to the floor. He had only been sitting for a moment when there was flash of movement as Marvin quickly approached, leaned over the box and motioned Mason forward. "I can't be here. Just plead guilty. Then wait at the jail." After the hurried and shocking disclosure the man was gone, scurrying out of the courtroom like a Titanic rat.

Mason felt a tightening below his rib cage, as his lungs fought for air. Abandoned by the shifty little lawyer was the worst and most unforeseen possible ending to this entire horrible affair. His back and shoulders began to tighten and knot due to the uncomfortable position and the massive increase in anxiety. He experienced startled relief when a loud deep voice ordered all to rise.

The experience with the justice system that day proved that any attempt to anticipate what the future may bring was futile. During the stay in jail Mason had lived and relived the trial with precise language and actions on the part of the legal personnel. He imagined the judge as stern and knowledgeable, the prosecutor dower and serious, his lawyer distinguished and wile, while the court proceedings were to be dignified and majestic. He inflated the time the process would take believing that days would be necessary to establish guilt or innocence. He saw lengthy objections, discussions of legal points, damning testimony with the inevitable brilliant cross examination and of course the hastily called recesses so the defence could discuss the situation with the accused. It was amazing how strong the power of the imagination was at preordaining events and how it was usually so totally wrong.

Reality showed the court procedures to be mundane and tedious, with an overall weariness that made Mason strangely sad. The judge, sporting a bad comb over, was a tall sliver of a man who appeared lost in the flowing robes. With a bored and unenthusiastic flourish order in the court was called for, accented by the loud hollow pounding of the gavel. The judge showed little concern for the continued talking, directing attention to the bailiff who called out the name of the prisoner to Mason's left. The prosecutor, a thinned lipped man with a drinker's nose, stood and read out the charges with disinterest. The accused pleaded guilty to the misdemeanour and was released with a fine. In similar manner all the other prisoners were dealt with except one man who was remanded in custody, as the charges were more serious.

Mason was the last and nervously stood facing the judge as the prosecutor read the charges. Public drunkenness and destruction of private property were the first two offences. He waited for the rest of the charges, but nothing further was said as the man sat down. The judge sat quietly for a moment and then turned the attention of the room towards the prisoner's box.

"Well how do you plead, guilty or not guilty?" the judge stated showing impatience at the delay in the answer.

Mason's brain stalled. He knew that following Marvin's advice was the only possible course of action. Surprisingly there was a burning desire to explain what had happened. The apologies and other speeches constructed in the quiet of the jail cell swam in circles around the inside of his head like milling fish. He attempted and failed to grab one of the slippery ideas or comments that could help everyone in the court to understand how he came to be in shackles. In the end Mason simply said, "guilty."

The gavel hit the desk with the speed of an involuntary muscle reaction. The judge was now all business wanting the slow and reluctant prisoner dealt with and removed from the court. The prosecutor, sensing the judge's impatience, rose and stated that a fine of twenty dollars and restitution of twenty-five dollars, for the damage to the restaurant dishes, was warranted. The judge, obviously needing to be a part of the proceedings and perhaps wanting to send a message to any other tardy defendants, upped the fine five dollars and stated Mason was free to go. With a final bang of the gavel his first court appearance was over.

Mason and the other prisoners were taken back to the jail to collect their belongings. He was confused and perplexed at the result of the proceedings. The serious charges anticipated had been dropped for an unknown reason. Marvin had hardly broken a sweat in his defence, only listening to his story, taking some pictures and then directing Mason to plead guilty. Whatever the little lawyer had done behind the scenes had resulted in freedom, conditional on paying a fine and making restitution, which were absurdly minor penalties considering the possible serious consequences.

After collecting his belongings Mason waited by the prisoner's exit as instructed. It was five o'clock before Marvin arrived driving a late model Cadillac and wearing a large smile. He wanted answers but Marvin simply waved a hand coyly repeating the word "patience". They drove to local bar where Victor and some of the men from work were in the process of celebrating Mason's return. All were drinking heavily. The doubles produced in his honour were appreciated and savoured with quickness.

During the first two drinks Marvin related what had happened. Mason realized why the little lawyer had waited so long to tell the tale. It became obvious that Marvin loved attention and thus needed a crowd. In addition, the lawyer could tell a good story, complete with facial expressions, body movements and an exaggerated analysis of the reactions of others. It turned out that Victor's cousin was a very expensive lawyer. Prosecutors commonly referred to Marvin as the "Bulldog" for the relentlessness and stubbornness in the pursuit of not guilty pleas for the expensive clients who hired the little attorney. Marvin was quick to state that without the request from Victor, there was no way Mason could have afforded the legal services provided.

The pictures taken at the interview were everything to the case, as the authorities did not want to be explaining the bruises from the beatings by police and the guards, especially under Marvin's scathing cross-examination. Dropping all charges after the police arrived at the restaurant was the price for the bruises. The prosecutor was assured that the pictures would be made public. In the end the man wanted no part of a messy examination of police methods and made the deal. The assault charge was more difficult due to the insistence of the offended party, the Major, to proceed with the complaint. Marvin had met twice with Sara's father, breaking down the resistance to dropping the charges, by threatening a long trial while assuring a most ungracious examination of the Major and his family's actions, specifically his daughter, once on the witness stand. In the end the Major had growled agreement, collected the missing teeth, the rest of the traumatized family and left for home. The restaurant was easy as Marvin was a very loyal customer and a heavy tipper.

"So that is the complete story. A couple of more things though before we're done. Do not attempt, in any way, to contact the girl. She has transferred to the school back home and will be living with her parents. Also, stay away from the restaurant. You are not welcome there. An important word of warning. The police are very pissed off and will want to put you back in custody for any reason. If I were you I would look to relocate to a different place. You should know that all I did for you was a favour to my favourite cousin who has stood up for me many times in the past. But I will tell you both this. I will not represent you again, even if you paid me. Now you lucky son-of-a-bitch, I want a triple of the best scotch in the house and doubles for all my friends."

The rest of the evening was spent drinking and telling stories. Marvin told the majority of the narratives. The man relished the spotlight and was not shy in sharing a large repertoire of legal tales. The little lawyer seemed to enjoy mocking clients and other legal professionals through the use of a biting sarcastic wit. The plight of past clients was of little concern as the entire table laughed at the funny, yet pathetic way Marvin portrayed the interaction with the downtrodden. The attorney did not spare Mason from the process as great care was taken to describe the look on his face in the prisoner's box. The exaggerated facial contortions and body motions brought howls of laughter from his drunken buddies. He flushed with embarrassment, but felt it best to laugh along.

Mason found out the next morning that he had been terminated for missing a week of work. Appeals to the superintendent and general manager of the plant were ignored. In the end he became resigned to the fact he had been fired. The rest of the day was spent at his small apartment drinking cold beer and examining future prospects. After careful analysis and eight beers Mason decided that it was time to move on.

Arrangements were made to take Victor for supper on the Saturday before leaving. A fancy restaurant would have been an insult. Instead a steak joint located outside of the city limits was chosen. The steaks were big and tender, with all the meat aged for twenty-one days. In addition, the clientele was less delicate than the last place he had eaten. The music was loud fast country, which Victor loved. Dancing was encouraged throughout the restaurant and on a Saturday the place really got jumping.

They ate, drank and talked. Told true stories and lies. Laughed at themselves and others. Even cried a little when the alcohol got them both sentimental. Victor began talking about a childhood in the old country, which was remembered with fondness and many toasts of strong sweet tasting alcohol, which were ordered from a buxom waitress who appeared to know the night was special.

At one point Victor leaned close and in a loud slurred voice asked, "Why you not ever talk about being a little boy?"

With a weaving hand movement Mason brushed away the comment as if attempting to part a thin curtain. "I got not much to say about that and it isn't really important anyways."

Victor grunted and took another drink from the large glass. "You be hurt as boy. I see that first time meeting. You try to fool everyone but you no fool Victor. Victor drink because he like drinking. You drink to forget things. Bad things. I no understand but I see."

No more questions were asked that night as soon the dancing began. The two friends proceeded to bump and grind with any brave women who would join them on the dance floor, between tables or in the hallways to the washrooms. They sang along with the canned country music using words and phrases that did not match. He sang all the words wrong but carried the melody well. Victor knew most of the words but could not match the notes, singing constantly off key.

At the end of the night two off duty waitresses came over to share in the last drink. One was older, one younger, both quite unattractive. From there the four went to an after hours bar and then to Mason's apartment were Victor took the couch and he the unmade bed. Noise from the living room kept Mason awake long after the woman in his arms fell into a restless sleep. In the morning Victor and his companion were gone. After a few uncomfortable moments, for both, a cab was called and the woman left him to nurse a pounding raging hangover. Although looking horrible in the mirror, beneath the queasy stomach and the pounding head, he felt quite content. After a long afternoon sleep he would complete one more task before leaving.

The letter to Sara was not a very smart idea, but it was important it be completed and mailed. The process should have been easy, however, similar to the last painful letter Mason had written, it took much longer than expected. It was three o'clock in the morning before the final mailing copy was completed and lay spread out on the rickety kitchen table, beside a stamped, addressed envelope. With tired sad eyes he read the letter one more time. It would never be what he truly wanted to say but at this point it was good enough.

> Dearest Sara:
> I know you probably never wanted to hear from me again, but I needed to write you and say my piece. I am very sorry for knocking your father's teeth out at the restaurant. I was very upset with everything that was happening and just reacted when he grabbed my shoulder. I did not mean to hurt him and I really never ever ever wanted to hurt you. You are the first woman I have ever loved. It is too bad you ended up hating me.

I never spoke about my past life much as I did not want you to feel sorry for me or run away from me. I have had a very hard time and have had to grow up faster then I would have liked. I have lost everyone that has been important and losing them has not been very pretty. But I don't want you feeling bad for me and think that I am making excuses, as I am not. Maybe that is why I drink so much. Victor says I drink to forget. He may be right. But no matter how much I drink I will never forget you. Ever.

I hope you have a long and healthy life. I do not expect to live that long myself. But you deserve it. I'm sure you will find a wonderful guy and have the special life you spoke and dreamed about. Sometimes when we were together I wished I could be that special guy, but I always knew I could not find that kind of happiness or make you that happy either.

I hope you have read this letter and not just ripped it up or burned it or thrown it in the garbage. Good luck with school. I know you will make a great nurse, wife and mother, someday. Maybe a long time in the future you will stop hating me and like me maybe a little bit. I sure hope so.

Love,

Mason was sure that putting "love" was appropriate but was not sure how to sign the letter. He did not feel comfortable with one of the pet names she had given him. After all the pain and bad circumstances the names seemed dumb and devoid of their former sparkle. Putting both his names somehow seemed too distant even through he believed that she loathed him. In the end he signed only Mason, folded the letter neatly, put it in the envelope, licked it shut and closed the contact on his first true love.

Morning came early and after a final hot shower he loaded up the truck and drove to the plant. The beef kill was already in process as he entered the employees' entrance, went up two flights of stairs and entered a heavy door that led to a cement and metal walkway that overlooked the floor. Victor noticed him first, giving up a loud yell and big bloody wave from the high skinning stand. Others turned and joined in, yelling and banging the backs of knives on metal pails and stands. Tears welled in Mason's eyes as the noise grew. He smiled large and waved back, blowing kisses to all. Someone below asked, in a screaming voice, where he was going. Mason thought for a minute and yelled back as loud as possible, to be heard over the deafening human roar and machine noise.

"Going travelling. See ya all later." And with a big victory wave walked through the door and out of the plant.

The term travelling connotes a journey from one place to another. It is a trip that has been planned with a prescribed destination. It is the going to a location for a reason, even if the rationale behind the excursion holds little purpose or purports no real sense of accomplishment. In truth the real essence of his travels was more of a wandering search, rather than accomplishing a purposeful passage. The search was certainly a part of his travelling lifestyle, which contained a spark of hopeful anticipation that missing personal emotional pieces could be discovered. Wandering was more to the point, as there was usually no specific reason in mind for changing locations. He had tried settling down to a steady job and woman, wishing to create a structured and meaningful existence. It had worked for a short period of time. The extremely poor results of that experiment had caused him to shy away from any new experiences that offered a whiff of permanence. As a result he kept moving, seldom staying in one place for any length of time.

Mason was not alone, as the late sixties and seventies brought on an intense migration of young people seeking to find themselves and experience an existence of peace and love or conversely sex, drugs and rock and roll. He was never much of a hippie, but did embrace the lifestyle as it made him a part of a larger societal group that proclaimed the necessity for a change in values and beliefs. While Mason looked like a hippie, it was more the gypsy lifestyle that suited his cynical view of settled down people. Therefore he embraced the transient life, hooking up with others for convenience and then leaving them for the same reason.

Mason met many great people on the road, full of idealistic thoughts and beliefs. There was often an unconditional sense of sharing and the understanding that all were vulnerable to unscrupulous travellers or hard headed authorities whose sole purpose was to impede a person's way. The good people helped each other offering real or emotional warmth when possible. He easily learned the language that allowed for inclusion and after a few months of letting his hair and beard grow, the appearance fit perfectly. Beads were worn and his ear was pierced by a large hairy woman whom he picked up hitchhiking.

During the wandering time Mason met many different people, packing and distributing many different drugs. He found the marijuana and hashish relaxing but restrictive as both caused him to retreat into his own confused thoughts. LSD was enjoyed as it resulted in belly-splitting laughter, followed by the desire to absorb everything around him. Textures and contours of object were amazing and pleasing, while being warped in size and shape. He enjoyed the strobe-like tracks that were apparent in broad daylight as he moved a hand or stared at a bird in flight. While the object moved, its past position remained frozen in his mind. At night the stoned view of a raging fire was magnificent, with trails of sparked lights shooting onward and upward into a black star-lit sky. There were all kinds of other drugs, mostly with simple letters and produced by inventive chemistry students bored with the college process. The drugs were mass-produced in dirty basements by combining dangerous chemicals and household products that one would never think to ingest, but would readily consume to obtain the promised mind-altering experience. Some drugs were natural, causing powerful highs, while others just made a person sick. Mason tried them all, liked only a few and once the drug experimenting phase was over continued to take none. Through the entire drug experience alcohol was a constant companion as the hippie life promoted ripple and homemade wine, tequila and cold beer.

At times the life was very hard. Mason lived out of his truck, sleeping in an old army tent that had been acquired in a one on one trade for his stereo. It may have been a poor swap, but at the time a roof, even if it leaked in a heavy rain, was more important than the more expensive stereo. Camping was done in isolated areas where a fire would not attract attention or in cheap campgrounds. Meals consisted of local produce that could be cheaply purchased or stolen.

The main fare was no name beans that could be cooked in the fire and eaten directly out of the can. He grew rakishly thin. When naked he looked like a mop of hair attached to pieces of bone and sinew. Former pride in appearance was discarded, as contact with regular washing facilities was a luxury not afforded to the existence. All other compatible travellers were in the same circumstances so one became oblivious to unwashed bodies, unclean clothes and the accompanying odour. The lack of personal hygiene was manageable under the stars and bright sun but was shunned by normal town and city people when limited contact occurred. Greeted by judgemental faces offering uncontained disgust became a challenge and brought out legitimate anger, which went against the peaceful, non-violent credo of the hippie culture. Therefore Mason was forced to accept the scorn, holding back a good ole boy's temper that lay bubbling under the surface.

The old truck was a means of escape and a tool to meet other likeminded folk as he often picked up hitchhikers. Histories would be shared and destinations discussed. If the new place sounded promising a change in course would occur, with the inevitable hope that perhaps an easy special adventure was just around the next bend in the hard difficult road. This was how he came to the Living Joy Commune.

Mason first heard of the retreat after picking up a homely young girl and her much older companion. The girl lied stating she was twenty-one while the man lied stating he was twenty-eight. They were both from different made up places designed to hide the past. The man was a city dweller finding the country life difficult, while the girl was from a small town persuaded to travel to San Francisco to experience the now defunct hippie phenomenon. On the way west they were going to stop at a commune located in the foothills of the Rocky Mountains. The girl spoke dreamily of the place as if it were the origin of great peace and love. The man envisioned it as a source of easy living where food, relaxation and women were plentiful. Mason's uncharted course was easily changed, becoming intrigued to see who was right.

On the way, they picked up a fellow who was more a boy than a young man. It was clear that the boy was running from the past. The boy too, had heard of the retreat on the edge of the mountains, believing it to be an appropriate destination, while secretly hoping to find safety. When they picked up a heavy woman in her mid-thirties, who stated with voiced venom that she had given up a hated secretarial life for the road, the troupe was complete.

The girl, having only sketchy directions, proceeded to increase the miles with wrong turns and bad decisions. After circling the general area of the commune on twisted pitching roads, Mason finally took control and using an old map, some grudging directions of locals and following a brightly painted Volkswagen van, arrived at the gates of a farmyard surrounded by a new chain link fence crowned in barbwire. The scene took on the appearance of an enclosed compound designed to keep unwanted visitors out while controlling the leaving of those inside. In the centre of the area stood an impressive three-story white house with a large veranda. It was located at the top a steep grassy hill in a sea of hills that rolled on like waves crashing upon the snow-capped mountains in the distance. A large barn was located to the left of the house, while the roofs of smaller buildings could be seen further away to the right. People were milling about on the veranda and in the yard. A group of bare-chested men and women threw a frisbee back and forth, while others lay on the grass.

The van drove through the gates unimpeded. Mason followed and was stopped by two large hairy men with upraised hands, asking their business. The men were carrying heavy hardwood staffs that were good for hiking or leaning but equally suitable as weapons. As the truck rolled to a stop, the girl and the older man leapt to the ground offering an excited greeting to the guards. Mason stayed in the truck not liking the feel of the men, as he could smell the odour of bully on both. He was about to order all back into the truck, when a short heavy man with smiling cheeks and a flowing brown robe, trundled down the dry, worn road and joined the discussion. "Welcome to Living Joy", the man stated with manufactured goodwill. "We are a commune that offers a peaceful and tranquil escape from the rigors of a hateful and brutal world. Let these weary travellers pass. You must be hungry after your long journey."

Mason watched closely as the man hugged the homely girl tightly and a little too long. Whispers were directed into her ears as she giggled and melted into the robes. There was a strength exuding from the man, who was obviously the leader, as the guards deferred to the directions, allowing all to enter. The boy also received a strong embrace, which was even longer, leaving the lad flushed and uncomfortable. The older woman was brushed off with a wave of indifference while the older man had already moved off to watch the bouncing and jiggling frisbee players. The men directed Mason to a parking area over the rise in the hill that contained other older beaten and dented vehicles. Nearer the house were two shiny new trucks that were separated from the lesser cars and vans. He parked and made his way to the large house.

After a simple but satisfying meal the five were called to an *orientation session*. They met in the living room of the house, which was arranged with comfortable chairs and soft mats to sit on. Quiet young girls with vacant eyes served mugs of strong tea and hard sweet cookies. After all were comfortable, the stout man, in flowing robes now changed to a brilliant white, made a regal entrance into the room. Behind the man followed three tough looking attendants sporting large knives clearly visible on their belts.

The delivery of the message involved good cheer and many smiles. The Living Joy retreat was a commune that had been created to offer a refuge for young people who were searching for the meaning of life. The creator, Benjamin Tuckel, who insisted that all call him Teacher, had inherited the house and land from his uncle who had passed away two years earlier. The commune was totally self-sufficient which meant that all worked together to provide for each other. The vision of cooperation presented offered a chance for lost souls to find a joy in living through the unselfish giving to others, hence the name. Physical possessions meant nothing in this place as the good of the group transcended earthly needs. Spiritual needs were met through daily lectures, meditations and individual sessions offered by the Teacher and his core of spiritual assistants.

Tuckel soon launched into an articulate oratory about the meaning of existence. There was no doubt that the Teacher was an educated man with a vast vocabulary, offering lucid comments and asking thought provoking questions. His voice was polished and soothing having a calming affect on the group. Even the hardened attendants seemed to escape into the words, unconditionally accepting the Teacher's assumptions as the total truth. As the Teacher continued to speak the room became quiet, until not a person was moving. All were transfixed, hanging on each word while longing for the next insight. It was as if a hypnotic trance had settled over the room with everyone dancing and moving to the Teacher's words and actions like a field of flowers swaying to the mastery of the wind. Time seemed to stand still as the Teacher pulled the audience close, capturing absolute attention and exerting absolute control while tying each tightly with an invisible cord of duty and obligation to the commune. It was magical, invigorating, liberating and of course it was bullshit.

Perhaps it was Mason's inability to properly focus on anything verbal for any length of time that saved him from the spell. In addition, being a visual learner he quickly became bored of the constant verbiage, losing the focus and the point of the well-scripted introduction. He did relax, but quickly realized that was due to the quality of the tea and ingredients that had been added to ensure that the listening minds were dulled and accepting of the messages offered by the Teacher. Mason's hardened nature and past experiences had resulted in the development of a suspicious nature. He had also learned that it was important not to allow the suspected person an awareness of the suspicions. Outside he sat still and watched the man with artificial interest as if enraptured with the Teacher's exalted message. Inside he watched the man closely, impressed by the way the lost souls were moved and manipulated. When appropriate Mason peripherally surveyed the others in the room. All were captured by Tuckel's magnetic personality. The natural ability of the man to ensnare willing souls with words and gestures was frightening. He had never met a man with a more imposing mental presence. The eyes captured the unsuspecting, offering the false promise of safety, security and the peace of belonging. He could see that the real object being sought was unconditional allegiance to the Teacher as ruler and master of the commune.

Mason feared most for the young man and woman to whom the oracle seemed to be directing the powerful statements. The vulnerability of the pair was scary as both had lost lots and were searching for a way to fill their empty emotional vessels. The older woman was quietly crying, enthralled with the Teacher. The older man was in awe of the power wielded by the charismatic leader.

Mason felt a tickle far down in his throat and rather than suppressing the irritation, allowed it to be released. The coughing fit interrupted the proceedings. He feigned an apologetic demeanour, showing appropriate humility and sorrow at disruption in the orientation. The Teacher was clearly upset that the enchantment had been broken, but graciously accepted the apology. The attendants were clearly not as forgiving, staring at him with a mixture of dislike and distrust.

Unable to recapture the spellbinding mood Tuckel moved on to speak of more practical items. The Teacher cleverly mentioned how all the money available was tied up in making the commune work, so any donations would be gladly accepted. The young girl knelt in front of the man delivering all the money she had, while kissing the outstretched hand. Likewise the older man and woman willingly offered up wads of bills. The boy had only change and was told, in a magnanimous gesture, to keep the coins. When the focus turned to Mason he shrugged weakly and with a downtrodden look quietly stated that the last of his money had been spent on gas for the truck. This intensified the scowling looks of the attendants.

The two young people were assigned sleeping accommodations in the house. The attendants took the older man away, while the older woman was directed to the female dorm located out the back door. Mason was allocated a place in the male dorm until they learned that he had butchering experience. That elevated his value to the commune greatly as the past butcher had left over a month ago and producing the meat had fallen to the attendants who desperately wanted rid of the job. Mason was given quarters in the barn. The small room was stark but clean, smelling sweetly of fresh hay and old manure. It was not unpleasant. He checked out the method for processing the meat and found a primitive yet efficient slaughter facility. After settling, Mason was left alone as no one wanted to be near the duties he performed. He was told early on that certain pieces of meat were to be wrapped separately and labelled TT. He showed no interest, knowing full well that the Teacher was hoarding the best cuts for private dinners.

Mason easily justified commandeering some of the best beef by believing it was appropriate to con the con man. This meant he ate well, often taking only vegetables at supper, retreating to the back of the barn and grilling a filet mignon or, if hungry, a porter house steak on a small fire. After so many months of frugal eating a constantly full belly made for comfortable living. There was also a replenishment of energy as the isolation of the job brought on a quiet peaceful existence, far from Tuckel's mutant realm and the brutality of the real world.

Living in the barn was pleasant and cosy. Mason did not mind sharing his dwelling with the mice and wild cats, which came to the barn for the hunt. At first the cats were spooked by his presence, but they soon accepted him after realizing they had nothing to fear. The shear height of the barn allowed a superior vantage point to observe the commune's activity. The loft doors faced the side of the large house with a small window facing to the north. He liked to sit in the soft comfort of the hay and watch the members do the appointed tasks. Every morning, very early, he would notice a small crew of attendants quietly leave the grounds and go north into a stand of evergreen and ash trees. They would not return until supper, tired yet laughing and relaxed. His curiosity needed satisfying, so on an overcast morning Mason arose in darkness, slipped into the woods and waited for the men to arrive. He had no problem following the noisy, easygoing crew that proceeded through the trees ending up in a large meadow completely hidden from the compound. Crawling into a thick bush he watched as the men began to attend a very large field of four-foot high marijuana plants. The crop was healthy and rich as was evident by the affects it had on the workers when the leaves were picked off the plants, dried by the fire and smoked in large cigar sized joints. The Teacher had a profitable little secret. The cash crop, upon harvest, would be worth a fortune once it was sold on the west coast. While secret knowledge of the Teacher's potential wealth was a powerful piece of information, it also resulted in a strong reaction of fear. The illegal drugs and heavy money involved made for the potential of serious violence should the crop and resulting profits be threatened in any way. This explained the security at the front gates and armed attendants.

Mason had stayed in the commune for over a month enjoying the isolation and plenty offered. Even the alcohol input had diminished dramatically as his smuggled stash of tequila sat hidden under a hay bale. The simple living, hard work and lack of alcohol brought on a strengthening of body and mind. He even began exercising, doing endless chin-ups on a heavy old water pipe that stretched across one corner of the empty horse stalls. Due to the acoustics of the cavern-like barn he began singing loud songs after a day's work. He enjoyed exercising his vocal cords caring little when the words to old songs were forgotten. The only communication Mason sought was with the other members of the original troupe. In the first two weeks he had seen the young boy often. At first the lad had been smiling and conversing with a genuine joy and excitement. The Teacher had been focusing on the boy's spiritual growth and the lad was grateful and happy. Unfortunately, during subsequent meetings, the boy had appeared distant and nervous, cutting the conversation short and leaving quickly.

When Mason began to run low on provisions he approached one of the attendants requesting money to go to town for necessary butchering supplies. The simple question resulted in a major reaction that went to the top of the command chain, ending in an audience with the Teacher. Tuckel demanded to know why the trip to town was required. In his best country bumpkin manner Mason explained that it was necessary to purchase spices, binder and casings for sausage making, along with other butchering needs. In addition, the useless bloody waste products needed to be deposited at the local garbage dump. He insisted that this should be done quickly as the bags of waste were beginning to rot. Mason requested one of the new trucks and an attendant to help with the stinking, crawling offal. When finished with the explanation he presented a leering, hillbilly grin and bowed slightly.

The Teacher asked why the waste could not be burned or buried on site. Mason laughed heartily stating that burning would not work but burying was a great idea. It could not be anywhere too close. Perhaps a spot back in the trees would work just fine. The "absolutely no" reaction from the Teacher was expected and welcomed. After quiet discussions it was decided that Mason would be allowed to go to town alone, as all the attendants wanted nothing to do with him or the disgusting cargo. He was given fifty dollars cash, told to bring back the receipts, the change and ordered to leave in one hour. In addition, he was to use his own truck.

From far back in the loft of the barn Mason secretly watched two attendants put the battery back into the old truck. Realizing that all the vans and cars were disabled brought about a feeling of anger and concern. No one was aware but all were prisoners at the commune. He did not like being held against his will and vowed that once through the gate he would not return. He was feeling healthy now and with the other members of the troupe comfortable with the Teacher's nonsense he could again embrace the open road.

Growing bored with the battery installation Mason glanced upward and caught a glimpse of movement in a third floor window of the house. There in plain view was the young lad who he had picked up on the road. The boy was waving his arms wildly. Mason waved back and smiled. Suddenly the lad was gone only to return a few moments later, holding a white object up to the window. Mason squinted, realizing something was on the white square. Moving quickly to the edge of the big doors he shaded his eyes and concentrated. The realization of what he was viewing caused Mason to shudder. The boy was holding up squares of attached toilet paper with the word HELP boldly printed in red. Mason hoped it was red marker, but knew down deep it was the boy's blood. The shock caused him to look away. Looking back, the boy was gone.

Shaken, Mason moved to the back of the loft and sat quietly in the hay gathering his thoughts. The plan of quickly moving on was still the only choice, however, the boy now consumed his thinking. A struggle of conscience played out in the dusty attic of the barn. Every part of his survival instinct agreed that running away was the best course of action. To try any form of rescue was laughable and just plain dumb. But he could not get the image of the boy's desperate appeal, carving and bleeding with the faint hope of release, out of his head. An unwanted yet strong ethical sense of responsibility for another person's safety was pulsing deep inside. This was not Mason's usual response to the possible plight of others. The feeling was new and strange, yet strong. At this time and place in his life the choice was undisputable and undeniable. Mason must stay and get the boy out of the commune. The determination and commitment to the boy made him feel light and strong like constrained piano wire ready to uncoil.

Mason's active mind began to create a rescue plan. The first step was to continue with the approved trip to town, as it was important not to arouse any suspicions. Perhaps there was assistance available that could make the rescue simple and non-threatening. This would inevitably involve going to the police. He had a massive distrust for any authority and did not believe that the local backwater cops would be effective in gaining release of the lad. Mason would do further examination upon arriving in the town, however, on the way an alternate scheme was conceived.

Mason's concerns about the local police were legitimate but understated. Not only were the town cops unable to help, it turned out they were on the payroll of the Teacher. According to the suspicious man who sold the supplies, the police not only left the commune alone, they also protected the place. On the drive back he finalized the escape plan.

Arriving back, Mason parked the truck. He told the two attendants who approached that another load of stinking garbage was to go in the morning. He had deliberately not washed out the box of the truck. As a result the leaked rot from the ripped garbage bags had accumulated in the grooves of the metal creating a pungent and sickening smell. A quick loud conversation, separated by fifteen feet, resulted in approval to leave the truck at the crest of the hill. The disgust on the attendants face told him that they would not be coming near the truck that evening. The escape vehicle was in place.

Returning to the barn Mason sat for an hour, smelling an aged odour and watching a multi-coloured wild cat as it watched him. The irony of the situation caused a weak smile. The one place that offered rest for the tiredness was the one place he could not stay. In an effort to gain closure before leaving this healing structure he propelled his favourite songs of strength high into the peaks of the barn, his voice loud and powerful. Mason would always remember the barn for simplicity and peace.

The plan was ready and it was time for implementation. Mason took a piece of heavy sticky tape used for wrapping meat and placed it gently on the sleeve of his shirt. The clear tape was invisible. He hoisted a heavy box of meat from the large cooler at the back of the barn, loaded up his last two bottles of tequila and made the way across the compound to the back door of the house. Resting the box on his knee he knocked on the door. From the outside he could hear the dead bolt open and was greeted by a red-faced older woman drying her hands with a small towel. She grunted access and Mason moved through the kitchen to a large freezer set in a recess of the wall in a long corridor that ran the length of the house. He put the meat into the freezer, closed the lid and moved down the hall. At the base of the stairs was a small room with a desk in the doorway. An attendant sat, while two others lounged in comfortable chairs further into the room.

"State your business," the man growled.

"The Teacher wanted me to return the change and receipts from the meat supplies I bought in town."

The man at the desk looked back at a larger man with brooding, drooping eyes and a boxer's nose. The leader scowled then waved a disinterested hand, dismissing both. "Top of the stairs, first right."

Mason came to the partially closed door and knocked quietly. The Teacher sat behind a large desk cluttered with papers. Tuckel's face soured some, addressing Mason with an annoyed look. "What do you want?" Mason offered the change and receipt. Tuckel tentatively took the paper and coin, quickly dropping it on the desk as if to minimize the contamination. Leaning back the Teacher said, "You don't like it here do you?"

With true sincerity Mason told the Teacher that the commune was the best place he had lived in many, many years. This seemed to perplex the man. The Teacher projected a long questioning stare, as if willing him to confess to a lie. It was easy to hold the stare as it was the truth, but unwilling to promote suspicion Mason looked away pretending submission to the man's wilting gaze. This seemed to relax Tuckel who was accustomed to winning any challenge in the commune.

"Yes it is a pretty wonderful place and you're doing a good job with the meat. All I require is commitment to the welfare of all the brethren that reside within the confines of this safe haven. The number of young people I have personally saved is staggering. Without my divine intervention they would be lost to drugs or a decadent way of living resulting in crushed spirits and destroyed souls." The man paused for a moment as if deciding whether it was worth continuing the sermon. Mason decided to assist in the decision stating, "I don't know about all that, I'm just a butcher" and then issued the dumbest look that could be mustered and believed.

The Teacher started to stiffen and then relaxed shaking his pink head and chuckling softly. The laugh was in response to the perceived belief in the great superiority he had over the simple and challenged butcher. It was with mocking pity that the Teacher said, "You can go and close the door. And for God sakes have a bath, you smell horrible."

In front of the closed door Mason soaked up the logistical information about the layout of the big house. Across from the office was an expensive looking door with a polished brass doorknob. That had to be the Teacher's bedroom. A railing separated the stairway down to the first floor and the second floor hallway. The third floor stairway was located at the end of the hall past the Teacher's room. At the other end of the hall was an open doorway with stairs that proceeded down to the main floor. This would be the servants' stairway in years long past. Having the design of the house locked in his head, Mason proceeded down the stairs to the security office.

He retrieved the meat box and turned to leave, then paused. "Do you guys drink at all?" he said in a quiet conspired way. The man behind the desk looked up quickly while the man in the corner put down a magazine. "I got some tequila you can have. My treat." The men turned deferring a decision to the leader whose eyes showed suspicion. "If you like it maybe I could get some more next time I'm in town and we could do some business." Anxious seconds went by until the man said, "Leave it." He reluctantly handed over the two bottles of good tequila to the salivating attendants.

Mason returned to the kitchen and coerced one of the kinder women into giving him some raw vegetables and a large chunk of fresh bread. He put both in the box and opened the door. With exaggerated struggles he manoeuvred the box to block the view with one hand, while pushing the deadbolt back into the chamber and applying the piece of tape over the opening so the bolt would not automatically slide into the door jam when closed. When the door was shut the assumption would be that the deadbolt was engaged.

Returning to the barn Mason relaxed and prepared for the night. Taking the Teacher's advice he had a long shower at the community facilities. He made a small, but hot fire and cooked a medium rare T-bone steak to eat with the vegetables and bread. He smoked a last remaining cigar and emptied the hiding place containing stashed money and the large knife he normally carried on his person.

The half moon was high in the sky when Mason moved. He quietly crept out to the truck and put his pack in the back. He moved across to the two new trucks and, unlike the last time, made quiet punctures in the four front tires. With the knife at the ready he moved to the back of the house and cut the telephone wire. Quietly he opened the rigged door and moved into the kitchen, staying low, concealed behind the counter. He moved through the kitchen and turned left at the hallway making for the back staircase. The sound of loud snoring was coming from the security room and not for the first time he praised tequila. Placing his feet on the outside of the stairs, to quiet the certain squeaking of the old steps, Mason made his way to the second floor. From there, hugging the wall, he went past the Teacher's door and up the third floor stairs. Fortunately the moon's light filtering through the hall window offered assistance in finding the door to the room where he had last seen the boy. In the diffused light he could make out a shiny-keyed lock. His heart sank. The door would most certainly be locked to keep the boy captive. He would have to break it down which would bring the drunken guards running. Mason paused for a minute, suppressing the urge to cry. Taking a chance he slowly turned the doorknob and to feelings of joy felt it turn in his hand. He could not believe the luck as the door slid open.

In the pale light of a small table lamp Mason realized why the door had not been locked. There was no chance for the boy to escape, as he was naked, trapped under the sickly pink bulk of Tuckel. The Teacher's hands provided a vice grip on the boy's thin biceps, while forcing the tiny shoulders into the narrow double bed. With eyes closed and wearing nothing but a toothy maniacal leer, Tuckel rode the boy with a pounding motion, reaming the lad with each uncaring and hurtful thrust. For a moment Mason froze as his mind attempted to absorb the overwhelming abomination. Firmly locked in lust the Teacher was not aware of Mason's presence. Neither was the boy who gazed at the far wall with empty lifeless eyes.

Rage helped Mason recover. He moved quickly to the side of the bed and, as Tuckel approached orgasm, grabbed the man's left ear, jerked the fat body to a stop and placed the sharp knife against the exposed throat. "If you make a sound it will give me great pleasure to spill your blood all over this room, you fat fuck."

Lust had turned to surprised fear as Mason moved the man back off the boy. The boy rolled away. With the knife very still, Mason looked into the boy's pale blue eyes and firmly told him to get dressed. When the lad did not move Mason repeated the request with a quiet urgency and saw a flicker of recognition. His attention turned back to Tuckel, tightening the grasp on the ear, staring into the teary eyes while silently imploring the man to make a sound that would justify a deadly attack. The Teacher read Mason's thoughts, remaining very mute and rigid, except for a slight involuntary shaking. He smelt urine and realized that the Teacher had wet the bed. The boy was moving like a bad mime, each motion stiff and choppy. It took longer than expected but the lad was soon dressed.

Every part of Mason wanted to slit Tuckel's throat. During those brief moments he came closer than he ever thought possible to killing another person. There was little doubt that the Teacher deserved the punishment that was only inches away, however, Mason had seen death and did not want to meet with it again in this tiny room. With a quick motion he brought the butt of the heavy blade down on the front of Tuckel's head. The man moaned but remained conscious so Mason gladly hit the bald man again, harder. He supported the heavy weight of the unconscious man as the body slipped off the bed and onto the floor. Leaking blood, the Teacher lay still.

Mason's attention turned to the boy, as he cradled the lad's head in his hands. "We are leaving. We are leaving now. I need you to walk and be quiet. If you do not do as I say they will catch us and hurt us both." The eyes woke at the mention of further pain. It was apparent that in the last two weeks the boy had received terrible abuse at the hands of Tuckel. Realizing escape might be possible, tears began to roll down the boy's cheeks. Mason brushed past the boy and then heard the sound of a heavy boot contacting flesh. The boy had kicked Tuckel in the face, probably breaking the man's jaw. Before he could react, the boy kicked the prone man again causing blood to fly from the Teacher's nose. Mason grabbed the boy's tense shoulders, moving between the lad and Tuckel. While he wanted to join in, each kick brought the two closer to discovery. He stuffed a sock in the Teacher's mouth and tied the hands by using the cord of the lamp.

Mason silently opened the door and the two slipped down the hall, descending the third floor stairs with only a small amount of noise. They came to the back exit and moved down the stairs. The loud creaks sounded like cymbal crashes to his adrenaline filled ears. He was now trusting that speed was more important than stealth. The boy stumbled on the last stair. Mason was steadying the lad when they rounded the corner into the kitchen, coming face to face with the homely young girl framed in the light of the refrigerator.

The slow steady ballet of escape came to an abrupt halt as she stared at them with surprise.

"We're leaving. Come with us now." Mason panted to the girl and the opened appliance. She took a quick breath and let out a short sharp scream. The second scream, longer and louder, was being prepared when Mason hit her flush on the mouth. Her body folded like an empty wallet. She was just settling to the kitchen floor when he and the boy hit the back step of the big house. He held on to the stumbling boy's arm as they headed across the compound at a full run. He had parked on the hill in hopes of a quiet rolling start but silence was no longer necessary. Mason turned the engine over and it caught with a roar as if it too wanted to be rid of the place. The three on a tree column gearshift was slammed into first gear with a grinding force. The gas was applied liberally and the clutch depressed quickly, resulting in the back end of the truck fish tailing as the rear tires fought for traction on the slippery dew soaked grass. The tires soon grabbed as he sped down the hill facing the last obstacle to escape.

The gate was locked down each night with a stout chain and heavy padlock. Mason had examined it earlier in the day on the way to town. The chain wrapped through a bracket of solid steel on the gate and then around a railroad tie buried deep in the ground. There would be little give on the opening side of the gate. The amateur engineers who had successful designed the system of strength obviously had a great deal of pride in their accomplishment, believing the design to be adequate. On one end it was. Fortunately, they did not build a successful design on the other end, which was only fastened to weak hinges attached to another railroad tie by four bolts. He had realized that hitting the obstacle hard on the hinged side would cause the gate to detach and swing the opposite way.

The truck hit the hinged side with the full force of the solid metal bumper causing the four bolts to give way. The gate swung wildly to the right crashing into the chain link fence, which caved inward. The fence bent to a certain point, absorbed the energy of the flying metal and then transferred the same energy back to the gate in a rebound affect that propelled it back towards the hinge side post. The gate hit the truck just behind the rear tires, knocking the back end towards the steep ditch. Mason cranked the wheel hard in the direction of the collision forced skid pushing the gas pedal to the floor. The tires sliding down into the ditch spun wildly searching for traction. The steepness of the lean caused the boy to slide across the seat ending up twisted around Mason and the steering wheel. He fought for control with a desperate strength that a man finds when faced with a sure and horrible death. The truck groaned as it reached an equilibrium, in which the force of gravity and balance met the force of the speed and mass. It was a moment where nothing could be done except see the thing through. The front left tire hit the edge of the intersecting road, which swung the physics of the life or death situation in favour of speed and mass. The lean was righted as the truck leaped onto the wide gravel road. Mason fought the tangled boy in an attempt to slow the racing machine, while trying to correct the constant skidding, first left then right. He was screaming for the boy to move as the truck began to travel into the other ditch. The lean of the truck in the opposite direction along with both occupants' efforts finally resulted in the boy ending up in a ball on the floor on the passenger's side of the truck. Mason pulled his foot off the gas, allowed the vehicle to slow and gradually pulled the truck back up onto the gravel road. Once firmly in the centre of the road he pressed on the gas peddle bringing the speed up to a quick but manageable pace.

 Mason rolled down the window and gulped in large draughts of dusty air. The dust stuck to the sweat of fear and exertion that was pouring from his body. He panted like an old dog in a hot sun. The boy laid in a tangled mess on the floor emitting uncontrollably heavy sobs. He left the boy to cry out some of the grief and pain as his vision blurred from the sweat running down his forehead. Mason's heart pounded against his chest threatening to escape or blow up. He watched closely in the rearview mirror, however, the only thing following was a dusty blackness. He travelled straight down the gravel road searching for pavement. Once found, Mason pointed the old truck south, kept under the speed limit and put as much distance as possible between them and the commune.

Mason drove the rest of the night as the boy slept, at first fitfully but soon deeply. As the sun began to rise he pulled into a secluded rest stop. The lack of motion caused the boy to wake. Mason smiled at the lad. "You slept well. We're a long way from the commune. I think we're safe. There is one more thing to do." He paused. "Do you really want to hurt Tuckel?" The question hung in the air like a bad joke.

The boy set his jaw and nodded. A burning look of hatred in the eyes overtook the sadness. Mason pulled a piece of paper out of the glove compartment. It was a directional map to the commune's location on one side and a drawing of the compound on the other. At the bottom beneath the drawing were notes written in his clearest hand, briefly describing Tuckel and the law breaking behaviours occurring. In capital letters was a description of the location and size of the marijuana crop, estimating the worth in hundreds of thousands of dollars. The corruption of the local police was also mentioned.

After a brief rest they travelled to a small city and following the signs, located the police station. It was still early so the parking lot was quiet. Mason wrote on the front of the envelope HEAD DETECTIVE and handed it back to the boy. "Go get the bastard," he stated quietly. The boy delivered the letter to a startled and sleepy desk sergeant. Then they headed east.

After driving for a couple of hours Mason pulled the truck into a quiet campground and set up the old tent. They camped for a week during which time the boy slept a great deal as the healing process began. Mason provided the meals and kept the fire going. During the first night he got quietly but seriously drunk on a bottle of whiskey. He slept in the truck offering the boy the privacy of the tent. The first few days they seldom spoke. He waited patiently for the boy to regain the personal control that Tuckel had stolen.

During the fourth day the boy began to talk. The lad's name was Jordan Milton. Jordan was fourteen years old and had run away from a small prairie city due to conflict with a strict uncaring stepfather. The biological father had left the family when Jordan was very young. No contact had occurred for many years. While the boy needed a place to go, back to the stepfather was not an option. An older aunt was a possibility, living four hours further east. After discussions it was decided that the last of the troupe would head for the aunt's home.

They remained in the campground for two more days during which time he bought the local paper and searched for any news of the commune. On the last day the police raid made the front page. According to the paper two police cars had gone to investigate an anonymous complaint. Upon producing a search warrant and showing special interest in the northern wooded area, a confrontation had occurred which resulted in shots being fired. One of the police officers was killed and one wounded. Three men were also shot dead. A standoff had occurred where the leader and a group of his followers, which included a young teenage girl, had barricaded themselves in a large barn. Reinforcements were called for from surrounding areas but the local authorities had been suspended while an investigation of corruption charges took place. After hours of futile negotiations, the police stormed the barn. The tear gas set the hay in the loft on fire. As the barn burned the commune members, now referred to as a cult, fought on. All of the cult members in the barn had perished due to the intense barrage of bullets and the raging fire that consumed the entire structure. Mason gave the article to Jordan who read it twice.

After the boy had gone to bed Mason sat at the picnic table using the last rays of the sun to reread the article and examined the large picture. A committed and brave photographer had breached the police lines and taken a photograph of the final moments of the Living Joy commune. The zoomed, black and white shot of the big loft doors showed Tuckel in a grainy white robe and swollen face carrying a rifle, while surrounded by fire and two zealous supporters. One was the droopy-eyed tequila drinker and the other was the young homely girl, screaming angrily while holding a handgun. In the end the girl had attained what he suspected she needed most; a place were she was accepted.

The drive to the home of Jordan's aunt was uneventful. For periods of time each would be lost in thoughts, reliving tragedies, while seeking relief. A natural bond between damaged souls had developed. Both had lived a great deal during the brief time of their friendship. Each respected the other's space and knew when the desire for silence was strongest. The death of Tuckel at the hands of the boy's delivered letter had balanced the scale some. There had been a piece of separation from the abuse as the boy would never have to imagine Tuckel living and hurting others. The boy took comfort in knowing that Tuckel could hurt no one while in Hell.

At one point the boy spoke up. "Why would he pick me out of everyone to hurt?" It was a valid question from a young man seeking to better understand the reason for the abuse.

"Probably because you are such a kind and innocent person. Tuckel had none of that in him and wanted all you had. The most important thing you must guard against in the future is not allowing that sick bastard to succeed in stealing those most wonderful gifts away from you." He did not know if that was the reason or not but the boy seemed very satisfied with the answer.

Arriving at Jordan's aunt's home they sat in the truck for a long time, each knowing the journey was at an end. After some small talk, the boy said, "Thank you for saving me," as tears began to run down the pale cheeks.

"I had to," he said quietly. "For you and for me." Mason offered a hippie seventies handshake, which the boy clasped with all the strength in the small arm. During that physical connection Mason attempted to project every bit of positive power and goodwill possible to the boy, as he knew the actions of Tuckel would make the boy's life difficult.

"I wish you were my brother", said the boy with strong affection. "I am and always will be," was the reply.

Mason drove slowly through the town until sighting a barber pole, went in and had the man cut off the long hair and trim the beard down low. Then he found a thrift store, buying two pairs of used jeans and three yuppie T-shirts. He checked into a cheap but clean motel, showered thoroughly and shaved. He threw his earring in a street garbage can, purchased a bottle of whiskey and in the safe but lonely confines of the hotel room watched sports and became passed out drunk. Mason Walls' hippie days were over.

Mason attempted to settle in one place and find a steady job. This was difficult as he was becoming more combative and angry each day. He began drinking heavily, craving the liquor. At the end of the day he would race from the poor jobs to the bar for an evening of drinking. He grew restless after a few days in any place. Staying a month was considered a long time. Mason embraced the life of a nomad, generally staying only short periods of time in any place, always choosing to keep moving. The wandering lifestyle caused problems with the police and, at times he was incarcerated for short periods for vagrancy, fighting or other local infractions. Although there was an ominous, fearful sound when the door of the heavy metal cell closed and the key turned, the fact there was no leaving was somehow soothing. The brief stay in a safe place was welcomed. Later he would read of lifer convicts who related a sense of security when in a locked cell, knowing the world was safe from them and they safe from the world.

This was experienced on one occasion when Mason was thrown in jail for two nights until the local authorities could figure out what to do with his presence in their small town. The emptiness and solitude was welcomed after an initial period of worry. The speedy assault of thoughts began to still in the hushed quiet. Soon the pace of thinking, both negative and positive, was slowed to a point where each notion could be examined and analyzed for content and meaning. Something strange began to occur, especially with hurtful self-defeating images. When looked at slowly and with an effort to define the significance of the mental picture, negatives would shrink and cower before the critique while the positives would grow leaving him feeling stronger. Human contact only occurred when meals were served. He was silent during the interaction, accepting the food and enjoying the flavours of the home-cooked meals. For two days he did not speak, causing peacefulness to settle over his spirit.

The release from jail resulted in a strange sadness. While he wanted out of the cage a large piece of his consciousness wished to stay and further examine the newly discovered potential. A wondrous surface had been scratched. An exciting possibility had been uncovered with the realization that the potential energy available was huge, provided the courage and strength could be committed to the task of personal exploration. For a brief period Mason enjoyed the clarity of existence, tasting fully the flavours of life, while living in the moment. The sun was brighter, the trees greener and the drive out of town in the old truck interesting as the entire contour of the road, with every bump and sway, was appreciated.

He moved on to the next town basking in the glow of possibilities. Taking a job as a dishwasher in a small diner he rented a tidy one-room motel cabin for a month and waited for the next step in the process. Each day Mason attempted to stay focused on the world around him. While initially stilled, the endless parade of negative thoughts soon began their incessant march. Each day the struggle to stay optimistic became more difficult. He sought the hidden message of salvation with an angry patience that was forced and contrived. The excitement he had felt after leaving jail began to be replaced by a caustic disillusionment as he bitterly strove to continue the process. He relentlessly searched his thoughts and with an unhealthy hope turned each corner or met each new person with the expectation that the answer would be given. Night and day his life became a compulsive search. The hunt was the sole purpose as his entire future became conditional on finding this one response from the world that would provide the direction. Unfortunately when no epiphany occurred he became overwhelmed and began drinking to excess.

Mason stayed drunk for three days going back to work on Monday morning hung over and filled with negative, angry energy. After two days of being miserable with everyone, including the boss, he was fired. With two weeks remaining on the rent he brought in many bottles of alcohol and drank away the time. In a horribly misguided sense of purpose his growing addiction willed him to believe that the goal of finding a positive path would be enhanced with a few drinks. Of course, the first drink slowed the thinking and captured moments of manufactured peace. To improve the sense of wellbeing he drank more with a false assurance that if one drink could provide some peace many drinks would bring about a lasting joy. Unfortunately, each drink found the prize more elusive, only intensifying the negative and depressive feelings.

On the twelfth day of eating little and drinking everything, he awoke shaking. Hot and cold sensations electrified his body causing nerves to scream, muscles to flex uncontrollably and eyes to roll. He just made it to the bathroom as his body began to purge. The retching was so powerful it felt as though major organs would be dispelled into the toilet bowl. With nose running and tears streaming down his straining face, bowels loosed. After the body's initial reaction to the appalling treatment, Mason lay in the filth attempting to catch his breath and slow a racing heart. The coolness of the bathroom tile eased the heat of his burning cheeks. The moment of calm was short as the retching soon began again, this time leaving the putrid water red. With desperation he held onto the toilet bowl as if it were a life preserver in a choppy, stormy sea.

He awoke blind, surrounded by a gothic blackness. Still clutching the porcelain he realized his arms were beginning to cramp badly. Releasing the grip offered a brief moment of relief until he slipped from the bowl and slammed his head on the adjacent bathtub. Groaning he tried to activate his mind and make a simple decision on what to do next. As the senses cleared the strong foul odour of sickness and decay covered him like a heavy, itchy blanket, stifling and choking. He fought to control the nausea as a deadly thought crept into his mind. The thought circled and intensified as his aching body lay in the putrid mess created by his inability to manage himself and his world. It was a question that captured his total attention. *If life is so hard, why Live?* The seven words formed a huge offensive billboard in his head, flashing and screaming out for attention as if attempting to overpower the landscape and take complete control. He attempted to rise and found it was only possible to get to his knees. The room spun causing the deadly thought to blur and recede. He stripped of the soiled clothes and turned on the shower. The hot water calmed his mind and cleansed his body. Shivering he climbed into bed and escaped into sleep.

Leaving the disgust of the motel cabin Mason moved on, travelling from place to place no longer searching for direction. His sole purpose now became avoiding the clear burning question that seemed to be lurking around each corner and jumping to the forefront of his thinking when he least expected. He no longer struggled to stay at a job, as he could not find one. In addition, the old truck began to make noises that seemed unnatural. He did not have the energy or money to ascertain the difficulties so, with a sense of futility, pointed the truck to the west and like a chased man atop a dying horse, rode the truck to its ultimate end. He left the good old steed on the outskirts of a large town in the western foothills. The engine had ceased due to a lack of oil. He received fifty dollars from a garage owner, who had a replacement engine, and left on guilty feet realizing that his neglect had killed his metal companion.

    He used part of the fifty to book a room for a month in an old motel. The owner, Grace Moore, was a lady in her mid-fifties. Her long hair was dyed to brittleness and frozen in place with multiple hair products. She wore makeup that looked heavy and thick like flesh-coloured putty. Her eyes were rimmed in black and projected loneliness. Her mouth was the reddest red he had ever seen and scarcely hid a hunger for companionship. She was the type of person who needed to tell strangers her entire story. As a result she offered her history, thoughts and feelings up to the public like samples of a new product at a grocery store. Mason learned that her husband had died in a head on collision a year ago, while coming home from a Shriner Club smoker, leaving her in financial and emotional distress. Just when she was ready to give up on the motel, an offer to purchase had been presented by a suited man with little glasses and small beady eyes, working for a large developer representing an even larger hotel chain. She quickly sold the land and building for more than she had ever imagined. The motel would be closing in a month and she would be moving to live near her sister in the east. As it turned out Mason was the only patron. She gave him a very cheap rate on a room, as the money was not important but the company was desperately needed.

    With swinging hips she showed him to the small room right beside the office. He asked if there was a restaurant in the area. Grace offered to make a sandwich for two bucks and he agreed, paying her and asking if she would deliver it to his room in an hour, as he wanted a shower. She agreed and with a twinkle in her hungry black eyes, left.

When the woman brought the sandwich Mason had wrapped a towel around his waist and was sporting a semi-erection. She had changed into a tight fitting dress that was two sizes too small. It was obvious she was naked underneath as the dress hugged the sagging flesh. He ate the sandwich with ravenous hunger and then inquired about dessert. At that point Grace removed her dress.

The rest of the day and into the night was spent in lovemaking. It reminded him of the sexual escapades with Sara. What the woman gave up in age and firmness of body she returned in enthusiasm. She left once and returned with a bottle of bourbon and two packages of cigarettes. During lulls in the sex the woman would talk about her life and adventures.

Both got quite drunk with the woman eventually staggering back to her own room, stating she would return in the morning for hangover sex. The sexual activity and release had relaxed him allowing a feeling of ease to overtake his body. Unfortunately, once the lady was gone his mind began churning with all thoughts returning back to the suicidal billboard that asked the question he desperately wished to avoid. The question insisted that an answer be given and when he could not find a reply that was suitable, the sign screamed "loser" in loud voices that reverberated around his head like very loud, poorly played, distorted music. Mason covered his ears and began to cry only ending when tears brought on the release of sleep.

True to her words Grace returned in the morning moving slower but wanting more sex. Mason accommodated her demands and then she left to run errands. He slept all day and when he awoke it was dark. The only light in his dark world was being offered by passing cars and the question that blinked on and off as his thoughts returned to it. He lay on the bed sweating, with a deep sadness building inside. He was totally alone in the world. That realization increased the despair to the point where an ache in his chest began to grow becoming physically painful and making it difficult to breath. He craved for a heart attack that would end everything, putting a stop the agony.

By the morning Mason was exhausted. Tears came easily with a remembered thought of loss or the prediction of an empty future inhabited only by the repeating haunting question. He began to believe that total insanity was his destination. Driving the despair was the realization he had nothing, would be nothing and, most damaging, believed strongly that he was nothing.

Later in the day, Mason dressed and walked to a shopping centre down the road, buying a couple bottles of bourbon and a length of rope. On the way back to his room Grace let him know she would not be home that night as she was staying with friends. He sat in his room drinking and smoking cigarettes feeling only weary, pounding despair. The question continued to grow in size finally pulsing like a beacon of intoxicating light reluctantly drawing him into its frigid, icy glow. With his body and mind steeled by the steady supply of liquor and a massive amount of hopelessness he surrendered and finally addressed the question that had been seeking an audience since its discovery. He faced the question head on, drinking and searching for an answer. When he could not find one he made a decision.

Moving around the motel Mason stumbled to a stand of trees. He attacked the trees with drunken motions, believing that everything would now bow to his purpose. Phantom branches, unseen in the darkness, slowed his progress whipping his head and stinging his face. Bushes became barriers as he attempted to crash through their bulk. Finally, the bush released the resistance, propelling him into a small clearing where he landed face down on the cold earth. He lay panting and sobbing, moaning for his losses and reluctantly wishing for someone or something to stop the final act and change the outcome. Silently the forested clearing would only watch as events had reached a point where the only one who could stop the process was helpless.

Mason moved slowly to the largest tree and after many tiring attempts threw the rope over a stout overhanging branch. At one end he made a sliding knot, while tying the other end to the base of a sapling growing beside its much older kin. His drunken mind began to clear as he measured the distances, climbed up on an old rotting stump, placed the rope around his neck and stepped into the air.

The nylon rope bit into his neck and swung him like a sack of twitching humanity. While Mason's mind had firmly set the course of action, his body involuntarily rejected the outrage, reacting in a violent way. He bounced and jerked while clawing at the rope. His eyes bulged, his ears began to burn and his mouth opened as his tongue attempted to escape. Fireworks of bright lights exploded in his brain as the muscle movements increased grotesquely.

Suddenly there was a sharp painful jerk, followed by deep total blackness.

Chapter Four
GRASS

Humanity has endlessly pondered the mysterious irrational outcomes of random or planned events since organized human existence evolved from the caves. Two ancient hunters are standing beside each other on the edge of a cliff searching for game, the ground gives way under one causing a death plunge to the valley below, while the other goes home and sires many children. The black plague sweeps through a medieval town killing an entire family, but leaves one of the children, with the same gene pool, untouched. A wire, common to many planes, shorts out in one specific plane causing it to fall from the sky. When the plane crashes all are killed but for one person or conversely all survive with only one dying. A man who braves the rigors of fierce prolonged combat comes home without a scratch but dies tragically, stepping out of the shower, when the one plane with one faulty wire falls on his home. What decides the course of a killer tornado and who decides where lightning strikes? Many leave the decision to an omnipotent being. Others see it to be a female decision as in Mother Nature or Mother Earth. Still others believe incomprehensible supernatural powers control situations. It could be fate, karma, luck, destiny, a fluke, an accident or a chance occurrence that would never happen again even if all the conditions were recreated. The most logical way to understand these enigmatic occurrences is to use the most illogical of methods. What usually works is simple and unconditional acceptance. This certainly was the case that morning and would often be repeated when Mason Walls attempted to understand the reason for the second chance offered on that drunken night of very bad decisions.

Consciousness told Mason that heaven had warmth, trees and a strange-timed, repeated ticking noise. It also had very deep physical pain. His neck was aching, while his eyes were swollen and burning. He looked around the small meadow realizing he had survived the suicide attempt. He remembered jumping off the stump and thrashing at the end of the nylon rope like a man whose pockets were filled with electricity. Rising slowly to his feet Mason pieced together what had happened. The weight of his body, magnified by the erratic movements, had caused the sapling, struggling to put down a solid roots system due to the competition with the large tree, to be torn from the ground. He had fallen, hitting his head on the base of the hanging tree, as there was blood on his head and on the bark. Strangely the most pressing question was the cause of the distant ticking noise that filled the air. It was as if a large clock was fastened to his ear. Gauging the direction of the sound Mason moved towards it, carefully making the way through the dense thicket and coming out the bush into a line of spaced tall trees living on a carpet of thick green spring grass. He walked through the trees and into an open field of shorter grass. His mind could not grasp what this place was. He began to think that perhaps heaven did have pain and that he was dead. He stood on the edge of the field and breathed deep, hurting his raw throat but inhaling the most wonderful smell of freshly cut wet grass. The odour was wonderfully pure reminding him of long ago joy. Suddenly a round white object landed in the opened grass and rolled to a stop. His legs buckled in amazement.

Mason was on a golf course. The sound that had drawn him was the revolving sprinklers, which moved in circles propelled by a metal spring-loaded flange attached to the spout of the sprinkler. The flange bounced endlessly against the stream of water, moving the direction of the flow in a circle, through small increments. Far away the system had one song. Up close, the timing of the sprinklers sounded different, causing each to have its own particular voice. It was beautiful music to his now alert ears. He sat in the short grass on the edge of the fairway and waited patiently for the owner of the ball to approach. The man noticed Mason and came over with a friendly smile. When close the golfer stopped and stood in shocked silence.

"Are you all right?" the man asked with the voice of amazement.

"Yes," Mason croaked, moving a hand to his throbbing neck and discovering the rope still attached. "Industrial accident," he stated with a painful snort.

"Do you want some help?"

"I'll be fine. Go finish your round," he whispered.

After the man was gone, Mason rose knowing that the strange presence of the rope man would make a nineteenth hole story and was sure to be investigated. He gingerly made the way back to the motel after removing the rope from his neck and coiling it into a tight circle. Thankfully Grace was not around as he went into the room, locked the door, stripped his clothes, climbed into bed and collapsed under the weight of the previous night.

Grace woke him two days later when she returned from the dance and a subsequent road trip to a gambling spot four hours away. She was stunned by Mason's appearance and medical condition. She responded like a favourite aunt rather than a lover, fussing over him in an attempt to ensure recovery. At his request, no professional medical assistance was provided. He had severe whiplash that took a week of stillness before any sideway head movements could be attempted. The neck skin was broken and torn from the coarseness of the nylon rope and he had a gash on the back of his head, but he was alive, as his nurse kept saying repeatedly.

Grace stayed with him almost constantly for a week. Mason believed partly it was to provide care, but mostly to ensure no further self-harm was attempted. She did not attempt to make him explain the actions, as if she had an understanding in a secret place of why a person would be driven to such lengths to find escape. After a week he was sitting up in bed and talking more then he had in a long while. At one point in the conversation Mason spoke of the night in detail. Grace sat quietly for the first time since he had known her and did not interrupt. When he had finished talking, they shared a common moment and then she slapped him hard across the face.

"Don't you ever try that again. Life is too precious." Her words spoke of tragedy. Mason knew of her husband's death but sensed another loss somehow deeper and more painful, hidden from all. At that moment he loved her for the gift of caring. They cried together for a long time and then she pushed him back on the bed, straddled his hips and gently rode him until both reached an intense climax.

The convalescence for the suicide attempt proceeded over the next days. Grace closed the motel, while managing to get a one-month extension on the possession date by the development company. After long periods of sleep Mason would lie in bed or sit by the window and listen to the soothing sound of Grace's voice speaking of nothing. When she was off running errands, he would think of the future. An idea had begun to form that was simple and hugely appealing. The most important part was the hope that it might possibly bring happiness.

Grace encouraged him to walk around the motel for exercise. Mason would pass the spot where his entrance into the bush had occurred. He physically shuddered when reliving the drunken moments of his near fatal folly. Grace watched the discomfort with each passing, asking at one point if he wished to go into the trees. He just turned away and continued walking laps around the condemned motel.

During the final weeks Mason sat quietly watching Grace put closure to twenty years in the motel business. She provided a commentary on the history of the building, the reason her husband wanted to buy the place, upgrades completed, rooms painted and interesting people that had stayed during their tenure as owners. She spoke of the two births that had occurred in rooms nine and eleven, bringing joy in the case of a young couple hurrying to the wife's parent's home and a worried sadness to the single mother, with three children under eight already in tow. She and husband Bert had felt joy in waving goodbye to the young couple and sorrow for the family who left quietly, but not unnoticed, in the middle of the night as the mother had no money to pay. A wonderful old man had stopped for an overnight and stayed three months before dying peacefully in bed. Bert had opened all the windows, flipped the mattress and put a travelling salesman in the same room that night. The next day upon leaving the man marvelled at the restful night sleep. They were not surprised as the old man was a gentle person and both believed that the kind spirit had stayed behind to welcome the next occupant. She told him of the two young working girls, who were wonderful guests, bringing extra business and welcomed energy. The girls plied their trade constantly, making the far end of the motel jump as paying customers lined up. The scarlet ladies, as their hired man named them, stayed for three weeks until all began to notice the uncustomary appearance of black and white police cars in the area. The girls too, left in the middle of the night with many giggles, providing full payment and a tip to the owners for being *too cool.* She laughed about the two little people who were so short in stature yet so large in the zest for life and the love they showed in every gesture and secret look shared. She cried when reliving the night where Bert had kicked the door down on number five after hearing a woman's screams. Her boyfriend was beating her for flirting with another man at the bar. Bert, a large man, attempted to intervene and was attacked by the man. Her husband had knocked the coward to the ground and went to help the woman who turned on Bert with a vicious misplaced anger. Grace lost her composure and hit the woman with the handle of the broom she had grabbed from the corner of the office on the way to the ruckus. The couple, now battered and bruised, ran cursing to their car and sped away in the night with the woman pressed close, hugging and rubbing the man's cheek. Bert had wanted to call the police fearing for the woman's safety. Grace refused, stating the woman got what she deserved. In the end, Bert and Grace hugged in the quiet of the night and were thankful they had each other. There were stories of conventions, marriages, funerals, birthday parties, conferences and other planned events. At times it was a very difficult existence, but she had loved most of it, disliked some of it and hated almost none of it.

"I like to think we helped a lot of people a little over the years. I know Bert believed we did. He always said, just to help one person is all that matters." She took a deep breath and let out a content sigh.

Mason watched her with blurred eyes. "Well you sure helped your last customer," he said quietly.

"And he has helped me say goodbye to this old place. Bert would have liked you, Mason. You have a very special something inside. Your biggest problem is you just don't know it." She paused for a moment letting the words hang in the air, as if hoping he would pluck them up, store them in a place of easy access, use them often and eventually believe them.

As was the practice every evening since closing the motel, Grace turned on the No Vacancy sign at dusk just to let motorists on the highway know that there were no rooms available. She said it also left the motel with some of the past glory, when it was the only place where weary travellers could get some rest. He listened to the fluorescent swirling letters of the sign quietly hum, attracting the newest spring insects to the glow. The companionship of the sign was somehow comforting, helping to fill a little of the vast emptiness he experienced each day. The moment offered the necessary courage to complete a task that had been looming since he began his walks around the motel.

Leaving the comfort of the light he moved around the building making his way across the now flattened field, easily finding the still trampled path. The large hanging tree was evident from the field, stretching above the line of the other trees, as if Lord and Master of all. Using the tree as a marker, he made for the small meadow, finding it easily. He stood quietly for a long time absorbing and becoming a part of the clearing. The scene promoted feelings of an oppressive empty sadness, while the gentle moonlight offered a sense of beauty and hope. The complex conflicting emotions pulsed through his body and mind changing direction with rapid speed and intensity like turning a hard shower from hot to cold. The coldness of death blanketed him with a chilling reminder of the past, while the warmth of living attempted to penetrate the covering and bring the necessary heat to commit to the future. The weight of both fell on his shoulders like a heavy falling object forcing his body to the ground. On his knees Mason waited as cold and hot sensations ripped through the sensitive, rapid-firing nerve endings demanding a commitment to life or surrender to death. No longer could he avoid the decision. The previous attempt at suicide had been impulsive and while drunk. He was now sober and thinking clearly. It was here that the haunting question must be answered. Thus, in the angelic moonlit surroundings of the beautiful little meadow life and death fought for supremacy. As an entity he seemed to disappear while ancient forces, vastly larger than one man, sought to dictate the future.

Ultimately the question *Why Live?* was left unanswered, while a more important decision was made with determination. In the end Mason simply chose to live, which would prove to be a more difficult decision. The heavy air seemed to lighten as the chill on his spirit drifted upwards and left the meadow. Death had departed, as it was not needed this night. With a heavy weight of tiredness resting on his person Mason rose and moved over to the sapling that leaned at a pitched angle. With his hands he dug out the wet soil around the young tree until it could be straightened. He pulled more earth from around the base creating a shallow hole. Into the hole, the nylon rope was gently laid, then buried. Mason pulled more earth and winter compost from the meadow's floor and placed it around the tree ensuring it was firmly anchored in the ground. Then using small heavy steps he packed the earth tightly around the sapling in a circled slow shuffling dance. He felt a connectedness and kinship with the tree. His actions that night had offered both a chance to live.

There were no more tears as Mason turned and faced Grace standing small and shivering at the edge of the meadow. She had watched the decision making process in silence, accepting the importance of the evening. Her cheeks were glistening in the moonlight. They embraced tightly, giving unselfishly a commitment to forever friendship and love. He put his coat around her shoulders leaving the meadow wrapped in the peace of nature and bathed in the magic of a spring night.

The next two weeks were a whirlwind of activity. The results of the impromptu ceremony held in the moonlit meadow seemed to free

Grace from worry, allowing for a release of previously held energy. She moved quicker and with a committed purpose, as if wanting to prepare the motel for its final rest. Mason marvelled at the pace she managed all day and the intensity of love making every night.

The last hours in the motel included a community activity. Grace had called an open house for any who wished to visit the place for the last time. A photographer and reporter from the local newspaper came for a story and took pictures of Grace and the motel. She insisted that Mason be in the photographs. He smiled warmly and genuinely for the picture, as that was how he felt the whole day. He was a part of a special send-off for a wonderful lady and the business that had allowed the community to grow.

They woke early and prepared for the arrival of the movers. Grace had eliminated many of the possessions so it did not take long to load the boxes and furniture. The movers, all burly in appearance, were polite yet business-like and the job was done quickly and efficiently. Mason helped load Grace's older model car and then she gave him a ride to the bus. Being early they waited in a small pretty park across the street from the bus depot. Little was said as they sat close together on a park bench and held hands.

As he prepared to enter the bus she held him close and whispered, "Just live. That's all you need to do, just live."

She handed him a copy of the daily newspaper for reading on his journey. Mason watched her closely as the bus pulled away. Soon she was gone from view. On the way out of town the bus drove past the old motel. Already men were on site pounding long wooden stakes in the ground. The red survey tape, tied to the tops of the stakes, danced in the dusty wind as the workers in shiny hardhats unloaded heavy machines, which would soon reduce the building to a pile of memories. Above it all was the presence of the hanging tree that looked down from its great height in safety. Mason began to experience a feeling of sadness until he opened the newspaper and there on the front page was a large picture of the motel, Grace and a smiling man who seemed not to have a care in the world. In addition, there were ten, one hundred dollar bills and a small note that read, *You are Loved! G.* Mason felt the smile spread across his face as the bus gathered speed and left the town behind. In so many ways he left a richer man for this amazing and almost deadly stop in his journey.

The realization that he had gone from almost certain death to a place that brought back so many childhood memories of fun and excitement was too much of a coincidence to ignore. The golf course was a place where the love of a father and son had been experienced. It had brought back wonderful memories of his Dad, chasing away the horrific and traumatic images of murder that had filled Mason's thoughts for so long. Memories of success and contentment were rekindled as he smelled the freshly cut grass and watched the small white ball effortlessly cut through the air. He had searched endlessly and with a self-destroying effort for some sort of message that would offer a much needed direction. Just when the final hope had been abandoned a strange and curious sound had led him to a place he never would have gone. He had not found any prolonged peace since leaving his birth city. Perhaps Mason could now find it on a golf course.

When making the plan it had been important to obtain employment, as it would be necessary to buy equipment and pay for the green fees necessary. Unfortunately many of the seasonal staff had been hired at the local courses. Mason eventually got work in a grocery store from four until midnight. With these hours he could play golf everyday in the morning. He used the generous gift provided by Grace to buy a used set of clubs and a new carry bag. His first trip to a driving range was both exciting and disappointing. He had not hit a golf ball since he was eleven. After a few whiffed swings he sat on a bench and struggled to remember everything Gus had said about the game. It was quite pleasant to recall his father as a teacher, showing him the fundamentals of the golf swing with patience and care. The memories turned out to be long on emotions and short on helpful techniques. He realized assistance would be necessary to develop a solid golf swing. As a result Mason spent the first two hours watching other customers practice. Most of the swings were accomplished with chopping and lurching motions. Some were very slow and ponderous, while others were fast and slashing, both in take away and follow through. He was becoming frustrated when an older white haired gentleman arrived. The man walked with a smooth confidence as if belonging at the range. Mason watched as the man approached the teeing area, stretched and then took numerous practice swings with the club moving in a smooth rhythm. It was a joy to watch, as the swing was so tension free and beautiful. He waited anxiously while the man delivered the first swing with a short, lofted club. Mason marvelled at the ball flight but was more excited about the solid click of the club striking the ball. While the swing appeared smooth it did not hide the power in the coiled body that made the ball explode off the club. He watched in awe, as each swing appeared identical to the previous effort.

Mason waited some minutes then approached the man taking the spot directly beside. Watching the man hit longer irons Mason waited for a pause and then spoke up. "Could you show me how to do that?"

The man looked up in surprise and then chuckled warmly. "I've been working on this swing since I was eight years old. But I can show you some things to do and not to do."

For the next three hours the two men stood talking and hitting golf balls. The white haired man would hit a shot to demonstrate a principal or make a point about the importance of a certain aspect of the swing or movement of the body. Once the man warmed to the process of teaching a very keen but inexperienced golfer, the information flowed out like contents of a spilt glass of milk. Mason soaked up the offerings with enthusiasm, storing and consuming the information until his head was swarming with the bees of golfing knowledge.

Mason returned to the range everyday hitting thousands of balls in an effort to improve. The natural athletic ability along with a determined commitment and prolonged practice assisted him in improving each day until he no longer worried about missing the ball. As he began to hit the balls hard, additional problems arose with the flight bending to the left or right. He recalled what the white haired man had said and changed his stance or hands while constantly checking the swing plane. Amongst the difficulties and frustrations one important thought kept surfacing. Mason was having a great time with each ball he hit. He realized that this would be a life long commitment as he could feel a growing passion each day to this silly but sensational game.

During the summer and early fall as Mason continued to work at improving, he found that the intake of alcohol decreased dramatically. He would have a few beers after each round, but was often too tired from golfing and working to drink much. At night he slept soundly, awakening refreshed and ready for another day of excitement on the golf course. Even work was acceptable as it offered the means to passionately play the game that seemed to help him make sense of the world.

When the snow had fallen and the passion rested, old ghosts from the past began to move in the shadows. At first Mason noticed interrupted sleep, awakening suddenly in the middle of the night and feeling fearful. He began to notice certain edginess in his manner at work. The appetite for food decreased while the desire for alcohol increased. Thinking it may be the lack of exercise he did push-ups and sit-ups until his muscles ached. In an effort to connect with the game, he bought golf magazines and putted for endless hours on the cheap thin carpet in the small living room. However, nothing seemed to suppress the growing uneasiness that began to build each day.

By early December Mason was getting drunk almost every night after work. He again became a solitary drinker, sipping straight whiskey from the bottle and putting ball after ball into a water glass placed on its side. The practice would still the thoughts until the one ball became two. Then he would put the putter away and just drink from the bottle. Mason would often awaken in the chair or on the old comfortable couch fully clothed and hurting.

He took another job in an effort to fill the time and make some extra money. He tried to avoid buying liquor in hopes that unavailability would make him want it less, but the plan proved ineffective, as he could not sleep, prowling around the tiny apartment angry and frustrated. The next day the apartment was restocked with whiskey as another alcohol-free night could not be tolerated.

Mason watched the weather reports each day, wildly cheering when the temperature rose. Lengthening days and the growing heat of the sun were celebrated making the time pass swiftly and happily. Black depression ruled when the weather turned sour and snowflakes filled the air. These days drove him to the bottle, seeking an artificial escape from the torment of waiting. Work colleagues and other acquaintances steered clear during the dark times as he emitted a toxic aura that people could sense and undoubtedly feared.

Just when Mason was prepared to seek medical assistance the weather turned sunny and the snow began to melt. At first, small puddles appeared but soon the water was running down the street feeding the hungry drains. Bare ground was sought and when found, worshipped with hopeful glee. Soon large patches of brown grass became the norm as the snow retreated and the weather warmed, bringing the first stinging spring rains. He watched the metamorphosis as the rains nurtured the ground causing the snow piles to shrink and the brown earth become flecked with bright green shoots, first quietly and then with a roar of colour. Hitting wedges in a muddy schoolyard were the first golf swings of the year causing the winter sleep to leave his body. The excitement of the coming of spring resulted in a noticeable decline in alcohol consumption. The fears that had lived in the darkness of his winter desolation were quickly expelled upon hitting the first golf shot of the season. The swing felt smooth and natural. He hit balls everyday and would spend the weekend at the range until the courses opened. As spring mastered winter and began its rule Mason played as much as possible. The better he played the more Mason searched for competition on the different courses. He looked for the best players at different venues, watching their technique while dreaming of being included amongst their number. He began to seek the best players, challenging himself each time he teed up the ball. With each success his golf game improved remarkably. Mason continued to work hard, playing and practicing every day. Gaining confidence in his golfing abilities he began to enter tournaments. At first he needed to adjust to the heightened competitiveness but soon became comfortable and began to win his share. If he did not win he placed near the top of the standings. The good play gave him recognition amongst the top golfers in the city. In mid-July Mason played the city championship and won the two-day tournament in a playoff. He cut the large picture from the front page of the newspaper's sport section. The photograph showed him smiling and kissing the winner's trophy.

The city victory provided the possibility of golf course employment. A tough-looking grizzled greens keeper, with a large potbelly, interviewed Mason for a maintenance position at an exclusive country club. The man asked him many questions and then offered the job. The hours were six in the morning until three in the afternoon. He would also have free golf and all the range balls he could hit. The happiness could not be contained as Mason drove home with the windows opened loudly singing along to the AM radio.

The summer passed with remarkable speed. The job was wonderful as it offered the beauty of experiencing a sunrise every morning, hard physical wonderfully dirty work and the smell of cut grass each day. Mason was quickly accepted by the other workers and enjoyed their company. He again had friends. Most importantly, every day after work he could play golf on a beautiful course. On his lunch breaks he would hit balls and on rained out days, when not doing maintenance on the equipment, Mason would don a rain suit and play thirty-six holes of gloriously lonely golf. He spent most of his time at the golf course. It became a place of sanctuary and escape from the outside world. In this green cathedral Mason understood the rules, which were ancient and confirmed. He could worship the beauty of nature and the simplicity of purpose. The job and venue suited his needs wonderfully and he began to believe that perhaps he had found a place in the world that could offer the contentment that had been so very elusive.

During this time his alcohol consumption dropped off noticeably. In addition, the nature of the drinking changed. Mason would still get smashed with fellow workers but the blackouts ended and the angry drunken meanness was no more. There did not appear to be the need to forget, as his brain became the thinking instrument it was designed to be, not some out of control machine bent on complete annihilation. The dreaded fear of living that usually prompted the bouts of heavy drinking seemed to have been shed. There was no place for the self-loathing in such a beautiful place, while doing such a pure and uncorrupted activity.

As autumn painted its colours across the land, a twinge of worry began to grow. On the last day of the year the crew had a going away party. It was a great time as many looked forward to the winter and new experiences. Mason hid the growing fear behind a cloak of good cheer, wishing everyone the very best. All he had was the golf course and he had no idea what to do without the nurturing its majesty and serenity provided. On the way home, in the privacy of his car, Mason cried the tears of a worried man. At one point he pulled off the road and sat sobbing, unable to continue the drive.

He got his job back at the grocery store for the winter and rather than fight the alcohol Mason gave in to the strong magnetic pull, accepting that without the golf course he could not fight the powerful urge. He worked everyday, saving as much money as possible and drank every night to quiet the thoughts, voices and self-defeating questions. The acceptance seemed to change the reaction to the alcohol making his emotions flat like a white piece of paper. He noticed a different emotional variation. There was no joy or excitement, nor were there any extreme negative reactions. The anger was not as prevalent and what there was did not explode outward or inward, but seeped like the constant ooze of heavy oil spilling from a broken tanker covering the beauty of the sea in disgust.

The days plodded by like an old slow-moving horse as Mason waited for spring. There was not the watchfulness or the count down of the previous year. He used the nightly drinking to dull everything in his world. Even the raging thoughts of loss and helplessness seemed to give up, wrapped in alcohol hibernation. The only energy available was for working and moving ghostlike through daily activities, drifting past the moments unaware and uncaring.

The coming of spring was not heralded by the normal small signs that brought a growing sense of excitement but rather by the appearance of three robins on a piece of a neighbour's lawn. The sight was like an alarm clock waking Mason from the four month drunken stupor. He watched the robins, stunned as if an evil spell had been lifted. The plunge into depression and sadness had been quick and merciless upon leaving the golf course. The soaring of spirit occurred when he returned. He felt rejuvenated upon attending the first day of work. The old feelings of self-worth returned along with a strong golf swing, offering an optimistic outlook for the coming season.

During his second year at the course, the social connections increased dramatically. Mason became well-known to members, both as a mower operator and a very talented golfer. Younger players wanted his company as he offered a challenge and a benchmark to gauge the state of their own game. Better players wanted the competition he provided. Mason enjoyed the game with anyone and approached each round with a singular purpose, not playing against the individuals in the foursome, but directing all his energy towards achieving the best score possible. This was the true measure of the game.

One evening after work, he started a twilight round with energy and excitement blistering the first seven holes in record time and with a record score. Moving quickly Mason caught the group in front on the ninth tee box where he was invited to join. The three older members were men of means. While two were quite pleasant, the third was a short-tempered gruff man with a large moustache who carried an air of superiority. The man was grudgingly inclusive until learning that Mason worked at the golf course. There was a noticeable change in the man's attitude, which turned from stern tolerance to non-acceptance upon gaining this knowledge. Mason was ready to leave the group when a golf cart pulled up and the most beautiful woman he had ever seen got out, approached, and hugged the moustached man he was beginning to dislike. The man's attitude changed again as a warm smile appeared and kind words were spoken to a loving daughter. Mason watched the young woman with fascination as she carried herself with grace and class, while looking at him with a haughty stare. He struggled to hold the challenging gaze, but soon turned and pretended to search out an invisible object located down the fairway. It was obvious the woman knew the other members of the foursome. The daughter asked his name in a bored voice. Mason replied too quickly. She knew that her beauty was having an effect and with exaggerated female mannerisms began to tease Mason in front of the three older men. Her father was noticeably bothered by the conduct. The man was especially bothered when the person receiving the attention was so far beneath the daughter's elevated social position. She was an astute young woman who sensed the uneasiness of both men and reveled in their discomfort.

It was very apparent why her presence impacted so powerfully. She wore very tight white shorts that hinted of transparency. As the men continued to play, Mason constantly and secretly glanced at the magnificent buttocks. Her sandals were simple, yet expensive, displaying a beautiful pedicure complete with painted toes. At times she took off the shoes and walked sensually through the grass, moving quietly and smoothly like a dancer or a cat tentatively walking through water. She wore a tight pink golf shirt with the top three buttons undone, showing off a tremendous cleavage. Her face was perfect, wearing makeup that enhanced the tanned beauty and brilliant white teeth. Her whole head was framed by naturally blond wavy hair, which moved in the wind but always seemed to return to the desired location. After four or five holes she suggested that Mason put his clubs on the empty cart she was driving. With shaking hands he loaded the golf bag and rode with her the rest of the round.

The focus of the conversation was mostly about her, which Mason accepted with total cooperation. Her name was Victoria Sanderson. She was a university graduate in business administration. College life had ended two years ago and she had accepted that it was time to work for a living. After six months in an accounting firm she developed hatred for balancing numbers and at the insistence of her father, Sam Sanderson, had joined the thriving family business. Her father had started a car dealership many years ago and parlayed the profits into a multi-million dollar company, diversifying into many different areas in the local community. Known in the city as Super Sam, due to starring in car commercials where "the Best Darn Deals in Town" were stalked and hunted, the man was well recognized and very powerful, with many owing a pay check to the diversified business ventures. She was quick to tell Mason that her mother was dead, she had no siblings and her father was very protective as she was very precious to the important man. Mason listened with a mixture of fascination and dread. She seemed almost daring him to become involved with her. He realized that she was playing him like an expert boxer, dancing nimbly about the ring, knowing the opponent could be knocked out at any time.

They continued to talk as the round proceeded. She seemed impressed with his golf game spurring him on with sultry words of encouragement or poses that highlighted her stunning body in a welcoming way. Mason began to feel intoxicated, as her movements made him feel dizzy and light headed. With her father watching and glowering she began a sensual seductive mating ritual full of innuendos. Mason tried to calm the rapidly rising passion but the intense promise of illicit pleasure, along with the woman's overwhelming beauty and the aphrodisiac of money and power, was too potent to resist. Beneath the strong emotions and burning sensations he knew that being with the woman in any way, either briefly or for a long period of time was very dangerous. Unfortunately, at that point there was no desire for objective, rational thinking. Mason was in love, in lust, enthralled and overwhelmed. She would become his passion. All other matters took a distant second to the need to be with her. This was the direction his life must take. There was no other alternative, no other possibility. The woman offered all he had sought for so long. Mason would win her and find the sense of total belonging that had eluded his long difficult search. Any gut feelings of potential danger or future harm were washed away by the intensity of the growing need to love this woman.

After the round was over Mason stayed with Victoria not wanting the evening to end. She absorbed his attention and commitment with a natural willingness as if they were quickly developing some form of relationship that neither could comprehend, but were absolutely compelled to experience. She encouraged the infatuation Mason displayed, finding his commonness appealing. Finally her father could stand no more and insisted that he and Victoria leave the clubhouse. She agreed, with reluctance and a flash of fury over her parent's unwanted involvement. To show displeasure at her father's intrusion she kissed Mason full on the lips allowing her tongue to move seductively inside his shocked mouth.

For the next two weeks Mason searched for her everyday. As the only connection established occurred on the golf course, he spent the entire day at work, arriving at six in the morning and closing the clubhouse lounge down at midnight. He played unfocused golf each day, responding with giddy excitement when happening upon any foursome containing women. The anticipation turned to crushing disappointment when she was not there. He found out Victoria's phone number, calling her repeatedly, each time connecting with an answering machine. He listened to her voice with a soaring heart, but quickly hung up without leaving a message, as he had no idea of what to say. It was apparent after many days that the level of anticipation could not continue. With resignation Mason began to realize the possibility of a relationship with the beautiful, wealthy and successful woman was ludicrous and laughable. He was poor with a future of manual labour ahead, while she walked with the rich and powerful.

Mason came upon her father while cutting grass. The others in the group acknowledged his presence, but Sanderson walked by as if he did not exist. To quell the pain of rejection he began to drink every night after work. On some occasions he would pick fights with other patrons believing the altercations would avenge the way the father and daughter were treating him. He often faired poorly in the fights due to his state of drunkenness. After one such unsuccessful evening Mason was working in a hole attempting to fix a leaky sprinkler hose. Sporting a black eye and a cut lip, he was in waist deep water tightening the screws on a hose clamp when Victoria appeared above him. With the sun behind her left shoulder a profile was silhouetted as she spoke in a playful voice.

"Hard work?" she teasingly questioned.

Mason looked up and stared at her for a moment as all the anger, the planned snub and arranged words disappeared like a quickly forgotten thought. She looked smashing in tight blue shorts. From the hole he looked directly up at her crotch, which she took no effort to conceal while standing with her legs apart. The snug fitting yellow tank top showed off her chest to perfection. The angle and the outfit offered a view that made him shudder in the cool water. Her face was beautiful and eagerly awaited his reply. Mason opened and closed his mouth trying to find words or a snappy, witty comeback. Unfortunately nothing came out but a small grunt.

Victoria giggled as he attempted to cleanup, futilely wiping muddy hands on his muddy chest. The action resulted in simply moving the mud around his body. Mason smoothed his tousled, thick hair, which simply made his head heavy with mud. She laughed harder with every attempt. Finally he gave up and asked her where she had been. Shaking her head she stated her father had insisted that she go away on business for two weeks and then had kept her very busy upon the return. "He did it to keep us apart," she said, gritting her teeth and issuing a frown that made her more beautiful.

At first Mason was not sure who the "us" was and struggled to make his brain process faster so a full interpretation of her comments could be understood. As he examined the simple words he began to realize that the "us" meant him and her. He desperately needed clarification. "Keep who apart?" he blurted out as if his mouth was full of the muddy water he sat in.

She looked at him strangely, glanced away and then reset a deeper frown on her face and let out a big sigh. "You and me, of course. Whom did you think I meant?" Her tone was laced with exasperation.

"We're an US?" Mason emphasized the last word with bewilderment.

"We were when I walked up. If you're not interested I can always seek out someone else." She turned to go and for the first time in his life Mason experienced the overwhelming and irrational emotion of jealousy in a relationship. The thought of her with another man brought him out of the hole quickly. He stood in front of her as water flowed down his muddy body, pooling at his feet.

"Us is very good." He said quickly and then began to profess his feelings. Mason knew it was wrong to be so direct, but he could not hold back the rush of words, as his feelings could not be suppressed. She listened to the outpouring of love with a small, satisfied grin.

"Why don't you call me, when and if you ever get cleaned up?" Then she was gone. Mason watched her walk across the fairway, admiring her swaying hips and realized that she had walked the golf course looking specifically for him. Both his heart and loins felt like they would simultaneously burst. All the while his whirling brain was screaming "US" in a silent voice so loud that the echo reverberated through his grey matter like a train whistle in a rock canyon.

The first real date went very well as did the second and the third. After a few weeks Mason was told that they were now officially dating. They began going to parties as a couple and soon after, when feeling comfortable enough, got drunk together. She liked to drink, which immediately was seen as an endearing quality. Mason loved all her flaws and imperfections, while his ego loved the feeling of walking with such beauty and charm. In this way he fell into a deep tempest of love, hanging on to her like a frightened sailor in a rudderless boat. He accepted everything about her, including her strange wish for celibacy prior to marriage. They found it difficult to continue embracing this arrangement especially during times of alcohol fuelled heavy petting, which left both frustrated. It appeared only a matter of time before an unexpected relaxing of the restraints would end in a coupling. That happened at a golf tournament where she had caddied for him and Mason had won. The celebration went far into the night with her basking in the champion's glory. After drinking to excess and with caution and clothes thrown to the wind they made brief and unsatisfying love by the eighth green. Both awoke with their pants down at their ankles embarrassed and disappointed in the quality of their first full sexual experience. Neither spoke of the night, except to agree that no repeat would occur.

Five weeks later Mason received a call that Victoria was coming over to his small apartment. She arrived agitated and worried. His mind whirled with negative possibilities, as he was sure that the relationship was over. Surprisingly she sat close with him on the couch, insisting that Mason profess his love in the strongest terms. With relief he dedicated his life to her and her alone. When finished, he sat winded, his heart throbbing. He moved closer, holding her hand tightly, while knowing she could not be rushed in what was needing to be said. After long, anxious moments she looked into his eyes with tears streaming down her cheeks. She opened her mouth to speak but only air escaped. Not knowing what to do Mason held her close attempting to encircle and protect her from whatever it was that had stolen her confidence and muted her voice. They embraced for long moments, with the only sound in the room being her quiet sobs, his ragged breathing and the loud ticking of the old clock that hung on the kitchen wall, noisily counting the seconds until the axe fell.

Finally Victoria seemed to steel herself as Mason braced for the unknown but inevitable emotional impact. He was frightened and somehow knew the next few minutes would be a turning point in both their lives. She pulled herself erect on the couch, looked into his eyes and stated.

"I'm pregnant, Mason." Then she began to sob.

Chapter Five
THE PUPPET

    Upon discovering that a man will be a father, certain reactions are unavoidable. No matter if the pregnancy is planned and eagerly anticipated, unexpected or unwanted there is some level of terror that exists when facing the responsibility of fatherhood. In cases where the conception is a natural progression of the relationship the doubts and struggles are hidden beneath thick layers of joy and celebration. Given that the commitment to the unborn child and the mother is strong, these threatening thoughts can be managed or discarded outright. Usually in strong men the voices of fear will be a natural part of the process in accepting the challenges and commitment of fatherhood. Weak men deal with the situation differently, often minimizing the necessity and importance of having an active role in the pregnancy and future parenting, somehow believing that since the baby comes from the mother it is the woman's responsibility to take on the major parenting role. Very weak and pathetic men walk away from the responsibility, offering no emotional or financial support to the woman or the child. These men choose not to accept any obligation and, with cruelty and total disregard, believe that their betrayal and abandonment will have no effect on the future of the children. Mason was not one of these men.
    The announcement of the pregnancy was stunning in many ways. The idea of fatherhood was a totally different personal concept and one that had not been previously explored. In addition there was the

very real worry that commitment opened up the distinct possibility of future loss. This fear had always lay lurking like a nest of wasps waiting to be disturbed. In spite of the dread, his reaction on the couch that day was strongly tempered by the love for this devastated woman. Mason would not avoid this responsibility, no matter how much emotional strain the commitment would generate.

There was a great deal of talking and discussion over the next weeks and months. The first decision regarded the commitment to the pregnancy. Victoria insisted on having the baby and Mason agreed to be present every step of the way, offering support and assistance. It became clear that the next step was to tell Mr. Sanderson. Mason wanted to be with Victoria when sharing the dangerous news. Victoria absolutely refused, insisting that she knew how to handle her father. He reluctantly accepted her non-negotiable decision, while bracing for the expected wrath of the man. The question as to the design of their future relationship was also introduced. In spite of his trepidation, marriage was an option that would be gladly accepted. Victoria had no reaction to his simple proposal. As a result of her flat response Mason became concerned that he may become a discarded sperm bank, having no further purpose. With great determination he stilled the negative thoughts, accepting the admonishment and quieting the increased feelings of rejection.

It took two more weeks before Victoria told her father of the pregnancy. All the previous discussions made it easier to say the words. Upon hearing them the man had said nothing, leaving the living room and moving to the den, staying behind the closed door for an hour.

"Who's the father?" Mr. Sanderson asked upon returning.

"You know who the father is," Victoria stated with little emotion.

"Are you sure about having this baby?" her father said, appearing to need to ask the question.

"Without a doubt."

"All right. What do you need from me?"

They spent the next few hours talking about her fear and joy. In the end her father accepted the inevitable. His daughter was now twenty-eight and a grown woman. On a family level, it was clear that Mr. Sanderson was only just containing the excitement of being a grandfather. Before leaving they discussed the position Mason would have in their lives. Sanderson agreed to unconditional acceptance while she accepted her father's conditions.

Victoria related the conversation and actions of the meeting in its entirety, only leaving out the final pact that father and daughter had sealed. Mason absorbed all she had to say. Perhaps he would be given a chance to prove he was worthy of taking care of Victoria. He would be a good father and, perhaps some time soon, a good husband.

The pregnancy rolled along like a large boulder crashing down a mountainside. While the ending was given, the trip was chaotic and turbulent. Victoria and Sam dealt with the disclosure of the pregnancy with all the subtlety of one of Super Sam's car commercials. Both presented ecstatic joy over the news. Victoria's friends began to plan baby showers, while she registered at all the local boutiques. The excitement about the birth grew in direct relation to her belly. Sam would call every night to see how the day had gone. A baby's room was prepared at the large sprawling Sanderson estate located in a beautiful treed acreage on the outskirts of the city. There was some talk of the father, but Mason's name offered no recognition in the Sanderson social circles. When asked what Mason did for a living, Sam simply said that he practically lived at the golf course, which was the truth. The initial excitement about being a father began to diminish as both Sandersons took control of the situation. At times Mason felt like an observer or part of the audience there to watch the father and daughter perform. It was truly amazing to witness the joy both received from being the centre of attention. While the performance was delivered Mason would usually attempt to find a quiet corner near the bar. He said little, staying in the background and out of the way. This seemed to suit both the Sandersons fine. Remarkably, Sam never treated him poorly in any way, including him in family gatherings, introducing him to friends and acquaintances in a respectful way.

The next major discussion, as the pregnancy entered the final trimester, was the living situation. Both had retained their separate apartments and after much discussion it was agreed that a house was needed to raise a child. Mason did not know how he would support a family on a grocery store wage, as the golf course job would soon end. Victoria did not seem worried at all believing something would come along. And her father did, mysteriously joining the debate and offering to purchase a house in a new development close to the estate. Victoria was thrilled. As usual, Mason agreed, unwilling to jeopardize the positive relationship he had with Sam or disappoint Victoria.

Two weeks later her father called and invited him to lunch. After eating, Sam got to the purpose of the meeting offering Mason a job in one of the car dealerships. Sam insisted Mason would have to start at the bottom and work his way up, but with perseverance and dedication, promotion was assured, in fact some day he may even be the general manager. Mason did not want to work for Sam. In addition, he would have to give up the golf course job that he loved. To bide time Mason asked for time to discuss the job with Victoria. For an instant there was a brief moment of darkening rage behind the cold blueness of the man's eyes, but then it was gone. Mason believed Victoria would support him in turning down the job. Surprisingly she was livid with him for not accepting the offer flat out. He was surprised and shocked by the display of anger and attempted to justify the decision by describing the uneasiness he was feeling about working for her father. She then began to waddle back and forth heaving her large eighth month pregnant belly from side to side and yelling that Mason's uneasiness would not put food on the table. Finally she moved in close and, with wild eyes and spit flying from her mouth, stated that no father of her baby was going to be a grocery clerk. Then she stormed up the stairs and slammed the door.

Mason was shocked having just experienced a new aspect of Victoria's character that he did not like at all. The worried doubts that had begun to build at lunch were expanding like the smoke from a growing fire. He rubbed his hands together and flexed his fingers to loosen the tension and chase away the tingle of the nerves. Then he poured a large Scotch whiskey wondering what to do next. He was on his second Scotch when Victoria came out of the bedroom.

She had changed into a long fleecy housecoat. She came to him and apologized for her behaviour, blaming the outburst on hormones, the length of the pregnancy and the size of the load she was carrying. He quickly forgave her, agreeing to take the job. Even in pregnancy there was a sexuality that she could exude when desired. As if to make up for the bad behaviour and angry reaction she undid the cloth belt and allowed the housecoat to open. Beneath the fabric she was buck naked and excited. Rather than listening to the voices of warning, Mason surrendered to the softness of warm flesh as she took him to bed, rewarding him for making the proper decision.

After finishing she fell asleep, while Mason sat by the bedroom window watching the streetlights, drinking Scotch and wondering about the quality of the lovemaking. After the discovered pregnancy he saw no reason why a healthy sexual relationship could not be solidly established. The more he pressed the more she resisted, offering lame excuses or relating health reasons. Mason became tired of pressing the issue and being made to feel like an uncaring sexual glutton. Soon he retreated and began to wait for her to make the next sexual advance. The initiative anticipated never occurred.

The topic of marriage was another issue that brought on a strange reaction. Incorrectly, Mason had believed that both Sam and Victoria would insist on legitimizing the relationship. He had decided that it was important, even though there were reservations, to give Victoria what she undoubtedly wanted. He bought a ring with his emergency money and presented it to her on bended knee. Mason had developed a brief ceremony, which was completed with the presenting of the ring. Looking from his face to the ring and back, Victoria softly closed the lid on the box, telling him she would not marry in this condition. Mason disagreed, stating that her condition certainly made this the best time for marriage. All his arguments were ignored as Victoria insisted that no further talk of marriage could occur. He had no idea what that meant, and when pressed for clarification she stopped talking and left the room. Mason felt deserted and confused. These were persistent feelings that were beginning to appear with increasing regularity. It was as if he was part of an unknown plan that others were orchestrating for their own purposes. The direction of the relationship, the pregnancy and now his position in the family, both as male figure and provider, seemed to be staged and organized by Sam and Victoria, the two puppeteers. While Mason felt the strong pull of manipulation, he was unable to change the process. Little power of persuasion was available and certainly no influence could be exerted on Sam or sadly, Victoria. He made a conscious decision to be attentive to Victoria's needs hoping for changes, while optimistic that the situation would become more tolerable when the baby's arrival would make them a family.

Little Samuel Bradley Sanderson was born at four o'clock in the morning. The labour had been very difficult for Victoria. Mason had remained with her the entire time. She was exhausted upon completing the birth, so Mason bathed his son and held the baby close. It was the most remarkable experience of his life. The idea that he was a father, holding a little life that would need guidance, support, direction and protection made for the light-headedness of overwhelming joy. Mason knew now that fatherhood would offer the personal fulfillment he had craved.

The next months were a whirling succession of learning experiences. Life at home improved as he had hoped. They began to do events as a family. Simple outings to the grocery or department stores were treasured trips as all received attention due to the baby. With puffed chest and a proud smile Mason accepted the public fixation. He treasured the feelings of belonging and importance that fatherhood brought. Changes also occurred at work where Sam gave him a promotion with a fancy title and new responsibilities. Unfortunately the job now included travelling to other cities and towns, selling or buying cars. Mason would often be away the entire week, which he found very difficult. When he spoke to Sam, the man stated it was critical that he build a future for his family and that meant commitment and sacrifice. Victoria accepted the travelling easily, saying how proud she was of his success. In the end, with the strings being pulled quickly and with rhythmic certainty, Mason danced to the tune set.

For almost a year and a half, life moved quickly. The baby grew rapidly and with a cuteness that surprised no one. Mason spent as much time as possible with the boy, but work became more demanding as Super Sam increased an already full workload. He was forced to work on Saturday and Sunday mornings. At times after a full Saturday at the dealership Mason would come home and find that Victoria and Samuel Jr. had gone to see grandpa and would be spending the night. At first he had been furious with these outings and heated fights occurred with Victoria. He soon learned that the confrontations only resulted in more prolonged visits to the Sanderson estate. With sorrow, Mason began to accept that for some reason he was being squeezed out of his child's life. The knowledge brought about an expected reaction as an increase in alcohol consumption occurred. He began drinking to endure the loneliness, while attempting to quell the rising tide of worry. Super Sam was nothing but supportive and pleasant in any interaction, but Mason was never invited to the estate unless the event was large enough to warrant an appearance of little Samuel's father.

Mason was building to an angry confrontation with Victoria when a shift in her behaviour occurred. After a long trip away he arrived home with an intense weariness. He struggled into the living room and was greeted by candles, chilled wine and Victoria wearing a see-through negligee. In a seductress's voice she told him that because he had been working so hard a reward was waiting. That night began two months of solid lovemaking. Every time they were together and Samuel Jr. was asleep or with grandpa they behaved like rutting beasts. She wanted him repeatedly in the course of a day when he was not working. Super Sam even appeared on board, lightening the workload and constantly offering to keep the boy so they could have alone time. For the two months Mason rode the wave of passion, adoring every moment. The lovemaking seemed to bring the couple closer together. All the past demons of concern were driven out by the sexual exorcism.

After two glorious months Mason arrived home from a buying trip and found the house full of people celebrating. He was bewildered by the pats on the back and drunken congratulations. Sam gave him a big hug, while Victoria was working the room seeking every guest's attention, glowing, flushed with excitement. He stood befuddled with a bogus jester's smile tacked crookedly on his face. The attention to the verbal banter of the guests soon paid off as one of Super Sam's drunken business associates hugged him to her grotesquely huge bosom, stating she hoped they had a little girl. Mason knew now that Victoria was pregnant thanks only to the vague reference by an unknown woman. He felt sick inside but said nothing until the last guest, Super Sam, had left. Then he confronted Victoria who was still basking in the warmth of the congratulatory mob. She had no idea why he would be upset as she had only received the news that day, giving her no time to let him know of the wonderful happening. Mason tried to explain the importance of being a part of the family. Finally, she ended his stumbling words, by throwing up her hands in frustration while leaving the room. That night he slept in the spare bedroom. The next morning the tactics changed to thick silence as the battle raged. After a solid week both grew weary and Mason attempted reconciliation. She saw the desire for communication as capitulation, accepting his apology. Later that night he attempted to rekindle the sexual activities, but was firmly repulsed. Unlike before no reasons were ever given for the firm, persistent and ongoing refusal. At the time Mason was not sure if the previous intense sexual activity had been used for the singular purpose of propagation or if the spiralling interest had been due to progression in the relationship. It seemed naïve that the sudden turning on and off of the sexual energy was due to fluctuations in Victoria's love for him. The whole debate left Mason desperately needing more discussion, which he knew Victoria would never allow. In the end, he paced the floor with tense Pinocchio-like steps waiting for his handlers to begin the next performance.

At some point a condemned man recognizes the fate that the judge, jury or life has dictated. In this way Mason began to accept that the love for Victoria, based on his own insecurities and the unrealistic desire to possess the life he so desperately needed to create, was in serious trouble. He further surmised that any attempt at overhaul was doomed to failure. The speculated outcome, preordained many years ago, that any relationship with Victoria would be disastrous, was coming true. Unfortunately Mason could not walk away and leave his son and unborn child. Realizing this fact helped him understand that he was powerless to create the relationship desired, so the only option was to accept the one available. In this way Mason fell into line and moved when the strings were yanked. Both Victoria and Sam seemed to sense his surrender to their unconditional terms as the tenseness around the home began to dissipate. Mason worked the long hours required with no complaints, even going in when unnecessary. He kept a bottle of vodka in the bottom drawer of the desk for the frequent lonely times.

The repetition of each day's schedule resulted in swift passage of time. Dates on the calendar represented appointments and business opportunities not the changing of the seasons. In this way the birth of Rebecca Victoria Sanderson came and went. Mason was away at the time as Sam had sent him by plane to represent the company at a national meeting. Super Sam had, not surprisingly, taken over his role and assisted Victoria. Mason accepted the missed opportunity with sad resignation, but said nothing to anyone, celebrating an individual joy late at night when alone holding his baby girl and rocking her gently.

The years moved by with remarkable speed as Samuel grew straight and strong, taking on many of the characteristics of grandfather. The boy had a determined confidence, quick to learn and take control of situations. Samuel Jr. was usually impatient and critical of any weakness, often showing little compassion for the plight or troubles of others. The boy was a superb athlete becoming accomplished in most sports. Mason was often too busy with work, so grandfather became the boy's mentor and supporter going to all the games and buying the most expensive equipment available. He attempted to connect with the lad at every opportunity, but the boy was often distant and uninterested in his desperate overtures. The father and son connection began to weaken early, as the distance between them grew. As age increased Mason realized that a great loss was occurring. Sadly he did not know how to prevent the disappearance of the love, while his son did not seem to care.

This also seemed the case with Victoria. Mason tried to believe that she cared for him in a way so special that no words or actions were necessary. As a result, for a while after Rebecca was born, he deceived himself into believing the relationship was healthy.

It was only a matter of time before reality crept in and delivered a hard, hurtful slap, wakening him from the delusion. Mason closely watched how she treated him or, more importantly, how she did not. Victoria seemed to accept his presence by ignoring his person. At times he would share thoughts about challenges at work or tell stories of how the day went. At first Mason thought her to be attentive. Later while quizzing Victoria on the conversations, he found she could not answer the simplest questions. In playful moments he would speak gibberish, throwing in foreign language words to see if she was paying attention. She never was. The only way he could get her undivided focus was mention Super Sam or the children, especially Samuel Jr. Mason unwillingly started to accept that Victoria had little time for him, his thoughts or needs, while seriously questioning her commitment to the relationship. In a brave moment he asked Victoria why they should stay together. She shrugged, looked him in the eyes and said that he could leave anytime, if that was what he wanted. Mason bit his bottom lip hard and for the first time thought he might want to put his hands around her thin, white neck and tightly squeeze forever.

While Victoria and Samuel seemed to accept the inevitable separation with little emotion or concern, from a young age Rebecca attempted to forge a bond with her father. From her first steps the little girl seemed able to sense Mason's unhappiness and need to be loved. She would seek him out in the early morning, insisting that he feed her breakfast before leaving for work. She would hug him when he came home and kiss him goodbye when he left. Mason would always get the call to tuck her into bed when he was home. The two developed an elaborate bedtime ritual full of secret thoughts quietly shared to chase away the bad dreams and the scary creatures of the night. As she got older, he would find scribbled notes in his suit pockets or crayon drawings left on the front seat of the car. He began to put the treasured items up in his office. The sight of the coloured abstracts brought him joy. They began to share special moments or knowing looks when Victoria, Samuel or her grandpa were doing mean or ignorant things. Mason marvelled at Rebecca's surprising strength and intelligence from an early age. He could tell that his daughter accepted her place in the pecking order and realized that gaining parity with her brother was not important or worth the effort. Instead she seemed to search for her own successes while finding fulfillment in activities of her own choosing. At times he would find her curled up reading or watching a wildlife program on television. She had superior intuitive skills, sensing and understanding the purpose of both good and bad behaviour. She developed an amazingly strong sense of right and wrong, always reaching out to help others. Perhaps it was a way to balance her brother's non-empathic view of the world. Mason encouraged her and cheered on the goodness that grew each day. While she cared for others, there was no weakness of character and she boldly stood up for herself within the family or in the community, either in physical altercations where she would never quit or a contest of wits where she would out argue and outsmart her brother.

When together, Rebecca felt comfortable in speaking about all matters on her mind. Mason noticed that she did not share her inner thoughts with the rest of the family. She was polite and loving, but carried a sense of cautious reserve with the others. They thought her to be shy, but he knew it was for protection. While she loved her family it became painfully obvious that she did not trust them. Rebecca knew her father would never harm her in any way. The relationship somehow answered the question Mason had asked Victoria. He stayed for the little girl, who offered him profound moments of contentment. It was these remarkable and special feelings, given unselfishly through the love of a daughter, that gave him reason and substance to his life.

There were a few magical times where he enjoyed the entire family. Unfortunately, these were rare as usually Sam came along at the insistence of Victoria and Samuel. There was one Christmas Day when grandpa was away visiting a sick older brother. With Mr. Sanderson gone the dynamics of the family seemed to change. For unknown reasons, on that special day Mason was totally included in the celebration by Victoria. From the first moment in the morning the family was connected with laughter and joy. He was never big on purchasing or receiving presents, but that year he had spent great care attempting to buy the perfect gifts. His patience had paid off as the children squealed with delight and Victoria gave him a large hug and wet kiss. The last gift to open was a small package wrapped in colourful red paper and sporting a golden bow. The two children huddled around him, watching with excitement as he slowly peeled back the shiny paper. Mason froze when the gift was unveiled. Sitting stunned in the chair he stroked the silver cigarette case that lay shining in his hand. The children must have polished incessantly as it shone with a brilliance that almost hurt his emotional eyes.

Even Samuel Jr. appeared excited by his reaction to the shiny expensive object. Both children hugged him close as he lavished attention on them for their thoughtfulness and good taste. He was surprised by the reaction of Victoria who had tears in her eyes as she pointed out the inscription which read, To The Best Husband and Father, Love Your Family. Tears flowed down his cheeks, because at that instant Mason totally believed the inscription. It was a moment he would always remember. Unfortunately other important events came and went, where he attended, was involved but never included. During these times Mason desperately tried to reconnect with the magic. No matter how hard he tried he never felt a part of the entire family again.

As the years went by the relationship with Victoria became more and more estranged. There were times when the couple would go days without communicating a word. Mason had given up on Samuel, leaving the rearing of the boy to Victoria and Mr. Sanderson. Rebecca offered the only spark of light in his dull existence and he created opportunities for their quiet talks and special moments of personal sharing. As she became a busy teenager less time was available for her father. He accepted this as natural and inevitable.

When the children were fifteen and thirteen, Mason made some decisions about his future. It was at work on a Sunday when the usual busy dealership was eerily quiet. He had completed the necessary work for the day and was preparing to go home. With a brace of straight vodkas churning inside he began to reflect on his life. There was one inescapable truth. He was bitterly unhappy. Victoria satisfied none of his physical or emotional needs, was not interested in him on any level and was becoming more difficult to live with each day. He had moved permanently to the downstairs bedroom, seeking to avoid her at every opportunity. With resignation Mason realized he was living in Victoria's house on borrowed time. His minimal and tentative place in the family was further threatened as the children grew into their own lives. He began to put money away in a secret bank account in preparation for the separation when it occurred.

In an effort to break the bonds of servitude Mason began to live his own life. It felt good to take responsibility for his existence again. Unfortunately he began to slip into old safe patterns of behaviour. A few of the single salesmen became every night bar buddies. The group would frequent clubs drinking heavily and attempting to pick up single or married women. He found the romantic interaction with women to be strange and difficult. In the past he had prided himself in being comfortable with the ladies. He now was awkward and shy. In frustration Mason sought other means of sexual release, paying exotic dancers for hours of satisfaction in cheap hotel rooms. At first he did not like the feeling of disgust after a session of sex, but soon the importance of the sexual satisfaction overruled any negative thoughts.

Mason began to play golf again, joining a men's league and playing every Thursday night. He golfed on the weekends, getting up early, playing a quick round as the sun rose, and then going to work for the day. No one seemed to take any notice of his absence. He began to miss any family gatherings, citing the importance of work. This caused conflict with Victoria who realized that the puppet was now moving to its own music.

Finally a week after Samuel's seventeenth birthday, which he had missed due to a golf game, a drinking session and a rendezvous with an oriental hooker, Victoria cleared the house of children and confronted him while he nursed a hangover in the kitchen.

"We need to talk," she ordered in her mean and nasty voice.

"We have nothing to say," he replied with equal venom.

"Oh yes we do. Your behaviour is unacceptable and I will not put up with it any more." She stood with her hands on hips as if addressing a guilty child. The whole scene effectively displayed the ridiculous nature of the relationship. Mason's only response was to react with laughter. This infuriated Victoria.

"Don't you dare mock me by laughing, you drunken, failure of a man."

"Don't like what you created?" He spit the words at her as the laughter died on his lips.

"What I created? You were a mess when I found you. I made you into something. I gave you two beautiful children who you don't give a shit about."

"That's not true, I love my daughter more than anything. As far as Samuel, your father took the boy away from me years ago."

Her eyes boiled with anger as her voice rose. "Don't blame my father for anything. He has given you opportunities you never would have had."

Mason scowled, "He worked me to death to keep me away from you and the kids. Both of you never wanted me as part of the family. You wouldn't even marry me, for Christ sake."

Victoria paused and got a sadistic little grin on her face. "You know why I didn't marry you? Because it was part of the deal with daddy. He would treat you nice, give you a job and accept you, to a point, if I never married you or gave the kids your name. I gave you a life and protected you from my father's power and you blame me? You are pathetic. You had nothing and look what I gave you."

Mason breathed hard through his mouth. "I was happy before I met you. I was doing alright." He screamed out the words.

"All right? You were up to your waist in muck and you're still up to your waist in disgusting muck, always drunk and fucking your whores. You have never been able to manage your life, always whining and crying. Be a man for Christ sakes."

"Like your father?" Mason said with a voice oozing out sarcasm.

"You could learn something about being a man from my father, because you never learned it from your own. Your father must have been a pitiful man and your mother must have been like the whores you visit every night. You are a disgusting and sorry creature. You know what you are? A loser, clear and simple. A big fat loser."

Mason stood quaking in the middle of the kitchen unable to decide what to do next. Then a comment seemed to develop from a series of small threads that had always been loose and separated, but were now coming together to form the fabric of a thought, that he somehow knew to be true.

"At least I never fucked my father, like you did."

The air went dead and heavy as only can happen when the intense human energy of bitter conflict reaches a breaking point. It was like an oppressive sky prior to lightning being released. The look on Victoria's face instantly told Mason that the comment was true. Her expression went from shock, to panic, to uncontrollable fury. She swung her arm with all the power in her muscled body. The blow caught Mason solidly on the side of his face resulting in a gunshot-like sound that reverberated around the elegant kitchen. The force immediately brought tears to his eyes as his head snapped sideways. In the past he would have taken the abuse with acceptance like a cowed wolf submitting to the leader of the pack. Perhaps it was the alcohol still pulsing through his body, the pent up rage that had lay dormant for years or the realization of the nasty secret shared by his abusers that forced his response. The puppet had finally had enough of the manipulation and endless dancing. Mason paused for a moment, as if thinking, then punched Victoria in the face, catching her between the eyes and knocking her to the kitchen floor. The puppeteer's strings had been finally cut.

She lay on the floor not moving. Mason's anger dissipated with the punch and the vision of Victoria lying prone with a trickle of blood on her forehead where the blow had broken the skin. For a moment he stood quietly and then with trepidation leaned over and felt a strong pulse in her neck. With deliberate purpose Mason went into the den and got out a piece of paper and a pen. Quickly but with calmness he wrote a brief letter to his daughter.

My very dearest Rebecca:

I have done something bad to your mother and will be in trouble for it. In the future your mother and grandfather will tell you many bad things about me. Some of them may be true, but many of them will be lies. I hope you will know the difference as you know me better then anyone on earth.

I am writing this letter as I know that your mother and grandfather will do absolutely everything they can to stop me from seeing or talking to you. I don't think I can fight them as they have so much more power than me. You know about power as we have talked about it lots. I will have no choice but to go away once they use all their power against me. I'm not going away because I do not want to see you so do not believe this even if they tell you so.

I must go now. You are the most amazing person that I have ever known. Do not let them hurt you, especially over me. Let them think that you do not care about me and do not support me in front of them as they may cause you pain. You are smarter and better than them so fool them like you have for so many years. I know you can do it.

Know this. You are the most wonderful beautiful person I know. You are special and I love you so very much. You are the greatest thing that I have ever known. Please be good and take care of yourself. Remember fool them.

I will write you letters and send presents when I can but I do not think that your mother or grandfather will give them to you.

I will miss you with all my heart and I hope we will see each other when you are older.

All my Love,
Dad

P.S. I have hidden this in your secret spot. I know you will read it, but don't let them know you have this letter.

Mason went to Rebecca's secret hiding place behind the loose board in the closet. She had shown it to him one day, making him pinkie swear on a stack of imaginary bibles that he would not tell anyone or access it without her approval. Once the letter was safely hidden, he went to his bedroom, placing a few items in a battered overnight bag. Mason moved through the living room where an eight by ten family picture stood on the mantle of the fireplace. Something caught his eye and he stood transfixed for many moments. He then smashed the glass front and tore the picture from the frame. Disbelief and anger rose in his mind as he grabbed his jacket and left through the front door just as Victoria began to moan in the kitchen. He opened the garage door and picked up his golf clubs. Once the golf clubs were loaded, he returned to the garage taking a rusty nail from a shelf and drawing a wavy line down the side of Victoria's latest present from Super Sam, a brand new black Mercedes Benz.

Mason drove directly to a local tavern located in the downtown area. The bar was old and seedy, offering the atmosphere that fit the mood. In addition, the food specialty was large steaks grilled to order. He requested a steak, baked potato, fresh rolls, a bottle of dry red wine and a double Scotch with water on the side. The meal was delicious and the wine was savoured with slow purpose. He bought drinks for acquaintances and for two working girls attempting to solicit his agreement in a business transaction. Mason regretfully told them not now, but would entertain both if he were still in the bar at the end of the night. They agreed to keep him in mind. With a constantly refilled glass he spent the night drinking and watching the front door closely. After all these years he was suddenly homeless again.

Inevitably there are choices, either good or bad, that change the direction of a person's life. People interviewed on glamorous talk shows speak of an impulsive decision resulting in success and fame when it was least expected. People in prison speak of similar occurrences. Everyone makes decisions each day that either knowingly or unknowingly propels a life in a different direction. Two friends stop for a drink in a bar. A woman comes over and seduces both telling them to come back to her home as her husband is away. One makes a lustful choice and leaves with the woman. The other decides to go home by way of a convenience store and impulsively buys a lottery ticket winning two million dollars. At the same moment a man decides to surprise his wife by not going to Tuesday night bowling, something he has been doing every winter for two years, only to find her in the arms of another man. The man then decides to shoot them both. Two men in the same instant making two different choices with two very different results, as one becomes a millionaire and the other becomes dead. Two drivers are side by side when the light turns amber, one decides to race through the now red light and gets T-boned. The other driver quickly stops at the light and becomes a witness to an accident. On a different road a similar light turns amber and a driver races through the intersection while the other slams on the brakes. The driver hitting the brakes is rear-ended by a truck that causes the gas tank to explode where the woman is incinerated. The driver going through the light is unaware of the accident behind. In this way one never knows when a decision will alter the set course of one's life, quickly and dramatically.

While Mason had been looking for changes, he had no idea when he woke that morning his entire life would look different by the time he went to bed. The rash decision to make a comment, that if false was horrendous and if true more horrendous, was not made consciously. Likewise, Victoria's decision to react the way she did was extremely impulsive. At that point the situation may have been salvageable. The final decision to strike Victoria, officially ending the affair, was done with awareness and calculation. Reliving the moment in the bar with a belly full of liquor Mason was sure he had made the right choice. The response had effectively changed his life. First he must face the consequences for the actions in the kitchen, knowing that the response from Mr. Samuel Sanderson would be swift and without mercy. The beauty of the situation was that Mason was ready, very ready.

At ten minutes to twelve the two police officers entered the bar. Both the officers looked Mason's way, noticeably tense, and then walked slowly towards him with hands resting on their guns. He drained the half-filled glass, threw a twenty-dollar bill in the middle of the table, stood up, caught the eye of both girls, shrugged an apology, faced the officers and extended his hands together with the palms up. As they applied the handcuffs Mason smiled, speaking pleasantly.

Once settled in the cell he began to plan out the next actions to be taken. Mason requested paper, pen and a telephone call to his lawyer. Unlike other times in jail, when it was necessary to rely on the charity and help of others, he knew whom to call. The lawyer was a golfing buddy that Mason trusted and who had a dislike for Super Sam due to past shady dealings where the man had been poorly treated. With the call made he settled down to write the letter. It was difficult as emotions kept entering the content and Mason desperately wanted the message to be one of clearly delineated facts. In a very direct way the completion of the letter brought about a therapeutic result. To see the words on paper brought on a clarity that shocked Mason with its truthfulness. In black and white there could no longer be any denial. While it was painful to feel the impact of the sentences, he knew the issue must be addressed for emotional closure and to attain personal safety. With letter copied and sealed in two addressed envelopes, he was ready when George, his lawyer, arrived later the next day.

"Man are you in a very bad spot," the lawyer started after staring at him with a pitied look.

"Tell me all that has happened," Mason stated in a knowing voice.

"Well," the man produced a sheet of paper from a brief case. "You have been charged with assault and battery, attempted murder, theft over one thousand dollars, destruction of private property and embezzlement of funds." The man took a pause and slouched back in the chair, waiting for a response.

Mason took a few moments before replying. Then he said, "Georgie, I have known you for a long time and you are a good guy, so I'm going to tell you what happened and then I am going to give you some very precise and direct instructions that I want you to follow." The lawyer sat up straight in the chair, surprised at the conviction and determination. The man had expected to find Mason distraught, over the massive amount of trouble he was in. Sam Sanderson was a very powerful man who was already calling in favours of other powerful men to ensure Mason would be pounded senseless.

"Victoria and I had a wicked argument. I said something that I'm glad I said and she slapped me hard across the face. I thought about my reaction and then knocked her out. Guilty as charged. The only thing I took from the house was some clothes, personal items and my golf clubs. Oh, and a picture. I keyed her car, to let her know that I despise her old man. Guilty of that too. I have never taken any money from the dealership other than my paycheck. Hell, I never even padded my expense account like some of those clowns. The embezzlement is bogus and a way to make me look bad in court. But that really does not matter. Here is what I want you to do. Take this sealed letter and put it somewhere very safe. If something happens to me that is suspicious I want the contents of the envelope sent immediately to the police and the local paper. Understand? Then I want you to go see Sanderson and tell him that I want to meet him here at the jail. Tell him to come alone."

"He'll never agree to that!" The lawyer was excited now, sitting on the edge of his seat, leaning on the table.

"I think he will. Tell him he had better come or the next time he sees me it will be at my trial where I'll have lots to say. Do not let him intimidate you and don't mention anything about the letter." He paused for a moment. "Is there anything you don't understand or are there questions you have?"

"I have a ton of questions but I don't think you will answer them."

"You're right. And Georgie, don't worry," Mason said in a passive self-assured voice like a man accepting an unchangeable fate.

It was two days before Sam Sanderson came to the jail. Mason was brought to a different meeting room where he sat waiting for more than two hours. The chair was hard and uncomfortable. After a long period of time he willed calmness, closed his eyes, quieted his breathing and sat motionless. With determination and stubbornness he vowed not to show any weakness in the encounter with Sanderson, as Mason knew the man was watching him closely through the one-way glass. Finally the door opened and in walked Sanderson and a solemn very tall man in an expensive silk suit. Both pulled up larger chairs, giving the men a height advantage.

"This is my lawyer, J. Arthur Ambrosse. He is one of the best criminal lawyers in the country and will be assisting the prosecution in convicting you. He will speak for me." Sanderson smugly stared at Mason, apparently relishing the moment when the destruction would begin.

With a snobby superior voice, refined throughout many successful years of constant victory over other men, Ambrosse said, "I told Mr. Sanderson that any meeting with you was wrong, however, Samuel is a gracious and compassionate man and has agreed to this brief discussion. Now, what do you want?"

Mason paused and then sighed long. "I guess my instructions were not very clear and for that I apologize. So I will make them very succinct. I will only talk to old Super Sam alone." He settled back in the chair finished with the opening comments.

The lawyer laughed quietly, "Not going to happen." The man offered him a smiling gaze, full of pity. "We will be leaving this room immediately unless you talk directly to me." The intimidation in the voice was clear and usually effective.

Mason waited many minutes. Both Sanderson and the lawyer wore their poker faces, showing no emotion. Beneath the stony façade Ambrosse was perplexed by the obvious composure of a man knowingly confronted with such power, while also facing very serious charges.

Finally Mason spoke. "Did Victoria tell you what the fight was about and what I said that made her slap me?" He posed the question to Sanderson.

"That has no real relevance. You attempted to kill a defenceless woman. That is the only thing that is relevant here," Ambrosse stated.

It was now Mason's turn to laugh. "First of all I did not attempt to kill her and second, the one thing Victoria is not or ever will be, is defenceless. As far as relevance, the comment that I made and further discoveries would be unbelievably important if I go to trial. The information would also be very, very public. But I do not want that in any way and will explain myself clearly to Sam, if you leave." Mason looked directly at the Ambrosse, who was not at all prepared to accept the dismissal.

"Let's go Sam, this discussion is over." The lawyer began to rise.

"You had better listen to me. I am just trying to protect you, Victoria and Samuel Jr." Mason deliberately left out Rebecca. "This is your last chance Sam. If you leave then I will not be at all held responsible for what will happen. But you decide, Sam, take your time. I'm not going anywhere, nor do I need to. I usually am comfortable in jail. As you can probably tell Mr. Ambrosse, I have been in this situation before. I didn't scare then and I am sure not scared now," Mason lied with conviction.

"Let's go. We're done." Repeated the lawyer, appearing less confident.

Sam sat quietly for a moment and then issued a hardy, hollow laugh. The man straightened and said with bravado to the lawyer, "Arthur, I believe I want to hear what this scum has to say." The lawyer began to speak, but Sanderson quieted the protest with a wave of his hand. "Don't worry. I've dealt with a lot tougher characters than this woman beater over the years."

"Be very careful what you say, Sam. I will be right outside if you need me." Mason could tell that the lawyer was very uncomfortable leaving the room.

Once the lawyer had left the two men sat looking at each other. Mason felt only sadness and betrayal, while Sam was looking for a weakness to be exploited. The man still did not understand what was happening. "Well? You have me here all to yourself, Walls. What is it you are going to tell me?" The sarcasm was thick like heavy morning phlegm.

"You first need to answer my question. Did Victoria tell you what I said that made her slap me?"

"As far as I know there was no slap delivered by her. You outright assaulted her and by God you will pay for it." For the first time since arriving Sam had become angry, as the emotions of the last few days began to surface.

"She did not tell you what I said?"

"Look. She told me there was an argument about your drinking and then you hit her. She even wanted to forget the whole thing and just let you go on your way. But there was no way that would ever happen. No one does that to Sam Sanderson's little girl and gets away with it." The malice exuded by the man saturated the air.

"Don't you give me that self-righteous crap, you hypocrite." Mason's own anger threatened to derail the entire purpose of the meeting. He paused, corralled his emotions, attempting to file them safely away.

Sam sat there waiting, as Mason gathered himself to say the words that had lived in his head for three days. "Victoria did confront me on my drinking and whoring, too. For once I was not going to accept her criticism and abuse. I confronted her back and we argued. She got personal, making comments about my mother and father, which were mean and in some ways more hurtful because they were true. Then, for some reason, your relationship with your daughter became very clear. So I said something that made her slap me." Mason paused for a few moments.

"Well, what did you say?" Sam attempted to sound casual and controlled, but there was sweat on the man's lip.

"After I said it, I knew it was true. Her face could not lie." Mason paused again.

"What the hell did you say?" Sam growled out the question with a dangerous redness colouring the man's face and neck.

"She said my father was pitiful and I said at least I never fucked my father." The words were like silent blows crashing into the old man. Sanderson exploded out of the chair, knocking it backwards to the floor with a metal crash. Mason had also risen and braced for the attack as the man's facial features changed rapidly and constantly like the shape of molten lava flowing down a steep hill. The door burst open and Ambrosse and the guard rushed in. Ambrosse went immediately to Sam as the guard, with baton in hand, advanced on Mason. He quickly sat down and put his hands flat on the table, eyes lowered. The guard stood over him ready for any threatening movement. Mason remained very still. Mason heard the chair righted and the heavy weight of a body falling onto the unyielding plastic seat. The electric tension in the room began to evaporate as the guard relaxed sensing that no physical force would be necessary to subdue the situation. Ambrosse also calmed and was the first to speak.

"This time I must insist that we leave this room." The lawyer attempted to help Sanderson rise from the chair.

As Mason slowly looked up, the older man said in a weak, stretched voice, "Please leave." Again the lawyer protested while the guard remained alert.

"Arthur, I need you and the guard to leave right now." There was urgency in Sanderson's voice that caused them to obey.

When alone, the two men sat quietly as if both were reluctant to continue what now must absolutely be completed. In a strange way there would always be an unwanted bond between the two. The moments stretched by with an agonizing slowness that threatened to freeze the proceedings, leaving the world suspended in a state of denial. Finally, with great unwillingness, Mason continued.

"You know there is more." The words appeared to rock Sanderson, whose body jerked upright at the softly spoken statement. Even Mason hesitated at the magnitude of what was coming next.

"I know that Samuel Jr. is your son." Mason said it with a matter of fact tone that he did not feel. Sanderson glared with a hateful malice that literally made Mason's skin shiver. The words hung like poisonous fumes as both men held their breath.

"I know now that all of Victoria's worry about being pregnant had nothing to do with me. It was hiding the secret that was the problem. So the two of you decided to create the charade. But you needed a gullible dupe who would go along with everything you two manufactured. I just wanted to belong to something and you offered the illusion that I did. After that the performance began, playing me like a stupid mark. You must have thought it was a big fat joke watching me trying to connect with the boy, while all the time knowing that he was from your loins." The words jumped out of Mason's mouth as if motivated by a bizarre challenge to get them said before gagging.

Mason took three quick breaths and began again. "I always wondered why you kept me away from the boy. I thought it was because I wasn't good enough for you and Victoria. That I didn't have the class or breeding." All the comments were an attempt to release the feelings of humiliation at his gullibility. It had been one more attempt at inclusion, resulting in another dismal failure. Mason stared into the corner of the room as Sanderson looked at the floor. Finally with resolve he said, "Enough about me. This is about making it work for everyone."

Sanderson broke out of his silent stupor and began to babble, "You have no idea what it is like to lose the woman you love only to have her reincarnated as your daughter. I never meant for that to happen. I was drawn to her and she encouraged our attraction. When she got pregnant, we needed to do something to protect our good name and reputation. I only wanted…"

"ENOUGH," Mason barked. "I cannot listen to your excuses or rationalizations about any of this. Nor do I want to wallow in my own self-pity. The time for that is long over. We just have to make it work out, especially for Samuel Jr. Now listen carefully because this is how it is going to work. I have a copy of a letter that I wrote and put in safekeeping. If anything happens to me that is in any way suspicious the letter will go to the police and the papers. I really do not want to see that happen. My sole purpose for dealing with this privately is to not ruin Samuel Jr.'s life. As far as you or Victoria are concerned I don't care. There are only three people who know the truth. You, Victoria and me. For what it is worth I will never, ever tell anyone what I know unless you come after me. Is that clear? IS THAT CLEAR?" Mason shouted.

Sanderson, muted, nodded.

"You continue to mentor the boy, make him your heir, and do what you want to Victoria…"

"That's over." It was now Sanderson's turn to interrupt, emphasizing the assertion.

"Whatever. I don't care at all. If you go near Rebecca I will kill you." Mason said, accenting the word *kill*.

"That is disgusting and sick. I love that girl. She's my granddaughter for goodness sake," Sanderson said with an outraged expression.

"I'm glad you feel that way. Just remember what I said. As far as Victoria goes, tell her whatever you want about what we discussed and how the situation got resolved. I don't care one way or the other. I am done with you and Victoria. You need to continue to take care of Samuel Jr. I don't think that is a problem as you're his father," Mason said with a sad certainty.

Sanderson had listened closely to each word. As a businessman, Sam knew when a deal was concluded and the man correctly sensed they were not finished with the negotiations. "What else?" Sanderson said suspiciously.

"You're right there is more. Here's what I want from you. First have all charges dropped, including the assault. I walk out of here a free man. I want two days and nights to wind up my affairs in the city with no hassles or interference by you, J. Arthur Asshole or anyone else. After I am finished with my business I will leave town. The last thing is I want access to my office to clean out my things. It can be after hours and I swear I will not take any items to do with your business. When you die, which I hope is sooner rather than later, I will destroy the letter I have in safekeeping. Finally, I never want to see your face again. Those are my demands and they are nonnegotiable." Mason stopped and waited for the response.

"Agreed. I thought you would want money," said Sanderson.

"I want nothing more from you. I just want to move on with what's left of my miserable life." Mason suddenly felt tired, wanting only to be away from this man and the situation.

"Then we are done here," Sanderson said with a final comment as if a car deal had just been completed. The man signalled to the glass and the door opened. Mason was silent on the walk back to his cell.

He was awakened the following morning by a new guard who told him that he could leave. George met him at the front door of the jail. The lawyer warned him that the press had amassed outside hoping to gain some understanding about what had happened over the last days. Initially the story had revolved around the assault of the heir to the Sanderson fortune by her live-in boyfriend. That news headline had gained momentum when Mason was taken into custody and later when Samuel Sanderson was seen visiting the jail. Just when the story was getting juicy and the sick vultures circling, all charges had been dropped and in a prepared statement, J. Arthur Ambrosse, the nationally recognized lawyer, had stated that the matter appeared to be a misunderstanding and that no further comment would be made. So the reporters had camped out at the jail hoping to get further information from the accused, now exonerated, boyfriend. The cameras clicked like the cracking of knuckles as George, obviously enjoying centre stage, stated that there was no story and no further comment.

George drove to a quiet restaurant with a private booth in the back. Mason was deliberately vague about the discussions with Sanderson, stating that the man had been cooperative and all had worked out well. George respected the privacy and did not press Mason for any details. Through the lawyer's sources it appeared that Victoria and Samuel Jr. had gone away to Sam's cottage for a few days and that Rebecca was staying with friends of the family. Mr. Sanderson had left that day on a private jet for meetings in New York and then for a much-needed holiday.

Mason had George drop him off at his car, which had remained in the downtown parking lot of the old hotel. He checked into the most expensive room, which was a remodelled suite on the top floor overlooking the city. Mason showered off the remnants of the jail, soaked in the tub until he was wrinkled clean and then ordered a light meal sent up to the room. He dozed until seven forty-five and then drove to the dealership for eight o'clock.

Entering the office Mason saw a figure sitting in the darkened room. Turning on the light he came face to face with Rebecca. They both cried and hugged until their arms hurt. Then, with Rebecca helping collect his personal items, they spoke of many things. At first she wanted to know all that had happened. With gentle firmness Mason refused to talk about the past. He was going away and there was nothing that could be done to change that fact. After packing his possessions, including all the artwork, the hour raced by like an angry wind. The security guard told them five more minutes as they hastily proclaimed undying love and commitment, although both knew that the separation would be absolute and lengthy.

The next morning, after checkout, Mason drove around the city for a couple of hours returning to old haunts and saying goodbye. He returned to the golf courses where old glories were relived. He drove by the dealership four times, never wanting to go back inside but somehow reluctant to leave a place where he had spent so many hours. He went to many of the bars he frequented and had final conversations with the owners or managers. Finally he drove by the schools his children had attended. He hoped that somehow Rebecca would be outside and they would talk naturally as if nothing was about to happen. Twice his heart jumped as Mason thought strangers were his daughter. Both times it was young girls who looked at him with fear, due to the expression on his face. He soon realized that continuously driving by schools could possibly result in a return to jail. After twenty years in this city, Mason was leaving for good. While there was certainly sadness there was a relief to forsake Sodom and Gomorrah.

The miles went by quickly as memories floated like clouds or roared past with the noise of a broken muffler. Mason tried to balance the good with the bad but found this difficult, until he forced Rebecca to the front of his thoughts. He was finally able to plan for the future. Since meeting Victoria seventeen years ago he had purposefully, and at times with total disregard for his needs, been pulled through life at the whims of others. In retrospect he found the manipulation disgusting, but at the time there had been a sense of safety of not having to think for himself. Mason realized it was a coward's way of dealing with life, but the failures experienced before meeting Victoria had driven him easily into a pattern of accepted servitude. He knew this pattern would have to change. Beneath everything was the hidden message he must find to show the way to lasting contentment. It became apparent that the time for the search was running out. At the rate the hunt was going, by the time he found the prize he would be too old to appreciate its worth.

For the next five years Mason moved from city to city again experiencing a nomadic existence. This journey was very different from his youthful wanderings. Before, each stop was an important opportunity. Unfortunately in his late forties, with the wall of fifty looming like a perilous foggy coastline, the prospect of any chance of success was becoming remote. The optimistic search of youth was being swept aside by the reality of middle age. He could also feel the spread of disillusionment and cynicism within his person.

While Mason enjoyed outside work, after seventeen years in the car business it was difficult to do other jobs. Besides, there was better money to be made when dealing with a profession he knew well. He worked for big dealerships and small used car lots. Some places Mason would stay briefly while at others he made a commitment for a period of time. He was comfortable with other salesmen enjoying their drinking habits. It took no time to establish his presence in the dealership, often quickly moving up the sales ladder. He did the best possible job, took the money and then went drinking.

Most of these stops resulted in no lasting relationships as Mason began to give less of himself to anyone. As a result, the alcohol became a familiar pastime. It was not long before the drinking provided all the information, as it became the answer. All that mattered was making enough money to live and drink. This resulted in a permanent sadness that began to engulf his nature. At times Mason sought emancipation through subscribing to the belief that this was his life and all was damn fine. Months would pass as he maintained the inner and outer façade, until the pressure became too great. Then he would internally crash into the pit of despair. The reaction would be foretold, as he would feel the listing, bending and inevitable implosion, as any structure built on a weak foundation of alcohol was apt to do. The booze caused the erosion of the internal concrete connectedness necessary for survival. At these very low points Mason would seek solitude hiding in his inexpensive dingy apartments, coming out only at night to drink in a dark bar or buy supplies for the long siege. In this way he lost jobs, acquaintances, and finally the will to care.

It was near the end of one these black pitiful episodes that he met the old lady. Mason had run out of booze on a winter's night and had slipped out to replenish his stock. Making the way to the liquor store had been easy and with a pretended sober walk and talk manageable, he purchased the necessary booze. On the way home, he had quickly slipped into a back alley for bladder relief, while consuming long pulls from one of the whiskey bottles. The shots of straight liquor, combined with the previous drinks and an empty stomach, caused Mason to become staggering drunk. It was one of those situations where he struggled to make the body parts work in unison. He would lean one way and his whole body would go in that direction, only stopping when he bounced off a stationary object like a fence or tree. After hitting the object he would then hit the ground, ending up in a ball of human misery. Mason did not curse the situation, as he could not talk due to the affect of the massive amount of alcohol on the brain. As a result Mason did not even hear the three teenagers approach him from behind and knock him down. He staggered to his feet and began to posture for a fight, but could not plant his legs as the drunken mind kept ordering the body this way and that. All the time Mason hung on tightly to the bag of alcohol in his left hand while waving his right arm in defense like a float sitter in a parade connecting with the crowd. The adolescents mocked his hilarious attempts at self-protection, calling out humiliating names and startling him with quick faked movements of aggression. Mason heard a higher pitched voice. Then he saw a blurry shape and heard cries of outrage, while his eyes began to sting and pour water. He gasped for breath and clutched the liquor bottles. Between bobs and weaves and leaking eyes Mason could vaguely see the teenagers flee the scene. A hand grabbed his arm, which caused him to stagger to the left, bounce off a tree and land hard on the ground banging his head. Then there was the retreat into nothingness.

Mason awoke in a strange place. The bright winter sun was shining through the window hurting his eyes and skewering his soggy brain. The headache started in the small of his back, went up the neck, past the left ear and ended in a pounding above his left eye. He moved slowly, feeling pains across his back, in his legs and in his arms.

Laying back down the cold sweats gripped him while saliva poured into his mouth. All he could do was swallow as quickly as possible to avoid drowning in spit. As was the usual case with his blackouts he would attempt to reconstruct the night, as if remembering would somehow legitimize the drunken amnesia. He remembered the trip to the liquor store and then there was a confrontation with someone. He paused as his tired mind attempted to track and capture images stored in hidden places. There were teenagers bugging him, he was ready to fight and then….

"You're awake. That's good. How are you feeling?" The high raspy woman's voice came out of nowhere and scared the air out of his lungs. There in a chair was a wizened up old woman with the whitest hair he had ever seen. She wore very thick glasses and an old lady's dress with a string of pearls. The way she was sitting showed no real body shape, just a round form of flesh that had been compressed by the powers of time and gravity.

"Where am I?" Mason asked.

"You are in the apartment of Margaret Addison, 553 Oak Rd." Mason briefly attempted to figure out how he had come to be reclining on this old lady's couch, but quickly gave up. He held both hands over his face as if hoping to disappear from the embarrassment that was surging through him with an icy tingle.

"What happened?" Mason stuttered, more to himself than to the woman.

"Well, I was coming home from the store when I saw you being accosted by three punks. I was appalled that they would attack a crippled man as you could hardly stand up. I told them to leave you alone and they laughed at me. So I gave the little bastards a shot of pepper spray. They weren't laughing then, I can tell you that. They ran away like scared little rabbits, howling and yelling. Sorry, I sprayed you too. You began to sputter and shake and then fell down and hit your head. I thought you were dead. I was pretty worried that I had killed a crippled guy. I'm too old to go to jail. But you weren't dead. So I slapped you until you woke up but you couldn't talk or tell me who you were or where you lived or nothing. I didn't know what to do with you. I could have left you but you would have froze.

I could have called the police but they may have arrested me for the pepper spray. So I brought you here as I didn't know what else to do. You staggered and babbled the whole way and when I finally got you to the couch and calmed down myself, I realized that you weren't crippled or retarded. You were drunk." She said the last sentence with disgust. "If I would have known that on the street I would have left you." The woman finished the long description and sat quietly as if not in the habit of talking to a person for that long.

"I should go," Mason said, attempting to rise again and facing the return of the intense sickness. He folded back into the soft old couch and caught his breath.

"You had better just lay still. I'll get you some water and aspirin." With surprising agility the woman moved her round body out of the large soft chair and went out to the little kitchen. She returned with a tall glass of water and four aspirins. "Drink all the water." Mason obeyed and settled back as she took the glass to the kitchen.

Margaret returned to the chair. "I'm going to make a cup of tea for us."

"Have you been in that chair all night?" Mason asked as the woman looked tired and somewhat disheveled.

"Yup. Wasn't going to undress and climb into my own bed with a strange man in my apartment. You could have woke up angry or you could be some kind of rapist. A man your age that gets himself in such a state, who's to know. I wasn't taking any chances, that's for sure." Mason noticed a large carving knife, a rolling pin and the can of pepper spray on the small table beside the chair. The woman was a pistol, he thought as a small smile appeared on his lips.

"What are you smiling about?" Margaret asked suspiciously.

"You are a brave young lady," Mason said with admiration and honesty.

Margaret seemed pleased with the comment. "That bang on the head must have screwed up your eyesight cause I sure am not young. I'm ninety-two years old. But I am tough and don't fear much. Momma always told me I had stupid courage for the things I had done in my life, but I've lived full and don't regret too much and what's the point anyways." She finished with a flourish and a wave of her arms. Mason liked this old woman and was glad he met her.

The aspirin was beginning to have the desired effect, suppressing the pounding in his head down to a manageable throbbing. While Margaret went to make the tea Mason sat up, fighting the dizziness that accompanied the abrupt movement. When his head had cleared he scanned the room. It was an elderly person's apartment complete with crochet throws, plastic flower arrangements and framed photographs, lots of photographs. Somewhat out of place was a modern stereo system with many CDs neatly contained in a large storage unit. Mason would like to see what kind of music the woman enjoyed. He wagered that he would be surprised.

They drank tea together after it had steeped. She respected his silence and just seemed to enjoy the presence of another person visiting in her small apartment. There was a civilized air to the tea drinking that Mason found comforting and pleasant. When the tea was gone, he rose on shaky legs, bowed gently, thanked her for the assistance and proceeded to the door. She collected his alcohol purchase, still surprisingly whole. Mason thanked Margaret again and with reluctance left.

Outside it took a few moments to realize that Margaret lived two blocks from his apartment. He had passed her street on the way to the liquor store the previous night. Locking the location into his now clearing, but still hurting mind, Mason made his way home. With a strange loathing he put the alcohol in the corner by the door and climbed into his dirty unmade bed. He lay awake for a long while attempting to make sense of the many feelings, thoughts and questions. The brave and caring intervention by the old woman perplexed him. Why would the woman risk her own safety for a stranger? She had obviously been concerned, but rather than seek the authorities, she had given a sleepless night to assure his safety.

It was three days of rest and baffling abstinence before Mason felt even a semblance of order, either mentally or physically. For some unexplainable reason avoiding a drink seemed natural and simple. During the recuperation period, when he felt driven to activity, Mason began to clean up his cluttered and dirty apartment. He took two large garbage bags of clothing, linens and towels to the laundromat, something he had not done for a month. On the way back, on an impulse, he got a neat short haircut. When he returned home he surprisingly still had energy so began the grueling job of cleaning his small but filthy apartment. On and off it took him three more days to complete the task, cleaning from the ceilings to the floors and everything in between. When he was finished he let in a winter breeze to clear the stale air. Then he poured himself a large Scotch. He had worked his way out of the winter blues and was prepared to live again.

After a great deal of thought Mason decided to visit the old lady. He did not know the reason for the attraction. Perhaps it was to prove that he was not simply a drunken loser. He purchased a bouquet of flowers and a gift assortment of teas and returned to the apartment. Margaret answered on the second knock and stood in the doorway with a puzzled expression.

She was the first to speak. "What is this…a date?" The question was delivered with surprise and good humor.

"More of a proper thank you for helping me last week."

"Well, I like the date idea better so you had better come on in." With the door closed she directed him towards the couch and went to put the kettle on to try one of the new packets of tea. Mason sat in the living room examining the order that the room offered. She was a tidy person, even though she lived alone. Mason was impressed by the practical nature of the room with the furniture arrangement, lighting and necessary items set out to satisfy a structured existence. The décor spoke of a person who knew what she liked. He also sensed a woman who knew who she was. He accepted the tea with thanks and sipped the boiled taste of apples and cinnamon.

She settled into the chair. "I do not want to appear ungrateful and I certainly do appreciate the company, but I must know why you came back?"

"Curiosity mostly." Mason studied the bemused face. He continued, "I just wanted to know what kind of ninety year old woman stops to help a strange man, then takes on three teenagers and finally brings the drunk home, stays up all night and then makes the guy tea. I think that person would be worth getting to know a little bit better."

"I guess when you put it that way it sounds like I'm crazy or have a wish to die. I may be closer to the first one, as I definitely am not into the dying part. Life is too full of surprises, cause you never know what is going to happen next." She paused, "Case in point. If you had told me that all of that would happen and the man would return, sober, cleaned up and wanting to know more I would have laughed out loud. See how strange and glorious it all is." She sipped her tea not taking her eyes off him.

"Tell me about yourself," Mason said quietly.

Not knowing where to start, she began at the beginning, telling him she was born just before World War One. She was a prairie girl with a hard-nosed, hard-headed, hardworking father and a lovely reserved mother. Margaret was the third oldest of six children. One of her younger brothers died at ten years old, while her youngest brother died in the Second World War on the border of France and Germany. Both deaths had been very difficult to accept, but she had persevered and shouldered on in spite of the grief.

She had left home at an early age to be an actress. The life had been hard as the troupe she joined traveled throughout the year playing small towns and obscure city theatres. She had loved the stage and the moments of magic it offered. The thrill of performing was all that mattered as the actors and actresses did the best work possible. She had loved being an actress and the personal importance of that fact shone through her description of the parts she played. Mason too felt the energy and marveled at how, after all these years, she still could grab that feeling and allow it to float her to a different place and time. Her description had left him with an exhilarated tingling.

She poured more tea and began again, continuing to glow from the memories. Her virginity was lost to an irresistible charming cad in the troupe. The actor was a beautiful man with a voice that could melt a girl's heart. They had stayed together for about a month and then one morning she woke up alone. Although the man had used her, she had not been angry, just pleased that she had been chosen. In the end the actor's beauty had been the cause of the man's ruin.

The handsome features had been destroyed when shot in the face by an outraged father while trying to slip out of a daughter's bedroom. Due to the laws of the time it was ruled a justifiable homicide and the actor was buried in a pauper's grave in the local cemetery when no one claimed the body.

She had met her first husband while on stage in a small city. She paused the story to tell him that once upon a time she had been a beautiful, high-spirited woman. Mason assured her that both qualities were clearly apparent even today. She listened to the words carefully searching for a condescending or sarcastic tone. There was nothing but complete sincerity, as he meant the words. Satisfied and blushing, Margaret continued with the tale, stating that her first was a plain man but wealthy, making incredible money in the development of farm equipment. The designs produced and manufactured sold very well with the blueprints subsequently being purchased by larger worldwide companies for large sums of money. Her first was older than her twenty-three years and desperately wanted company and someone to operate the large house at the edge of the city. She agreed and the couple was married. Her father was ecstatic, but on the eve of the marriage her mother had concerns, not for the quality of the man but for the impulsiveness of her daughter. The mother believed that after the novelty of the marriage wore off Margaret would not be able to tolerate a settled existence.

After four years and one miscarriage the relationship appeared destined for trouble as her first was insisting on children and she was ready for a new and exciting adventure. Just when she began to realize that change was necessary, her first husband was killed in a freak accident when a tractor slipped off the jacks holding up the machine, crushing his thin chest. She received a great deal of "widow's money" and went back to being an actress. There were many offers of parts, mostly due to greedy producers wanting the rich widow to bankroll the usually unsuccessful play. After many failures and the loss of much of her wealth she discovered what was happening and angrily left the theatre life. She invested the rest of her money in a trust and in some ventures that were initially profitless but paid huge dividends in the 1950's.

By 1942, with war raging all over the world, she joined the army nursing corp. She spent the next seven years in Europe. During the war she was decorated for bravery due to her excellent work in combat zones. When pressed on the story of these adventures she became quiet and large tears grew in her eyes. "Let's just say I saw things that I would not be able to describe and if by some chance I could describe them it would be unlikely that you would believe me. It was so awful, but I grew up in a big hurry."

She met her second husband in western Germany after the war. They had become involved at a hospital for Holocaust victims. He was an excellent doctor. They were married by an army chaplain and returned home in 1949. The plan was to stay a few months and then go to Africa, however, she became pregnant and the doctor began to drink. Her baby girl was born nine months later and was healthy in every way. She loved being a mother, content in postponing the African plans. Her second husband never seemed able to manage the raw and overwhelming war memories. The man would wake up at night screaming and thrashing about clawing at the air. She would grab hold of the flailing body until the sobbing started, which would signal the release phase of the night terrors. By the time the episode was complete the sheets would be soaked with tears and sweat. The dreams became so bad that her second husband began to drink in the evening. When drinking, the man was never abusive or angry in any way. At times she wished for anger, as it would have been a sign that some fight remained, but the war memories had stripped the gentle physician of the will to live. All the attempts of intervention by her and others proved useless as the man drank himself to death within five years of returning home. Mason listened very quietly as she told this section of her history. When she was finished the two sat without moving in the now darkening room, as if waiting for a knock on the door or the ring of the telephone to break the trance. Neither interruption came, so neither spoke for long minutes.

Finally, they looked at each other. Margaret smiled and with wet cheeks, spoke. "That is enough for today. I'm tired and you must have had enough of an old woman's silly stories." Mason went to speak, but she held up her hand stopping the words in his throat. "If you have time we can talk again tomorrow. I can tell the rest of the stupid old story then, if you would like. If you have heard enough then you don't have to come back, you know."

"What time tomorrow?" Mason asked quietly.

"About ten o'clock would be fine. I'll have the tea ready."

Mason rose from the couch, went to her in the chair and took her hands. With a slow movement he bent at the waist and gentle kissed the back of both. She approved of the gesture and a simple bond that had been initiated on the night of the pepper spray now appeared to be forged with iron strength. After bowing for a moment Mason straightened and left the apartment.

The route home was long with unintended detours due to the preoccupation with thoughts of the old woman and her incredible story. As she told her story he had felt the joy and sorrow. Mason could relate well to the losses she had experienced but Margaret talked with excitement and wonder, as if she would not change a single second. Here was an old woman telling her life story to a virtual stranger and sharing the tale with brutal honesty. At certain points in the telling she seemed to become unaware of his presence, dissolving into the distant moments struggling to glean every shade of the image and the subsequent feelings, cherishing both good and bad. It almost appeared as if she was doing more than relating the adventure to him. It seemed the most important part for Margaret was to embrace all the life moments, whether bright or dark, good or bad, right or wrong. All the remembrances were necessary for her to gain a total picture of her life. Her ability to unconditionally accept all the happenings of her long and remarkable adventure was amazing to him as it spoke of fulfillment.

In contrast, Mason fought the losses in his life with fury and the singular purpose of destroying the memories. When the attempted amputation of the painful area was unsuccessful, he would obsess on eradication of these recollections through the use of alcohol. The method would be successful until consciousness was regained. Then the memories would come back, lingering at first but soon growing stronger ultimately taking control like a bully who is alone in a room with his victim. He kept searching for a method of salvation that had never proved effective. Margaret may be the one person that would guide him through the emotional maze that had been created over the last forty years. With a great expectation Mason bounded into his apartment, poured a large Scotch whiskey and made an elaborate toast to an old woman, hoping she was the great sage sent to lead him forward out of the darkness.

The next day Mason was up early and returned to the old lady's apartment arriving at ten o'clock. Margaret let him in with a fond greeting and good cheer. He returned to the couch and settled as she brought in freshly made tea and a plate of store bought digestive biscuits. They visited for a while talking weather, news and health. The hot tea was delicious as they sipped quietly. Finally Mason's patience disappeared as he asked after her daughter. She laughed merrily, looking at him with a mischievous spark in her very gray eyes.

"Are you sure you want to hear the rest of my wandering story?" It was as if she was challenging him for encouragement like a rock band insisting on an audience's thunderous applause before an already expected and planned encore.

"I would love to hear the rest. You have a wonderful story and tell it well. But only tell it if you want. I do not want you to continue if it is too hard."

"Too hard? I have never met a person yet who finds it too hard to talk about themselves. Besides it is a good story."

After her second husband's death she was left in bad shape. The drinking had caused the physician to lose most of the money they had and all of the patients. As a result there was no practice to sell. By then her daughter, Martha, was three years old. Martha was a remarkable child who was busy and brilliant, learning with quickness and confidence. Margaret wanted only to stay home and raise her girl, but as a single mother went back to work so the two could eat. She continued to work as a nurse in a hospital close to her home. Margaret's younger sister had moved to the same city and babysat Martha while she began working as a nurse in the surgical ward. Soon Martha started school and did very well, enjoying all academic challenges. The girl grew straight and strong while participating in all sorts of sports. Mother and daughter shared the activities with the girl participating and Margaret cheering her on in a loud supportive voice. Margaret seemed to relish in this part of the tale, describing in detail track meets, basketball games, skating competitions and gymnastic events where her daughter excelled. Margaret's images and remembrances were crystal clear, recalling the moments as if they had just happened.

Mason was smiling large as Margaret was reliving a winter basketball game where Martha had scored the last basket at the very end of the game. The buzzer beater had provided Martha's team with a victory, which propelled them into the city finals. On the ride home, both were celebrating, enjoying a wonderful time, when coming over a hill Margaret was blinded by the lights of a fast-moving car passing a semi-trailer truck. She had reacted quickly swerving to miss the car. Just when she thought they would make it past, the oncoming car clipped the back end of Margaret's car, spinning it in out of control circles. The car skidded off the road, hitting the shoulder and flipping over as it rolled down a steep incline. The force pulled the wheel from her hands and she was flipped about the car like a rock in a shaken can. She woke up in the hospital four days later. The doctors were amazed that she had survived the crash. Martha had been thrown out the window, landing at the bottom of the ditch where the rolling car had crushed the girl in its unstoppable path. Her baby girl was dead at fourteen.

"That was in, let's see, 1964. Nobody wore seatbelts then. Stupid really. I was never sure if staying in the car would have saved her or not. But do you know something about that night?" Mason sat stunned unable to answer. "I will never ever forget that basketball game. I know the colors of the uniform, the number she wore, and can always feel the excitement and joy when she made the winning basket. The look on Martha's face was golden, just golden. The most special thing was that after she made the basket she looked right at me in the stands and gave me the biggest smile. I didn't even think she would notice me, but she knew exactly where I was the whole game. That instant is the most special moment of my entire life." Mason could not believe the beautiful smile on Margaret's face as she reached into her vivid memory, holding her long dead daughter close while letting untainted love flow into the room. The openness of a mother's love saturated the air as Margaret suggested more tea.

She scurried off to the kitchen, her smooth soled slippers making a scratching sound against the slippery floor tiles. Mason could hear her humming as she turned on the tap and filled the kettle. He relived the story in his head, experiencing her joy of the game and then the stunning impact of the accident. He was amazed at the powerful sense of emptiness that swarmed his thoughts, activating the vast reservoirs of ruin that lay constantly bubbling under the surface. He felt like crawling into a bed or bottle forever.

Mason waited until Margaret returned with hot tea. Once both were settled she appeared ready to resume. Just before she began to speak, he asked a question. "When you told me about Martha, you seemed so happy?"

She smiled broadly. "That basketball game was so wonderful. Yes, it makes me happy, very happy, even after all these years. The other part is not so good, but the look on her face was so special. And to give that moment to me, well that is just glorious."

"Doesn't it make you sad?" Mason asked, attempting to make the comment sound like an innocent question rather than an accusation.

Her eyes narrowed very briefly, as he realized the attempt had failed. "The accident part.....always. But the basketball part is much more important. Why would I want to live in the pain of a crash, rather than with the joy of a smile?" She laughed a little and shook her white head gently as if feeling sorry that a concept so simple could not be easily understood.

"Did they ever find the other driver?" Mason asked.

"I don't think so. I never really heard for sure." Margaret shrugged her shoulders.

"Weren't you angry?"

"Yes, at first I was. There was lots of blame towards everyone and everything, especially myself. But that just took too much out of me. If I had stayed there I would have become lost in bitterness, a place that offers nothing but pain. I had enough pain, both physical and emotional, that I finally got to a certain point and decided that I would live with the basketball memory." She paused for a long moment, cocking her head to one side. "You know, you're spending far too much time with the accident. It is minor in the entire story, a side bar only. The essence of my life can be found in the smile and that is where you should be looking too. I think you have spent far too much time with your accidents and not enough with your smiles."

Mason went to speak, with the purpose of defending himself from Margaret's simple comments, which he perceived as wrong and somehow threatening. But she shushed him before he could say the defensive phrases forming in his whirling brain. "Let's just sit quietly for a moment. I really like your company. I want to thank you for listening. It is so good to be in those memories again. We can't talk any longer as I am going shopping with a friend soon." Mason sat still and confused until both finished the tea and she showed him to the door.

"Why not come back in three days and we will finish the story. I'll have lots of time then." She looked directly into his eyes. "Remember the smile." And with that whispered suggestion she gently closed the door, leaving him standing in the hallway with his conflicted feelings.

As was the pattern after the last visit Mason wandered home using a crooked path. He was experiencing deep turmoil, attempting to understand the old woman. The story was simple. Joy turned into intense sorrow by the total injustice of one moment in a long, long life. It was the cruelest of occurrences, when a mother loses a daughter. That was not causing the confusion. It was the way Margaret chose to react that was so puzzling. To him the basketball game with the winning results and the final connection with her daughter was a pleasant and heart-warming moment, but it was not the story. The important part of the evening to him was the accident. Perhaps the basketball game had a place in the telling of the story as background information, yet Margaret seemed to mention the accident nonchalantly, stressing the importance of her dead daughter's smile. Mason began to think she did not care for the daughter. This caused an angry response to well up inside. In his usual manner, when he could not comprehend or accept an event or another person's emotions, the typical reaction was anger. He was fuming upon arriving home, his mind whirling with accusations directed at Margaret. He began to see her as an uncaring mother who refused to continue to grieve for her lost daughter. The pain was critical in keeping her daughter's memory alive.

His head began to hurt. He saw Margaret's lack of pain as a betrayal to him and most certainly her daughter. A decision was made that he would not go back in three days. He would never see the woman again. Any person who would not perpetually grieve for such an overwhelming loss must be cruel and callous. Mason began to think of the accident, visualizing in his head. Anger, bitterness and the desire for retribution blossomed forth like sick mutant flowers of pain. This was what the old woman should be feeling because this was real and how the world worked. With a sense of purpose he allowed the pain to wash over him while reaching for the bottle of Scotch beckoning from the center of the kitchen table.

He awoke lying on the floor behind the couch. Mason struggled to rise, finally deciding it was better to remain on hands and knees until the spinning slowed. Around the room was a chaotic scene of destruction. All his trophies were mangled and lay in heaps where they had struck the walls of the apartment. The wooden bases were scorched where an attempt at setting them on fire had occurred. A large butcher knife was stuck in the wall, just above numerous fist holes. He pushed himself up from the floor, feeling the pain in his knuckles, which were covered in blood. Looking about the lightening room Mason realized it was dawn and he was in the midst of destruction, with overturned furniture and emptied drawers flung about the room. Knowing what to do, he staggered and kicked through the rubble, somehow finding his bed.

Mason missed the meeting with Margaret, due to remaining in bed for a week. The hangover continued for much too long and was finally replaced by a tiredness that would not leave. He made trips to the bathroom, ate plain bread, blackening bananas, soft mushy apples and drank warm tap water, but mostly he slept, thankful for the blackness of unconsciousness. Finally after eight days he found the strength to have a shower and begin the reluctant clean up.

Mason managed the alcohol, in the daytime, for the next six months as he moved forward. Spring came and he took a job driving a gravel truck. The hours were at times long, but the money was good. He attempted to rekindle the interest in golf, but played poorly and soon spent his leisure time drinking. As the summer passed he began to think of Margaret. Mason thought about dropping by to see her but did not find the courage until the snow had fallen and freeze up had brought a shutdown in the gravel business. Having a few days before beginning a new job selling cars, he decided to go see Margaret.

Going to the apartment, Mason was greeted by an older woman who was clearly a sister, as the resemblance was remarkable. He asked for Margaret and saw the woman's face change.

"You knew my sister?" The past tense resulted in him tensing.

"Yes. More acquaintances really. I met her in the winter and have been busy working and haven't been able to get back to see her, but I thought now would be a good time as I'm laid off and have time to see her now." He delivered the untruthful words in a stumbling fashion. For some reason he was sweating and very nervous.

"Are you the young man she saved with the pepper spray?" There was a knowing look on the woman's face.

"Yes, ma'am. That would be me." Mason looked at the floor wondering what the woman knew and what she thought of him. The insecurities began to flow like water from a pump.

"Margaret spoke about you in our telephone conversations. You had meant something to her, because she was quite worried when you never came back. She thought she had hurt your feelings." The woman stared hard at him and he could feel her disapproval.

"Nothing like that, just busy is all." Again the lie came out hollow and empty sounding.

The woman stared at Mason and paused as if unsure of what to do. Finally, and with regret in her voice, she asked if he would like to stay for tea since a pot had just steeped. Mason thanked her and sat at his place on the couch.

The woman returned with the tea and said, "My name is Ellen. I'm Margaret's sister. Margaret died two weeks ago." Mason was not surprised as he had sensed the recent presence of death. Ellen went on to explain that Margaret had steadily weakened over the summer and had finally been taken by pneumonia after getting a chill. "She was very old, you know." Ellen paused.

"Margaret was a very gentle soul and always tried to help others. She had felt the pain of loss, very, very deeply. Did she tell you about Martha?" Mason nodded. "Well, after Martha's death she had an awful time. She had survived a World War and had buried two husbands but the loss of Martha was too, too much. She started drinking and was fired from the hospital, which crushed her. I tried to help but my children were young and I was so far away. She became involved in all types of bad things and we thought that she would wind up dead. Late one night, I'll never forget it, she called me and woke me up. She was so excited. I thought she was drunk or something, but she assured me she was sober. She kept saying, "I remembered" over and over as if she had discovered a secret treasure or something. I never did find out what it was. When I asked her later she would just smile or laugh as if I would never understand. All very strange it was. But the most surprising thing was that she quit drinking that night and never touched a drop again. She even remarried twice more, enjoying her husbands and helping both with the pain they were feeling. She could tell, you know. She had lived with it so much, she could tell. Buried both those men. Was very sad about losing them, but was strangely content with each of their passing. She sure helped them both too, and they knew it. Both worshipped her and she deserved it. She was special, that's for sure. More tea?" Mason shook his head, lost in Ellen's words.

"Which brings us to you. As you can see I am just finishing up with her things so I don't have too much time right now. My bus leaves for home tomorrow. So I will be clear. She believed that the best way for a person to learn about himself or herself was to gently move them in the direction they needed to go. Got that from our mother. I got more of Daddy's side of the family. Quick, direct and to the point. I do not have the patience of beautiful Margaret." Ellen cocked her head, catching Mason's eyes and holding the stare with a firmness that made looking away impossible. "She spoke about you in our telephone calls, hoping that she could give you something that would help you deal with your addiction." The words cut deep. "She was at first hopeful but after you did not come back she felt that she had disappointed you in some strange way. I told her that she should forget about it, as you were just another drunk who would disappoint her, but she would not let it go, hoping you would come back. And you have, but too late for her," Ellen said, releasing him from the stare. She waved her hands gently in the air as if to somehow touch her sister. "Anyways, it's too late to get anything further from her, but it is not too late to change where your life is at. You are too old to be behaving the way you are and too young to die. But you need to decide. If I thought it would help you I would slap you on the head and knock some sense into you. But I know what Margaret would say. Everyone has to make their own way in life. We can only offer help to direct lost souls back on the right path." She finished the imitation, which was quite good, sighed and sat for a minute with her hands folded.

Ellen rose from the chair as if silently directing that it was time to leave. Walking Mason to the door, she paused and then moved into the kitchen, returning with the ornamental teapot that had just been used. "Take this, as she said you seemed to like tea. She probably would have liked you to have it."

"Thank you," Mason said, feeling the still warm teapot in his hands.

"Good luck," Ellen said with a sad expression, "and think long and hard about what my sister said. She was a loving, caring person but underneath she was tough as nails. She had been there, so if she told you something I would listen. Those words are of great value." With that, Ellen closed the door of the apartment. Again Mason was left with thoughts and emotions jumping about his head like excited children on a trampoline.

Over the next few winter months he worked at the car dealership and drank. Mason found it hard to be positive about anything in his life. An optimistic voice of hope arrived at strange times and disappeared just as quickly. At these times the voice seemed determined to make a difference, ready to fight multitudes of negative hosts that rose up to do battle. The feelings provoked by the thoughts were welcomed and seemed to give him energy and courage. Then it would be gone, leaving Mason searching his being for a reconnection. When none could be found he would fly into rages where anger would be released. The anger remained so strong it lived close to the surface with others sensing its essence and avoiding personal contact. At work customers chose other salesmen, even when Mason put on a most accommodating smile. The angrier he got the more his messed up mind encouraged the drinking. Thus the circle was complete with the pulsing anger making him drink more, causing greater difficulties in his life, which caused more anger.

It was on a cold day in February that Mason received his eviction notice from the apartment. It was hand delivered by the caretaker and his two brawny nephews. The man was curt and to the point. Mason's angry loud behavior was scaring the other tenants and he would have to leave. The date of moving was set for the end of March, so Mason had six weeks to find another place. All damage must be repaired or the damage deposit would be forfeited. If the noise and yelling continued the police would be called and eviction would be immediate. The man, who was obviously nervous, said there was no other choice. It was apparent that there was no regret in the two young nephews, who appeared anxious for an altercation so they could teach the old guy some manners. The caretaker turned to leave while the two nephews scowled, with the last one pointing an index finger menacingly and then a middle finger skyward. Mason closed the door and slumped against the jam. His image was caught in the small smudged mirror hanging crookedly on the wall. He absorbed the image for a long time and then looked down in defeat. Making his way to the couch he lay quietly in the fetal position until he was able to drag his tired body to work.

As soon as Mason reached the dealership, he knew something was wrong. The usual pretended hardy hellos were tempered or nonexistent. He did not have his coat off before the telephone rang and the general manager requested his attendance immediately. The voice on the phone spoke of reprimand. Presenting himself he was informed that the situation at the dealership was requiring some immediate changes. The sales manager that had hired him had been fired and Harry Morrice had been promoted. Mason and Harry went way back, working together off and on for years. The man was a puritan who hated Mason's debauched lifestyle and callous disregard for religious values that Harry held sacred. Mason would have one week to make the changes Harry wanted or he would be unemployed.

"Better sober up and get to a church by Monday," Harry commented with a smirk. Mason would be done at this place by next week and both he and Harry knew it.

Knowing that he was finished at work, Mason could not stay and watch Harry's greedy eyes watching and waiting for the anticipated and soon to be savored firing. Telling the receptionist he had a doctor's appointment, Mason left work, cashed his paycheck and headed for the roadhouse. Perhaps Sid the bartender would be in a more pleasant mood this Wednesday evening and not cut him off like last month when Mason became involved in a fight. A person never knew what to expect when walking through the doors of a bar. Mason was certain of one fact. The situation could not get any worse.

Chapter Six
BOOZE

The walnut color of the liquid was an interesting contrast to the frothy amber tone of the malt beer. Mason sat on the bar stool, with hungry gaze shifting from one to the other. In civilized drinking establishments this was called a "boiler maker". He had followed the customary process, whiskey first, many times in the past, but he had just as often switched the order depending on his frame of mind, which had to do with his level of inebriation. Tonight, being middling in his drunkenness, Mason quickly picked up the shot glass with his left hand and effortlessly poured the whiskey down his throat. His right hand found the beer glass in a fluid motion, brought it to his lips, and drained the contents. No wasted effort, no spillage, no burning sensation or body shudders anymore, just spreading warmth through his midsection like a belt too tight.

Mason removed his arms from the bar, straightened his shoulders and waited for the spreading tendrils of numbness to reach the balls of his feet dangling off the stool. Usually the resultant muted tingle meant that he was in control of the liquor. Check that. Mason was never "in control" of the dragon, as it would suffer no master. This was the liar's game Mason had played with the beast for the past thirty-five years, becoming quite proficient at both lying and drinking. It was unfortunate that the one endeavor in which he truly excelled was probably the one thing that would eventually kill him. Or would it be sooner, an internal voice posed. The queries were coming with greater frequency as of late. Mason knew how to silence these difficult to manage inquiries. Unfortunately, that often led to extremely painful mornings, followed by further alcohol therapy to cure the cure, and chase the common sense knowledge away.

His musings were interrupted by a sudden introduction of cold air as the side door of the bar opened. A stranger looked around the room, dusted off snowy shoulders and walked over to the bar. Mason quickly looked away wanting nothing to do with socially acceptable chitchat, having no interest in his fellow man. Leaning on the bar, the short, balding middle-aged man rubbed together his cold hands.

"Sure is getting ugly out there," the man stated in a friendly manner.

Mason remained frozen, as a child who believes stillness is invisibility and waited anxiously for the next sentence. Fortunately it never came as Sid arrived and quickly served the man. He liked Sid. No idle conversation or probing feeling questions like "how are you today?" just simple straightforward service. To this end Sid held up his index and middle finger, wiggled them up and down and sideways. The response was a slight nod of the head. That was the type of conversation Mason appreciated, with no niceties or pretense that Sid or he cared even the slightest bit for the other. Unfortunately Sid did care some for him. This barkeep would not want him to drink too much as that could result in problems and Sid did not like expending energy on anyone else's issues. Some regulars were not to be worried about, but Mason's doorway to trouble was never too far away. Sid knew it and had seen it recently. The bartender had carefully assessed the situation and soon the empty drink glasses were replaced.

Mason reached into his coat pocket, searching for the recognizable square. He found it with greedy fingers, while the familiar nicotine craving began deep in his darkened lungs. His left hand formed around his ancient Zippo lighter and soon both were on display. He examined the worn silver case remembering a distant time when the box was new and shone with a brilliant sheen, especially when displayed on a sunny day. Rebecca and Sam Jr. had been amazed and believed him a magician, when he danced the reflected light around the large backyard of Victoria's house. Mason rubbed the case, secretly hoping that the shine would return, but it remained tarnished and sad, a concrete example of his life. He could still make out the letters of the inscription in the corner, but chose not to read or remember the significance. The longing for something of substance appeared and, like a wisp of smoke on a windy day, was gone leaving only a stinging moist irritation in his eyes. Suddenly the oxidized silver square disappeared and was replaced by the hairy back of Sid's large hand. Mason stiffened with rage, as his head snapped upward meeting a piercing, cold stare.

"I told you before, no more smoking in the bar. It's the law and you are just going to have to get used to it."

"Fucking law," Mason growled through clenched teeth.

"You don't have to like it but you do have to obey it," Sid stated with finality.

"I know, I know," his voice softening. "I was just looking at the case."

Sid grunted and having made his point moved away down the bar.

"It was a present," Mason said to no one. "It was a present."

Mason slowly moved the case back into his coat pocket and clicked open the well-worn Zippo. It made the familiar, metallic sound he associated with the lighting of a great many cigarettes over a great many years. Unlike the case, the lighter was a prize. He had won it in a golf tournament years before. While any other trophies had been misplaced or destroyed in fits of drunken rage, he had somehow retained and cherished the lighter, which was a reminder of past victory. Mason had not won at many endeavors in his life. Strangely enough it was an activity he chose to participate in sober. For some reason drinking and golf did not mix on his emotional plane. Playing partners would often ridicule him for not having a few drinks on the course. He would gladly take their money and then make up for the abstinence at the nineteenth hole. He did not play much now, sensing his one bastion against alcohol was in danger of being corrupted. As a result avoidance won out. Another loss, another defeat, another wound healed only through cauterization by the whiskey dragon's breath.

Mason forced his mind to return to a long ago happier, healthier time when the land was alive and the game of golf gave structure and reason to his world. On the golf course the task was simple. All that mattered was getting the ball in the hole. Unfortunately, while simplicity was often the most wonderfully rewarding endeavor, both in life and golf, it had become increasingly difficult for Mason to obtain on any level. The finding of the answer was now elusive and confusing, like catching fog or comprehending a quickly spoken foreign language. There had been so many failures he had almost stopped searching and mostly stopped caring. He struggled to suppress the negative thoughts, breathing slowly through his nose feeling his chest rise and fall. The emptiness slowly began to leave like the relief found when stale hot air suddenly moves. He began to settle, experiencing a slight melting feeling. This was the occasional calmness he had felt in life. A weak decision was made to get in shape again and play lots of golf this year. This may offer a way to find the elusive space inside where peace, contentment and stillness may still exist. The search for a simple existence was becoming absolutely necessary and would begin on the golf course. A contented smile pulled his eyes slightly close as a lightness of body and spirit brought a strange peace to his troubled soul.

"Don't you fall asleep on me or I'll throw you out in the snow bank!" barked Sid in a voice quiet enough not to disturb the other patrons, but loud enough for most to hear. Snickers and the shrill laughter of a woman followed the comment.

"Don't worry," Mason angrily slurred.

Any attempt at a peaceful moment was lost and his brain began to work again at full capacity, dragging and dredging up self-defeating images of what he had become. He started wondering what the other patrons thought of Sid's comments. Slowly he turned on the barstool and in an exaggerated, nonchalant manner panned the Wednesday night spectacle. He specifically wanted to know if the shrill laugh had been directed at him. If someone were mocking, then perhaps the ugliness would be released. No one appeared to be paying undue attention, but he did notice a dark haired woman at a corner table. As their eyes locked she smiled warmly. Mason self-consciously looked away.

Beneath his hardened exterior had always lived a very sensitive soul, extremely susceptible to any perceived judgments or criticism. Unfortunately, once others planted a seed, through an innocent gesture or comment, Mason would nurture and tend the sprout until there was a flourishing crop of distrust, insecurity and self-loathing. Over his fifty-two years he had become an extremely proficient and accomplished farmer, producing bumper crops of self-conscious worry that would at times paralyze him with fear and indecision. Compulsively, his mind would not stop, forever seeking negative control through endless self-hurting messages about what he had done, was doing or would do wrong in the future. Many, who cared, had offered support. Rather than disappoint and expose his weakness, he would withdraw into the anger of alcohol-induced nights and the fog of the next day hangover.

Knowing all this why not change, reason interrupted. Lately the voice had become louder as the drinking, his pain of past loss and bad life events had begun to spin faster and faster like a violent storm building to an ugly conclusion. Mason could feel it inside and wondered if this was the last stand of that inner essence that had no real name in his language. The resulting feeling appeared with the possibility of hopeful change. It was as if this third party had joined the war, with some strength and determination. An increase in this positive voice had resulted in a reaction. The alcohol intake had increased. So had the negative messages and resulting outbursts of anger. Even old drinking buddies were beginning to stay away as if sensing an impending crisis event. A major battle seemed inevitable that may determine the entire conflict and the resultant postwar landscape. Unfortunately, Mason was not optimistic as to the outcome and had a vision of a barren emotional state, if any state remained at all.

He closed his eyes and allowed his head to lean back and rest on his shoulders. Tiredness settled as he lolled his head from side to side. No more debate. No more thinking. No more searching for salvation in a place little understood and not even fully accepted. Given the eviction and the impending loss of his job Mason could not tolerate any more self-examination. It was time to seek oblivion. That was enough thinking for this evening. He lowered his head, picked up the beer glass and drained half the contents. The whiskey was tossed off without a thought and then he dumped the remaining beer down his throat.

As his stomach settled Mason began to feel the effects of numerous beers. He always put off the first visit to the washroom as long as possible, knowing that once he started, many trips would ensue. Unfortunately, he could no longer wait, so accepted the first challenge of the evening and gingerly lowered his five foot ten inch frame off the stool. He planted both feet before letting go of the arms, turned slowly and marched on straight legs to the facilities located in the back corner of the bar. The first steps were the most difficult due to the paradox of being drunk while attempting to walk sober. This gave a wooden quality to his gait, making it appear that he was drunker than was actually the case. Later, when more intoxicated and less concerned about the opinions of others, his body movements would loosen. At the same time Mason began to smile, knowing full well that people were somewhat mollified if an obviously inebriated man was happy. However, he needed to be careful not to resemble the village idiot, grinning and laughing over a long forgotten joke.

Mason straightened as he moved through a small visiting crowd standing beside a double table. The congestion allowed for the briefest of pauses, during which he made his appraisal of the dark haired woman. She was not as young as he had first thought. The makeup was liberally applied and tended to hide some of the facial road map of life's experiences. His acute powers of observation quickly saw through the fluff realizing this lady had seen hard living and had experienced lots of pain, as the small scar above her left eyebrow attested. Her teeth were straight and probably a most prized feature, as she was quick to smile. The gesture was an attempt to camouflage the hurt and it probably fooled most, but Mason was a professional observant of pain, having many strategies to hide his own true feelings.

Mason looked away while sliding by the bottleneck and, with a final jerky movement, stole a second quick glance. She was with him, locking on with suggestive eyes, while hiding behind the bright white curtain. The inviting offer caught him off guard. He felt a slight pulling at his crotch, which was pleasing.

Mason continued on with more deliberate steps, as the encounter with the Smile had put additional pressure on his already full and constricted bladder. He hit the door with outstretched arms and heard rather than felt it hit the wall. The smell of urine assailed his nostrils as he entered the brightly lit room. He quickly unzipped his fly and relaxed. Nothing else was needed as his body did the rest. A gentle sigh escaped as his shoulders slumped in submission.

When finished, Mason turned to the row of sinks on the wall. He was careful in saddling up to the white basin, wishing to avoid the carelessly splashed water. The movement of hands under the spout brought on a short, cold burst of water. The soap dispenser was useless, as it hung open and empty, a small pool of pink liquid congealing on the counter. He rubbed his hands together as the water stopped and avoided the image in the polished metal mirror bolted to the wall. He did not want to end up back in the fetal position. Mason deliberately looked down, received more water, cupped the contents and vigorously worked his hands up and down his face. He moved to the paper towel dispenser and, upon finding it empty, brought the sleeves of his shirt down both cheeks. An oily stickiness began to form making him feel unclean. With hopelessness building, he sadly thought that his appearance didn't mean a damn anyways.

Arriving back at the side bar, Mason settled on the stool. He desperately needed a drink and motioned to Sid. While Sid noticed the gesture, the response was slow and deliberate. The evening's first serious evaluation had begun. The only choice was to show patience, as if it did not matter how long it took for a beverage. Suppressing the desire to jump over the bar and throw a useless punch at a now useless bartender, Mason swiveled casually. The Smile was gone. Her replacements were two surly, slightly disheveled looking men. Both noticed Mason's interest, meeting his stare with challenging scowls. He quickly spun the stool back to face the bar. His emotions changed from sexual anticipation to the gnawing sensation of fear in one quick moment. The fear was real as he could tell the men were knowledgeable, in both creating and happily dealing with trouble. In one of his ugly attack moods Mason may have held his own for a while with one, but with both any confrontation would be short and messy.

"Hey, Sid. How about a rum and Pepsi?" Mason asked in his best business voice. The inflection sounded good, as the bartender approvingly responded.

"What kind of rum?"

"Black"

"Black?"

"Black rum. Navy rum, and make it a double in a large glass," he added in a casual voice, attempting not to sound too anxious.

As Sid shrugged and went off to pour the drink, relief replaced all other emotions. Mason would get his drink but not without the inevitable struggle to keep himself in control. It was becoming more difficult everyday to interact with others. Each of his emotions seemed exaggerated lately. When he was excited or happy, the behavior was often manic, bringing on exaggerated movements and laughter. Sadness brought on lethargy and at times uncontrollable sobbing. Anger brought on quick, violent verbal and physical reactions, steeped in mountains of blame towards any he erroneously believed had done him wrong. Disappointment or worry resulted in periods of black depression, where the only goal was to lay quietly in a darken room and attempt to exorcise the heavy emotional pain throbbing deep in his chest. The solution to these emotions run amuck, was to blot out all feelings with a liquid anesthetic. The alcohol solved nothing, but it did dull the emotive process through fogging the senses or by offering the peace of the frequent blackouts.

The double black rum landed on the bar with a restrained thud, resulting in a slight splash on the already soiled cardboard coaster. "I'll need you to settle up," Sid stated as he quickly moved down the bar to fill a server's order. Mason removed the straws, picked up the drink and took a large gulp. The rum taste was strong, sweet and pleasing. He was feeling better. Sid returned and offered Mason the tab.

"Take care of this one and we will start another," the bartender stated in a matter of fact tone. Buoyed by the realization that there would be no stoppage in the flow of alcohol for the next while, Mason brought out his wallet. Opening it resulted in a good feeling, as he had just been paid. As was custom he took the entire amount in cash. Even though most would go towards rent, expenses and the little food he ate, for the evening the sight of the cash deluded others and sadly himself into believing he was wealthy. Mason glanced at the tab, while removing a hundred dollar bill.

"Hello," came a deep, throaty voice over his right shoulder.

Mason swiveled slightly and there was the Smile beaming at him. "Well hello."

"Anyone sitting here?" she questioned, motioning to an empty bar stool.

"You are," Mason said with a cocky, silly smile. Her giggle put him at ease as she moved the stool closer to his, and then parked her tight jean encrusted behind.

"I've seen you here before," she said while motioning to Sid.

"I usually drop by after work for a couple," he lied.

Sid arrived quickly, took her drink order and left after giving him a look of suspicion. Mason returned the look with one of impudent triumph. Steadily he attempted to calm his sexual anticipation. He would need to woo her and get her somewhere alone. It would be necessary to slow down and do this right. Mason suddenly realized she was speaking and refocused his attention on her face.

".....and I usually meet a couple of girlfriends here later in the evening," she said as he picked up the conversation. She appeared not to have noticed the lapse.

"Are they here now?" he asked politely.

"I don't think so," she stated swiveling the stool. Mason glanced over her shoulder, even though he had no idea what he was looking for. His eyes picked up the two men in the corner who were in deep conversation and oblivious to his observations.

She rotated back, extended her hand and stated her name was Janie. Mason introduced himself as they began the polite and yet probing verbal mating ritual. He felt good about the conversation that covered safe areas such as work and current events, while at times slipping into risqué topics with vague sexual innuendo. In addition, physical movements took on a suggestive intimate quality.

Mason soon realized he was having fun. Janie was pleasant company and as the drinks kept coming she became more attractive and his need to be with her became more urgent. She was making him feel better and better. This may be the start of something special Mason thought as she launched into a long-winded story of faraway summer romance. His mind drifted, offering the naïve possibility of new love. This allowed the alcohol and libido fueled delusions of contentment to take him further into the outrageous fantasy. Mason refocused again.

"That was great. You're a natural story teller." He stroked her ego with kind words.

"It's because you're so easy to talk to and such a good listener," Janie stated as the verbal massaging continued.

In the past few years, Mason found this phony niceness appalling and would end it after a few minutes. But tonight was different. This woman was different. Janie was pleasant, interesting and made him feel good. There was a nagging pull of caution inside, but the combination of alcohol and desire, both sexual and for peaceful tenderness, resulted in him totally disregarding any concerns.

Mason liked Janie more and more as the night proceeded. Nursing her drinks, she was quick to order him refills. Sid became the obedient bartender, as her presence was somehow intimidating. She began to move closer after laughing at each witticism or quip about a person, experience or real life situation. The alcohol and her attention began to wrap around him like a comfort blanket made of soft cloth. Mason talked quickly now hoping to share everything before each refreshing moment was somehow lost. After an especially long story involving opinions and philosophy, he paused and with a sigh said, "I am having a wonderful time and by God you are beautiful." Mason sensed and saw the sadness for a brief moment and then the smile returned, brighter than ever.

"You deserve to have a good time, you are a remarkable man."

He grinned shyly. No one had ever called him remarkable. But coming from her he was remarkable. Mason certainly had blemishes on his character but they could be healed through the right combination of remedies. She was the elixir that could begin the process. Mason felt a glowing sensation building inside.

She patted him gently on the face and then allowed her hand to rest with her fingertips lying against the front of his ear. "You are so sweet," she cooed. Mason closed his eyes as the hand slowly slid forward off his face leaving a lingering sensation of warmth. When he opened his eyes she was sipping her drink, while gazing over the top of the glass.

"You wouldn't happen to have a cigarette would you?" Janie asked.

"I sure do." Mason slurred through a widening smile.

She leaned closer and into his offered ear she whispered, "Why don't we go outside for a quick smoke, finish our drinks and head to my place for a nightcap?"

"Sounds great," Mason panted while sliding into the arms of his parka. "Let's go." He hit the floor in one motion, unconcerned that he appeared over anxious. She joined him with her jacket on, linked his arm and leaned her ample bosom against his eager bicep. Janie giggled as they headed for the side door.

"Just a smoke break, Sid. Be back shortly."

As they made for the door, he began to believe that this was the start of a wondrous journey. This chance meeting with a bar angel could begin a process that would finally make him whole. She had been sent to save him from the world and more importantly from himself. Janie was what he had always been searching for as she had the answer.

Walking out of the bar, he could hear an unfamiliar, yet instantly pleasing song playing over the sound system. It made him feel even better. This was going to be a great night!

Chapter Seven

A Sobering Moment

Janie pushed the crash bar and suddenly they were outside. The burning cold February air seared Mason's lungs. The coughing bout was severe and profound, bringing tears to his eyes, causing his nose to run. As the coughing subsided Mason wiped the moisture from his nose and eyes with the arm of his jacket, leaving trails of fluid that froze instantly, resulting in frosty tracks on the nylon surface. He must be a pretty sight, Mason thought, as Janie physically supported him through the fit.

"You OK?" She questioned with a voice full of concern.

"Never better." Mason gasped. "Where should we go for the smoke?" he asked, hearing the foolishness of his own words.

"Where's your car?" Janie asked, her words significantly muted by the howling wind. This was some kind of serious weather, Mason thought, lowering his head and shoulders.

"Are you sure you want to stay out here in this blizzard?" As much as he liked smoking Mason was not prepared to freeze for a cigarette. In addition, there was a certainty that a drag of smoke would get him coughing again, something he was positive Janie would not see as appealing.

"For sure. I really need one. Please!" She yelled, begging.

Mason grabbed her by the arm and proceeded across the parking lot to his car, resting in a snowdrift. He opened the passenger side door and pushed her in, sliding in behind onto the front bench seat. Both were shaking. After the screaming of the wind the sheltered front seat offered an exaggerated stillness that was almost spooky. The air in the car was very cold and seemed to crackle as they breathed rapidly, out of breath from the fight with the storm. The chillness of the still air made the warm expulsions from their lungs crystallize instantly, freezing to the windows, creating swirling designs of random patterns that were caught in the faded glow of the parking lot lights. They rested for a minute, both attempting to slow the pace of breathing.

Pulling out the silver case Mason took out two cigarettes. The Zippo caught on the first try. He allowed the flame to offer some warmth that reached out into the frigid air. Both cigarettes were lighted and Janie took a long, nervous pull. He watched the amber flare as she dragged the smoke into her lungs. Even the burning of the tobacco gave off an icy glare appearing frozen and unreal. There was a deliberate hesitation before Mason took the first drag of his cigarette. He was no different than any long time smoker who knows with certainty that coughing will be assured if a cigarette is smoked. The pull of the cigarette brought the coughing convulsions back with an intensity that started to scare him. As the fit incapacitated Mason, he could feel a slight movement as Janie slid across the seat towards the far door. Finally the spasms in his lungs began to subside. He sat shaking and exhausted, trying desperately to catch his breath.

Mason was again wiping his eyes as the roar of the storm entered his ears with a suddenness that took him completely off guard. At first he thought that the woman had left through the driver's door. Through blurred eyes Mason could see that Janie was attempting to get out of the car, yet the driver's door would only open a foot as the wind packed snowdrift would not allow for further movement. She was frantically pushing against the door in a futile effort to escape. In his slow moving rum-soaked mind Mason found it odd that she was in such a hurry to get out of the car. He also wondered how the small opening of the driver's door could allow so much wind and snow to enter the front seat. Still looking across at a now flailing and screaming Janie he noticed another dark figure outside the driver's side kicking snow and pulling on the door. A Good Samaritan coming to help, he thought with acceptance. It would be just as easy if he exited the car and let the woman out the passenger side. Mason reached for the door and could not find the handle. In fact the whole door was gone and then in slow brain time, he realized that the door was somehow open. At the same instant, Mason felt a heavy hand grab his jacket. The whole situation made no sense until he felt the edge of the knife under his chin.

"Gimme your wallet, asshole, or I'll cut your throat," came the loud words that were muffled by the storm but echoed around the car.

As with any threatening gesture or action, once identified, the body will react with speed and strength brought on by the intense injection of chemicals into the blood stream. The situation was no longer confusing, it was threatening so Mason's body took over. Instantly, both hands grabbed the arm and, with leverage and power on his side, slammed the hand against the frozen front window with a quickness and force that broke the surface and perhaps some knuckles. The grabbing of the arm caused the lighted ambers from the burning cigarette to explode across the inside of the car. The quickness and painful nature of the attack caused the man to drop the knife, which landed on the dashboard and then fell into the darkness of the floor. Mason heard a deep howl of pain and knew he had not produced the sound, as the noise coming from his throat was a low growl. Still holding the arm Mason pulled the weight of the stranger into the car and then with a sudden jerk pushed outward with all his strength. The force propelled the man backwards. The slippery new snow resulted in the attacker upending and crashing to the frozen parking lot. Mason was out of the car quickly and advancing on the man with only one purpose. His caveman instincts were aroused and he attacked with a sustained purpose that shocked the younger man. The man was attempting to rise when Mason kicked the mugger just under the chin sending the man sprawling. Mason was quickly on the mugger throwing wild punches with both fists. After a few connected blows the man began to turtle, rolling over and covering his unprotected head. Mason was beginning to stand when he felt a crushing impact to the back of his head. It was the hardest punch he had ever experienced, having the feel of iron.

The blow was so powerful it removed his legs and Mason fell to his knees in the snow. On his knees he felt a sharp pain in his back. The scene began to move very slowly. Janie stood above him with a knife in her hand, screaming. The look in her eyes would never be forgotten as the hurt that Mason had seen in the bar flowed out of her and presented itself in violent ugliness. Beside her stood one of the dangerous men he had noticed earlier in the night. On his right hand was a set of brass knuckles. Janie moved in, slashing with the knife, catching Mason on the cheek. She continued to scream, but he could hear nothing due to the loud drum beating rapidly in his head. As Mason moved his head to avoid the knife he noticed the other man rising from the ground. In an instant it suddenly became very clear he would probably die.

Moving to protect his head from the knife Mason brought his arm up to his face as Janie came down with a stabbing motion and stuck the blade into the heavy jacket and through the muscle of his forearm. The pain caused Mason to jerk away, tearing the knife out of the woman's grip. The movement also exposed his face to the brass knuckled fist that crashed into his left cheek, making a horrible sound and sending him face first onto the parking lot where he landed on his nose. Then the kicking started as the attackers became bent on retribution. The sensations of the blows began to deaden, as pain and time began to disappear. Mason knew the impact area and identified that serious damage was being done, but a peaceful drifting had begun to occur that was not unpleasant. Mason remembered feeling a hand on his back and was never sure if it was one of the thieves taking his wallet or the gentle touch of death letting him know that it was time to go.

Mason floated above the bloody scene while all three thieves kicked his helpless body. There was no connection as the trio tired of the exertion, took his possessions and turned to leave. As if wanting one more piece of revenge, the bloodied mugger kicked at the disconnected head and then the whole scene abruptly stopped, going black like the breaking of film in a darkened movie theatre.

Over the next endless period of time the only sensation was the motion and movement of air by dissevered bodies or the sounds of faraway noises. There was never any assurances that the disruptions were humanly made, as the minor disturbances were delicate and ethereal, making them difficult to comprehend and impossible to analyze. None of the action was coherent, often making little sense. Attempting to understand what was happening became too hard and usually, after a few simple flashes, the entire system would shut down and the nothingness would return. When the movements would start again Mason would become aware but quite disinterested. There was no recognition of self, situation or circumstances. The existence became a spread out series of quick electrical jolts that would appear suddenly and be gone just as quickly. At one point there was the impression that he was rolling, faster and faster. At another time there was a far off beeping that was spaced and then constant and then gone. There was a numb feeling of violent shaking with none of the discomfort. In fact there was no unpleasantness or pain at all. There was no impression that any trauma or physical hurt had been incurred. It was just an emptiness filled with the rare drifting connection of a physical world so fragile that too forceful a hold could result in the most tentative union becoming fractured and lost.

Very gradually the coupling grew stronger. Initially it was a buzzing sound that came out of a shadow land and stayed for a period of time. At first no ideas were generated as to what the sound was. Strangely the image of a common housefly penetrated the curtain. There was an additional thought that disagreed, stating the sound was too mechanical. Then the thinking process flashed to flowing water and promptly shutdown, leaving the question of the buzzing unanswered. The next time it was the barking of a dog and then the realization that the observation was wrong, with a suggestion that the sound, while distant, could be that of a human being coughing. This analysis was immediately understood and accepted as the right answer. Mason heard a woman gently singing and the sensation of his head moving. He heard the clatter of a metal object hitting a concrete floor. Then one night Mason woke from a long sleep and was able to open his eyes. At first all was blurry, with no discernable shapes apparent. There was a small red light blinking off in the distance. It was difficult to tell the size or how far away the light was but as he watched it for a time the image began to clear somewhat, causing Mason to believe the light was very small. He was not sure if the glow meant warning or was some sign of welcome. Later he woke again, opening then quickly closing his eyes due to the brightness of the light coming through the window. Mason repeated the procedure again and again until his eyes were no longer bothered by the sunlight. Then he scanned the room, moving only his eyes, encountering a blurred picture on the wall, an open door that led to an out of focus hallway and a white smoke detector with a small red light difficult to see in the brightness of the sun's energy.

At one point Mason woke in the middle of the night. He suddenly began to think again, attempting to put lost pieces back together and make sense out of what had happened. He thought this was going to be an easy task, yet for some reason the images were in no order and offered no progression. Mason knew he liked bike riding, especially the feel of the fast-moving air on his face. For some reason he remembered that he needed to move by March 31st. He had a strong urge to check a calendar where he knew the information would be contained. After recalling other information he became exhausted, with sleep halting the quest for information.

There was a sense that he was getting better as the pain began one morning. In this way the structure of the days and nights began to take shape. In addition, he began to communicate again. Up until that point Mason had avoided any contact keeping his eyes closed when others were in the room. He was not sure why he chose this approach. Once decided he stayed with the method until a nurse surprised him early one morning, coming into the room and finding him with eyes open, staring at the rising sunlight.

"Hello, Mason. I see you're awake. Good for you," she said with warmth and encouragement. Mason liked her immediately as she seemed very genuine. "How are you feeling today?" He attempted to speak but all that came out was a baffling rasping grunt. "Oh don't worry about the talking, it will come as your throat heals." The young nurse buzzed about, straightening up the room and checking all the equipment that was attached to him in one way or another. When she had finished doing the necessary tasks, she cranked up the bed so Mason was sitting up, brushed back his hair with her hand and looked him in the eyes. "Good to have you back. I'm sure the doctors will want to talk to you soon."

The plural of doctor made Mason slightly uneasy as it clearly meant that the beating had been serious. Wait, now he remembered. A woman and the two dangerous guys had robbed him in the parking lot of the bar. There had been a blizzard and lots of snow. Wait! He had been stabbed and hit with brass knuckles. Then many memories began flooding back. Most of the remembrances stung like a red-hot knife laid flat on the skin. Mason attempted to take deep breaths to calm the many emotions triggered by the memories. Each intake of air brought about a severe pain in his chest. He began to gasp for air as two nurses rushed in. One spoke calmly to him as the other injected a liquid into the tube protruding from his wrist. Mason felt a coldness travelling up his arm and through his shoulder. Then the sensation went through his entire body, resulting in an instant relaxation as his breath became regular and the speed of the loud beeps from the machine slowed and sounded less frightening. Mason began to melt into the bed, his body becoming limp. Whatever it was that had been injected into the tube was remarkable, removing any concerns. Soon his eyes were heavy and he drifted into the peace of sleep.

Early the next morning a group of doctors, nurses and other white-coated individuals trooped into his room. A white haired man who seemed to be the boss examined the chart. "Well, Mr. Walls. How are you today?"

"Good." Mason attempted a croaky lie. It came out more like, "Gaaa."

"Still hard to talk, huh. Well that will get better soon. You need to drink lots of water to assist with the healing. I want to explain your condition, so a few of us will be back later for a chat." The doctor turned to leave and then stopped. "Is the pain getting worse?" Mason nodded. "Great." Then the entire entourage left the room, leaving him and the machines.

Mason began to doze again, waking up later with numerous sharp uncomfortable pains. He was attempting to isolate them all when the nurse came into the room. "Are you starting to feel pain?" she questioned. Mason nodded. "Good," she said with the same tone as the doctor. Perhaps it was the perplexed expression on his face that caused her to continue. "Why is feeling pain good, right?" He again nodded. "Well, you have been in an induced coma for about three weeks, due to the brain swelling from the assault. We have kept you sedated and pain free while the swelling went down. Now we need to back off on the use of painkillers or you may become addicted and we wouldn't want that. Besides you're strong enough to handle the pain now. But you must remember. While you are healing you must.... hear me....... must stay calm. What happened yesterday must not happen again or you may pull out the stitches in your lung and that would result in more surgery and believe me you do not need any more surgery. So just stay calm for awhile." As usual, she bustled about the room.

While Mason waited for the doctors to return he began to think of the future. He believed most of his memory had come back. If there were recollections still forgotten that was probably for the best as many of the memories were definitely not pleasant. He would wait for the doctor's assessment and then it was time to get back to his life, although what he remembered was not encouraging. He was being evicted from his apartment while some guy at work was going to fire him soon. He liked to drink alcohol, which seemed to be a critical part of every remembered experience and probably the reason he was in this hospital bed with tubes inserted into his body. Mason was beginning to feel better and while the pain was difficult at times everyone seemed to think that was a positive sign.

The doctors returned about an hour later. There were three men and a nurse. The white haired doctor's name was Mendelson. The man began by saying that Mason was very, very lucky to be alive. If it had not been for the coldness of the evening, he would have bled to death in the parking lot. His injuries were serious and numerous. The most concerning had been the internal bleeding caused by the stab wound to the lung and the ruptured spleen. The knife taken out of Mason's arm was a thin bladed stiletto that had entered his back, gone between two ribs and punctured his lung. The thickness of the winter jacket helped as the knife did not go as deep as the blow warranted. In addition, the severe beating, probably from being repeatedly kicked, had ruptured Mason's spleen. The other big concern had been the severe concussion he had received from the blunt trauma to the back of the head. It had taken twenty-six stitches to close the wound and there had been some brain swelling. Luckily the swelling had gone down before surgery had been necessary. Mason had two cracked and three broken ribs. There was damage to his right forearm where the knife had been lodged. Fortunately the blade was thin and while causing some muscle injury, there appeared to be no permanent tendon or ligament damage. He had a fractured ankle and broken left wrist resulting from the probable force of a large foot. There was some damage to his testicles that would hopefully heal over time. Mason had frost bite on his fingers, which needed to be watched closely so gangrene did not occur.

The doctor paused for a moment. He pointed to a young handsome dark-skinned fellow, introducing the man as Dr. Ramshad, and stated that the surgeon had removed Mason's gall bladder and appendix. The gall bladder was taken out as it was very inflamed and the appendix because it was damaged and about to rupture from the beating.

"And then there is your face but we will talk about that later when you are stronger. I will leave that to Dr. Scarletti, as that is his department. You really are a lucky man, Mr. Walls. We almost lost you three times, once in the ambulance and twice here at the hospital. You owe your life to Dr. Ramshad." The dark-skinned man nodded and smiled. The next comment surprised Mason. "You are a very tough guy with a strong will to live. I think we are done here for now. Both of these doctors will be talking to you in the next few days as there are other things to discuss." The men went to leave, but Mendelson stopped and turned while the others left the room. "Oh, by the way, the reason you're having difficulty speaking is because of all the tubes that were down your throat, during surgery and afterwards while you were in a coma. As your throat heals you will begin to get your words back. Remember what I said, lots of water."

This time, Mendelson was almost out the door when the man stopped again. "Almost forgot. The police want to speak with you once you can talk well enough to be interviewed. That will probably be in a few days. Get lots of rest as this afternoon we will start getting you moving."

Mason lay motionless for a long time attempting to absorb all the information. He had really been severely beaten. With the scaling back of the painkillers his body was beginning to send him the message loud and succinct, he had been hurt and hurt badly. In addition, the tentative voice that had been questioning his destructive and dysfunctional lifestyle now had centre stage. The strong and demanding presence of the alcohol dragon had been eliminated, for now, by the length of the coma. His usually overactive brain was stilled and sheepish as if knowing that the illusions it had fabricated had driven Mason wantonly into a potentially fatal situation. The voice of reason and potential wellness now had a chance to grow and expand, unimpeded by the other two negative influences.

Over the years, in stronger moments, Mason had researched addictions, especially examining alcohol and its insidious effects. There were many stories of drinkers hitting bottom and finally addressing the problem. He could feel something small growing but was not sure what it was or what to do with it. The spark was there, albeit weak and distant. The force of it had been responsible for some of the simple and profound questions that had entered his thoughts lately. These searing streaks of inquiry had demanded answers and attention, no longer willing to be relegated to unimportance. In some ways Mason had seen the queries as a last chance before a total submission and submersion in the quicksand of alcohol despair. The kernel of change was present but would require massive encouragement and energy, things he had always lacked. The huge challenge Mason would face was to somehow find the courage and strength to change. He suddenly became exhausted from the information delivered by the doctors and the initial beginnings of a critical process. He soon fell asleep.

The next week was full of more doctor meetings, hard physical work and introspection. Dr. Ramshad arrived one morning and pulled up a chair as if settling down for a long discussion. Mason's whispering voice had returned. The doctor spoke slowly and carefully as if conscious that the thick accent may result in misunderstandings. The surgeon went back over the information shared by Dr. Mendelson, focusing further on the results of each surgical procedure. The lung surgery had been the most difficult and had taken all the man's skill to ensure success. Unfortunately, due to the positioning of the wound, it was necessary to complete emergency surgery twice. There was another issue to be discussed and that was the condition of his lungs due to prolonged and heavy smoking. The doctor paused for a moment and then proceeded in a direct and forceful manner. If Mason did not quit smoking immediately he would die or have his life severely restricted by a respiratory illness. There was a chance for some recovery if he did not have another cigarette. This was an absolute given with no chance of any mistake. If Mason chose to deny this fact and keep on smoking all the surgery that was completed would be a waste of time, as he would soon die. When asked if there were any questions about his lungs, Mason shook his head, as he knew the prognosis to be true.

    The man then talked about the removal of the spleen and examined the angry red but healing scar running from his lower abdomen to his upper chest. The zipper-like quality of the incision was due to the staples applied to close the wound. The removal of the spleen was necessary due to the internal bleeding. Ramshad stated Mason could live without the spleen but would need to be vaccinated against pneumococal pneumonia and other potentially dangerous bacteria. In addition, Mason would need to be very careful of any infections and immediately seek antibiotics to control the bacteria. The gall bladder had been removed due to inflammation from drinking, which led the doctor to another forceful and direct observation. While opened during the surgery Dr. Ramshad had examined his liver and kidneys. The surgeon looked Mason directly in the eyes and told him with certainty that if he continued to drink alcohol in the future eventually his kidneys would shut down and he would need dialysis. His liver would not be able to handle much more liquor input, as the damage was substantial. It was a certainty that continued drinking would cause death. If he quit both drinking and smoking, and got his body into better shape then there was hope for a normal, albeit possibly shortened, life.

The room remained very quiet while the two men sat watching each other. The doctor appeared relieved that the information had been given and received with thoughtfulness. The force of change seemed to relish the knowledge, knowing now that any denial or continuation in the self-destructive behaviour could only be seen as total disregard for personal wellbeing and inevitably an act of suicide. The silence continued as each man became lost in his own thoughts.

Finally the doctor spoke, asking if there were any questions. Mason shook his head and in a quiet voice thanked the man for the medical help, the direct explanation about the injuries and the blunt, yet realistic, appraisal of the future. With an encouraging smile the surgeon wished Mason luck with the necessary decisions. Dr. Ramshad knew that while on the surface the decision to stop drinking and live seemed simple and automatic prolonged abstinence would be extremely difficult and involve a strengthening of many life areas.

Mason reflected and dozed throughout the day, attempting to sort out the situation first critically and then emotionally. Critically it appeared an easy case of problem and solution. The facts were clear. If he did not stop drinking and smoking, he would probably die. The voice of change halted the procedures with the first debate, not probably, the man had said very clearly that a continuation would bring about a fatal situation sooner rather than later. Clearly there was no choice from a practical sense if he wanted to live some kind of quality existence he must quit smoking and drinking.

The decision then became a simple matter of committing to a healthier life style that removed alcohol and cigarettes, while adding exercise and positive emotional activities. That would be the challenge. Just thinking about the process brought on the desire for a large Scotch and a smoke. The longing began to strengthen as the voice for change shrunk into the recesses of his mind. It was at that point that Mason began to realize how difficult the massive alterations would be. The internal debate had now advanced to the emotional level, where in fact it had always been fought.

In the next few days Mason's room continued to be a hub of activity. Dr. Scarletti, the plastic surgeon arrived to discuss the damage to his face. The back of his head would be fine once the stitches were removed. Mason would have to watch washing his hair, as the scar would take a good deal of time to heal. His face had received extreme abuse. The swipe of the knife had sliced the right side of his cheek from his lower chin to his temple. The blade had been razor sharp leaving a long deep but clean cut that would heal very well. There would be no cosmetic surgery available to assist in hiding the scar, however, normal time would fade it to the point where it would present as a pencil thin, long line on his face. His nose had been broken in two places. The man seemed quite hopeful that no breathing problems would occur. The nose would never be straight given the severity of the breaks. He had lost three teeth, fortunately none in the very front. The loose front teeth would probably stabilize. The real damage was to the left side of his face where the brass knuckles had shattered the bone and severely perforated the skin. While the surgeon had done the best work possible, the damage had resulted in disfigurement of the cheek that may require further surgery. Unfortunately the surgery was dangerous and could result in a more severe, permanent deformity. It was too early to be certain with more healing time necessary. The trauma to the cheek had resulted in a weakening of the muscles that caused his left eye to droop badly.

"Whenever you like just ask the nurse for a mirror and you can see for yourself. It is up to you when you look. We have been shaving you every couple of days, but that will now end. You are very lucky. Your eyes appear to be fine, which is very good. How they did not break your jaw is a miracle. Like Dr. Mendelson said you are one tough customer."

"Thanks, I think." Mason quietly answered.

When the doctor left Mason analyzed the assessment. People had said he was tough all his life. There was the incident way back with the bike where he had never given up. The sneering kid's gang had grudgingly seen him as a tough fighter with no give. The fat sergeant at the police station after his father was killed had clamped him on the back and marvelled at Mason's strength. The powerful Tuckel had been destroyed by his actions. Even with this latest in a list of damaging life experiences, Mason had not given up, fighting the three younger adversaries until they had believed he was dead. He died three times and then didn't die. Maybe he was tough enough to take on this next and probably most difficult battle.

Mason spent the rest of the morning and early afternoon thinking about his toughness until the physiotherapist arrived. The woman's name was Lottie. She was eastern European. Ripped with muscles, the woman helped him into a wheelchair and moved Mason down the hall to the physiotherapy room. There she began with his legs, giving him lifting and strengthening exercises to build up the atrophied muscles. She encouraged him, yelled at him and threatened him. By the end of the session Mason was sweating profusely and breathing quick breaths. The lung was healing well as he felt no real pain, just a throb deep inside.

Later in the afternoon Harry Morrice arrived at his room. The greeting was short and terse. Harry was all business as he told Mason that because the incident happened while he was still working and because the assault had received so much press, Mason would be receiving full benefits, including long-term disability until ready to come back to work. Harry made it clear, that on the first day back to work Mason would be promptly fired. Then the man left. Mason lay chuckling, thinking how it had been a painful way to spoil Harry's fun. He would never go back to the dealership and never sell another car.

It was not long after Harry departed that his caretaker showed up with the two nephews in tow. The generally well-meaning man was noticeably shaken when confronted with Mason's appearance. The man seemed to feel badly about the eviction. It was made clear that the notice had been rescinded, due to the media coverage, and because the caretaker was a sympathetic man. Mason thanked him for the reprieve and received his mail that included all five weeks of newspapers, neatly stacked and tied with cord. The man left quickly, still apologizing, followed by the nephews who were not in the least sorry for Mason's situation, giving the appearance that he clearly deserved exactly what had been metered out. Mason could almost sense the two thugs' disappointment that they had not been able to be the ones doing the metering.

Mason passed the time catching up on the news, taking particular interest to the front-page story of the assault, complete with a large parking lot picture and an inset of his old face from a dealership sale newspaper ad taken a long time ago. Due to the especially brutal nature of the assault, the heroic rescue, the remarkable fact that Mason lived and the subsequent manhunt as it was learned that the thieves had escaped from a medium security prison, the story was popular and well documented. The heroic rescue had resulted when the bartender, Sid Chakovic, had wondered why he had not returned and on a break had looked in the parking lot, finding Mason in a pool of frozen blood. Sid had rushed back and called 911. Then, the bartender had attempted to keep Mason warm by draping a spare bar coat over the unconscious man and shielding the body from the wind by lying on top. This was surprising, as Sid's manner had never appeared compassionate or heroic. Mason would need to go by and pay his respects to another man who had saved his life.

The physiotherapy continued every day. Mason found strength returning and was receiving hints that soon he would be leaving. The thought of leaving the hospital began to concern him due to the fear of returning to the old habits that had resulted in so much recent trouble and past pain.

It was after a physio session that a different white-coated person appeared in his room, introducing herself as a psychologist from the psychiatric ward. The lady was in her mid-thirties and appeared very confident, almost to the point of cockiness. With clipboard in hand the woman began asking a series of questions about his past. Mason did not know this lady at all, but that did not seem to matter as the woman forged ahead expecting private and honest responses to the personal questions. At first he thought she was kidding. Soon she became annoying and intrusive, not really listening, asking the battery of questions quickly as if being on some kind of self-imposed deadline. At one point Mason stopped her and asked the purpose of the interview. She showed obvious frustration and impatience while telling him that Dr. Mendelson had asked her to meet with him to assist with his addiction. She spoke slowly with a condescending tone as if he were challenged or just stupid. Mason could feel the anger begin to well inside, a feeling he had not experienced since the parking lot. After she had completed her ponderous explanation he asked her to leave. She seemed confused, so Mason spoke slower, emphasising each word as she had done. When she asked for clarification, he closed his eyes and did not move. She then became indignant at his uncooperative manner, stating that she did not have time for wasting. That was when he told her to go fuck herself. After saying it, Mason realized that she had never been spoken to in that manner.

She had left in a huge huff and he found himself getting angrier at the attempted invasion into his life. By the time supper arrived Mason was sullen and non-responsive, sensing a brooding feeling enter his body. He was angry with the woman and was craving either more conflict or some drinks to quell the pain that the emotion had released. He was too upset to eat, leaving the food untouched on his tray. He became uncommunicative with the nurses, most of whom he liked. A fitful sleep appeared ahead when the door opened and in walked a man he had never seen before.

"Hello. My name is Dave. The nurses asked me to stop by and see how you are doing," the man stated with a steady calm.

"Why would they do that? Is there something wrong with me?" Mason glared at the man, clenching his fists.

"Well, my observation skills would tell me you're very angry with something or someone. The nurses are worried about you, I guess because they like you and wanted to know if it was something they had done." The man took off his white coat and tossed it on the floor, stretching and waiting for an answer.

"No, it is nothing they did." Mason paused, seeing if the man was interested. The fellow was hanging on every word so he continued. "I guess I'm just sick of this place. I've been here a long time and am just a little worried about getting out."

"Worried about what?" The man asked with interest.

He began to speak and then stopped. "Excuse me, who are you again and what do you do?"

"I'm Dave and I'm a hospital social worker," the man said comfortably.

"First a psychologist and then a social worker. Jesus Christ," Mason said with frustration.

"I'm not the first person to see you today." It was more of a statement rather than a question. "Was the other person a psychologist in her mid-thirties with black hair and glasses? Not half bad if it's midnight at the bar. Sorry, that wasn't called for. Been a long day." The man paused. "So the lady psychologist comes to see you and asks many questions. You don't know why she is here to see you and soon the interview goes south with you getting pissed off and her becoming disgusted with your lack of commitment and, let me see…..your choice of language?" The social worker stopped on the question.

"That's about right." Mason waited to see what the man would say next. The social worker seemed like an all right guy who thought along the same lines. Before the psychologist had gotten him angry he had wondered about her looks. The description the man had used about the bar was perfect.

"Well. To tell you the truth I was supposed to see you today. Dr. Mendelson had asked me to meet with you and find out if I could assist you prior to your discharge. Then I got busy with a bad car accident and didn't get a chance. I was going to see you first thing in the morning. I guess Dorthea jumped the gun, probably to impress Mendelson. He is a big deal around these parts." The social worker rubbed his eyes and made eye contact. "There, now you know all I know. I was asked to see you because the doctors are very worried, especially Ramshad, who is a very good surgeon. According to the report I got if you do not quit drinking you will die, probably in six months to a year. The smoking has got to end too, as it is putting too much pressure on your heart. But I'm sure they have told you all this stuff." The man slouched in the chair.

"So what do you want from me?" The comment came out as a simple question free of sarcasm or anger. Mason was feeling himself slowly calm.

"I want your commitment to meet with me tonight and three other times. I would like you to be as open and honest as you can. I promise you I will listen and give you open and honest observations back. Through the process we will build a relationship and see if you can become strong enough to deal with the extremely difficult, but possibly very rewarding task ahead." The social worker waited for a reply. Mason watched closely for the social worker's reaction, expecting some form of impatience. The man showed no concern, making appropriate eye contact, at ease with the quiet. Mason realized it was his choice whether the conversation would continue or be terminated. Finally he nodded, giving the social worker the approval for the interview to proceed. The man straightened in his chair, leaned down and produced a clipboard from under the lab coat.

"Just so I can get your words down correctly," the man stated. "Tell me about yourself."

"Where do you want me to start?" Mason asked, now for some reason ready to comply with the wishes of the man. His anger was gone. He felt ready to proceed with the interview, anxious to see where the process would take him.

"Wherever you want. Past, present or future or simply who you think you are under the layers we all present to the world." Mason liked the sound of the description, as that was certainly how he operated in his life, protecting and avoiding, worrying about the unknown, and reacting to anything that made him anxious, with anger or alcohol.

"Let's talk about anger and alcohol." Mason said it with a clear voice wanting to talk about these two addictions.

Once Mason began talking about the two A's he was unstoppable. The social worker allowed him to speak, only interrupting to ask a clarifying question or reinforce a comment. It took an hour and a half before Mason realized that his voice was becoming hoarse and his throat was hurting. Then it took another half an hour for the social worker to share the observations of the many statements he had made during the conversation. The man used the written comments to ensure the descriptions were accurate. Mason marvelled as his own words were read back to him, reinforcing positive observations made by the social worker. He thought that sharing would result in the man identifying his many weaknesses. The social worker had surprisingly chosen positive descriptions, at times pulling and stroking the personal images until strengths of character lay exposed and glowing. When Mason's own words were read back to him, followed by comments from the social worker, he began to notice some beauty that he had never seen before. Among the negative comments came words such as courage, caring, sensitivity, loyalty, compassion and intelligence. The gentle probing of the skilled clinician brought out a sense of worth, confusing him and threatening the concept of deserving despair that he had built the foundation of his life on. Here were words and descriptions, self-generated, that focused on powerful images of strength and endurance. This could be the beginning of a strong scaffold from which to build a hardy existence free from self-doubt and the self-fulfilling prophesy of failure.

The amazement showed as he stared at the social worker. The man was looking at him with a noncommittal face, gauging Mason's reaction with knowing eyes. "Was any of this helpful?" the man asked with a genuine questioning tone.

Mason hardly paused before saying, "Yes, very much."

"Good," came the reply. "Would it be all right if we meet again tomorrow?"

"Ya. That would be fine," Mason said in a distant and hesitant voice. It was as if he had casually opened a curtain, unexpectedly entering a new and mysterious world containing an immense potential for a golden treasure. He did not fully understand but believed if he had the commitment to cast off the bonds of the old ways a rebirth may occur. The tingling of excitement circled him as he experienced a powerful, sobering moment, when his past life was laid bare before him showing the blackness, while he stood in an entrance filled with light and gazed at the possibility of a new and wondrous beginning.

The social worker distracted him as the tired man rose from the chair. The interview had been hard work after a hard day of assisting others in their journey. "You have a lot to think about. I can see it in your face. You need to be patient. Take your time with what you need to do. I will be back tomorrow morning. Do you read?"

"I used to like reading. I haven't read anything but the paper in years."

"Well, it's time you started again. It is never too late." The man paused and leaned over, resting a warm hand on Mason's shoulder. Using a quiet forceful voice, while emphasizing every word, the social worker said, "It is..never..too..late." With that Dave picked up the lab coat and left the room, leaving Mason sitting alone, with only the humming of the fluorescent light shining in the corner.

Mason went to bed excited as a child on the eve of Christmas day, anxiously anticipating the wonderful surprises the next morning would bring. While dozing he reviewed all that the first counselling session had yielded. He also incorporated additional reinforcing experiences that had been triggered by the observations made and recorded during the interview. Images of Grace, Margaret and Jordan popped into his head like the kernels of dried corn exploding from the heated oil of a lidless pot. For the first time in a very great while his father appeared, not bloodied and rattling, but smiling and encouraging as they played golf or ate breakfast in a small town restaurant. His mother arrived in his thoughts, baking cookies in the old kitchen and passing a still hot gooey good circle that melted in his mouth as he gobbled the morsel down. There was no hatred or anger, just a slight melancholy for a time that was gone but never lost unless he chose to throw the memories in a pit of misery. The discussion had shown him that he was much more than a defeated drunken loser. Mason lay very still and let the images scan over him like a beam of red light. The pulsing of the smoke detector bulb seemed to blink out a beacon of hope as he surrendered to sleep, hoping the morning would bring a continuation of the fantastic revelations.

The morning began with optimism that quickly evaporated as Mason's hopes were eroded by a series of events. Dr. Mendelson arrived stating that with the cast off his arm and leg, his lung healed and the physiotherapy needing only two more sessions, Mason would be discharged in two days. The news hit him hard as worry began to land on him like ash from a volcano, sticking to his body and weighing down his soul. Just when he was beginning to understand and discover a possible escape from the self-imposed oppressive and tormented living conditions, he was going to be cut loose to find his own way. Mason said nothing until the doctor left and then cursed loudly, banging his still tender hands on the firm hospital mattress. He noticed the good feelings beginning to break up and disappear. He struggled to catch the slivers of warm thoughts as they shot through his mind. Pieces were captured, except there appeared no place to put the images. The helplessness began to build as anger grew and hopelessness returned.

The nurse soon arrived and told him that the social worker was caught up in a very serious situation and had sent regrets, promising to visit as soon as possible. After that a police detective arrived to discuss the assault. Mason was asked to relive the events of the evening with the officer taking notes. For the record he proceeded to identify his three attackers from the pictures provided. The two men were cousins and petty criminals known for law-breaking behaviours that had been linked to violence in the past. Both had escaped from a halfway house while on day parole and were on the run when the scam had been set up. It was a method used before. It turned out that the woman was the love interest of both men. The trio had been cornered three days later in the next time zone east, after robbing a gun shop and shooting a liquor store clerk. A high-speed chase had ensued with one of the men being shot to death at a roadblock and the other drowning when the stolen vehicle had crashed through a guardrail and landed in the middle of a river. The girl had miraculously escaped the submerged car and had been dragged out of the water, more dead than alive. She was currently in hospital, under guard, facing a multitude of charges. She had already confessed to the assault and robbery, so the officer did not even think it would be necessary for him to testify. Everything taken from Mason was in the car and unfortunately nothing had yet been recovered. The authorities were having difficulty raising the vehicle due to the depth of the water and swiftness of the current. Finally there was one last item. The man asked him if there had been any cigarettes or matches burning in his car during the confrontation with the convicts. Mason nodded and told of the cigarette that had broken apart in the fight. The police officer commented that the scattering of the cigarette embers would explain the fire that broke out in his car early the next morning. The embers must have landed on the seat and smouldered undetected all night finally bursting into flames. A passing motorist had seen the smoke and called the fire department. By the time the fire trucks arrived the gas tank and all four tires had exploded. The car had been completely gutted. The golf clubs in the trunk had been melted into an unrecognizable mass. There was nothing left. The officer had him sign the statement and left the room.

After the man left Mason became sullen and quiet. The great hope that had been present at the beginning of the day had dissipated with no chance of revival. He was angry and agitated wondering how the hope, recently strong, could be so easily destroyed. Rolling on his side he feigned sleep for the rest of the afternoon, ignoring the nurses and refusing to go to physiotherapy by causing an angry childish scene when Lottie had insisted. By the time the social worker arrived Mason was in a foul mood, spoiling for a fight.

The interview began poorly. Mason lashed out at the social worker, soon including the entire hospital staff in the attack. Others were solely to blame for what had occurred today. He had sought support, surrendering to the promised assistance in good faith only to have the offer of help pulled away at the last minute like the removal of a rope to a falling man. The tirade continued to expand and began to include his father, grandfather, grandmother, mother, sister, Sara, the Major, Victoria, Sanderson and past friends. He had expected help in finding a direction and had received nothing, being abandoned by all. Disappointment after disappointment was the only support ever given. And now just when he thought there was a promising opportunity, he was being kicked out of the hospital. No one gave a shit what happened to him. The voice of self-pity and complaint flowed out of him like thick syrup over the edge of a plate, heavy and choking. Mason felt the sob begin in the depths and rise slowly but with vast power. He continued to speak hoping the talking would contain the emotion. The speech patterns began to break up as the sob overtook the words. The wracking cries of pain issued forth uncontrolled like barks from a child with croup. He thought of Samuel Jr. with the betrayal by Victoria and saw the face of Rebecca crying. The thoughts stuck fast in the glue of pain causing the sobs to come faster and faster as the emotions were set free. There was no control now, just release as all the loss, anger, pain, hope, desire and despair turned into one large hair ball of emotions that stuck in his throat threatening to choke him. He tried to swallow the emotions back into the depths, attempting to impede the flow, but the pressure was too great. Soon the force became overwhelming as the dam began to weaken and the emotions poured out in an immensely powerful rush of pent up feelings. Finally Mason released everything inside. At first the discharge involved uncontrollable crying and wailing which he believed would never end until his heart stopped. As the pressure weakened he began to speak, at first using only one-sentence phrases to describe whatever thought was to be set free. As the crying lessened paragraphs of emotions blasted out. Initially the words were spontaneous and impulsive, somehow directed to the social worker, but soon the attempted dialogue became a monologue with the man forgotten. The process became a discussion, a debate, an argument and a means of talking to and through himself. It was crazy talk, but it was critically necessary. The words slammed around the room, bouncing off the walls and reflecting back to him, being absorbed and then bouncing around his head until either understood or discarded. Time was unimportant as the mental operation took on a life of its own, peaking and waning, ending and beginning again and again until amidst sentence it stopped.

    Mason sat slumped in the chair panting as his heart wound down like the slowing of an unplugged spinning motor. His hospital robe was soaked with tears and sweat. He was only just aware of the social worker and the two nurses who began to strip the soiled hospital gown from his body. One nurse supported him while the other washed him with a warm cloth dipped in a pan of hot water. The sound of the water drips wrung from the cloth was clear and sharp like the notes from a finely tuned piano. He marvelled at the clarity as his weakened physical presence swayed against the supporting nurse. The cool air caressed the moisture on his skin, causing a trembling to occur. He did not mind as it gave him a sensation of living that was strangely pleasant. His senses seemed to heighten to an extraordinary level as if he could hear the separate beating of a bird's wing or see the moisture droplets of a cloud. The sensation lasted while he stood weakly in front of the three strangers, unconcerned about his complete nakedness. It was as if he was a newborn child being cleansed from the fluids of a traumatic birth. He felt light and empty, for the first time since childhood, devoid of a nagging hurtful pressure that had constantly attempted to wrestle him from the world and pin his spirit to the mat.

Once the nurses had wrapped him in a dry gown they led him to bed. He staggered like an infant taking its first steps. Everything felt new and indescribably different. He was tucked in with care, remembering a time centuries ago when his mother would hum to help him sleep. Sleep began to overtake his empty mind as a very peaceful feeling settled lightly, soothing and comforting. For the first time since riding his bike Mason Walls liked who he was.

Mason woke early and starving. The feeling of hunger had never been very prevalent during his adult life. The alcohol and cigarettes had often dulled his appetite and destroyed his taste buds, making food necessary but lightly consumed, offering no particular joy and provoking no serious interest. This morning he waited with anticipation for the dry toast, weak juice and runny eggs. Mason was not mistaken as all came in the expected condition and were consumed with robust enthusiasm. His senses appeared finely tuned, his mind was alert, not consumed in an inner prison of debate and mindless discussions, but aware of everything around him. He sat by the window, soaking up the sights of the outside. He had been in the hospital six long weeks and during that time nature had given birth. Spring had arrived and was building to its zenith as the flora had been awakened from the winter respite. The last remembrance of the outside was of a smothering cold that attempted to consume everything, freezing all in a state of useless limbo. That was how his soul had felt. Now Mason could only see the beauty of warmth and growth, which strangely enough seemed to emanate from within his person. He glowed with a strong connection to the awakening occurring outside. He started feeling his own vast emptiness. Yet the emptiness was not a negative, brooding bitterness filled by anger or despair. It was a clear void, an empty easel, waiting for any creative strokes he wished to paint. It was neither good nor bad, it just was. Nothing was necessary, nothing expected or demanded. The entire limitless cavern seemed to offer endless possibilities and opportunities, while presenting a soothing message of patience, wanting the experience of the creation to be joyous and savoured. It was a delectable meal to be prepared at his leisure and with as much care as he wished, as the feast was for no one but him to enjoy.

Mason spent the morning gazing out the window, letting the bright sun soak into his eyes, filling him with warmth and light. Every motion on the outside was exciting and interesting. Inside the hospital room there were other wonders that began to interest him. He examined his scarred hands and how they moved at an instant propelled by unseen mental directions. The gentle licking of his lips, the moving of his arms or the focused touching of his skin brought on new sensations to old experiences. He began to sense a slowing of his world. For once it could be absorbed with simplicity truly encountered, rather than racing by in a blur of random aimless noisy activity.

When the nurses came Mason watched them closely, listening carefully to their words as if getting to know them for the first time. Each radiated an energy that he had not seen before, as he had been caught in his own web of self-absorbing need. Mason asked one politely for a razor and some cream, as his face had not been shaved since the nurse's had left the job to him three weeks before. He had not looked at his face since the mirror on the wall of his apartment and somehow felt he had not clearly seen himself for many, many years. When he finally had the courage to look he was shocked at the appearance. The scars created by the knife and brass knuckles were red against a pale sickly white flesh. The difference in the colours screamed disagreement and conflict. The length of the knife scar was amazing, appearing as an attempted face painting abruptly terminated. The sagging of the left side of the face reminded him of a butcher friend who suffered from Bells Palsy. The drooping was made worse by the impact path of the brass knuckles with still angry, yet healing, breaks in the skin. The whole defeated mess was covered in a mat of dark facial hair. His nose looked swollen and there was a crookedness that would never disappear. Possibly the most shocking display in the mirror was his eyes. When he had last looked, a lifetime ago, the eyes were weak and sick, issuing pain at every glance. Now they were bright with the pupils colourful and the whites clear of any red. While the rest of his face appeared broken and abused, his eyes were challenging and strong. Mason quickly looked away and then was drawn back, not to the damaged face but to the eyes that made his body straighten and a smile grow on his lips.

He was beginning to feel new inside and he now had a new look outside. One fact was irrefutable. Mason would no longer suffer problems with the ladies, as his current appearance would definitely not encourage interest from women. Moving his head from side to side he accepted the fact that his face now definitely had character. The thought brought on a giggle, which soon escalated to uncontrollable laughter. Mason had not found anything funny in a very long time and vowed that would change from this moment forth.

He greeted Lottie with an apology that took the physiotherapist off guard. The woman had entered the room ready for a resumption of hostilities and was pleasantly surprised by the cheery welcome. Mason worked very hard on the exercises demanded by the woman. This day he did the tasks for himself, delighting in the tautness of his muscles once the regime of exercises was completed.

Dave showed up in late afternoon. They spent two hours talking. Mason had many questions, especially about what had happened yesterday. The man seemed more interested in getting Mason's opinion than providing an explanation. The social worker spent most of the time building on these explanations. Near the end of the interview, the man related that there appeared to have been some form of primal event where Mason expelled past destructive emotions through release. The social worker wondered whether the reaction was just the culmination of a process that had been going on since leaving Victoria.

Dave had secured an extra day at the hospital and wanted to have two more sessions before he returned home. When the session ended the man also offered some books to read including a Bible, with five post-it marked passages, a copy of Joseph Campbell's *The Hero's Journey*, a book by Eckhart Tolle, a thin, very small book on Zen Buddhism and the big book of Alcoholics Anonymous.

Mason spent the rest of the morning and all afternoon reading. He read the five marked sections from the Bible that quoted Jesus Christ. The passages were short and easy reading. He had never spent much time around religion, often very suspicious of the underlying motives that spanned centuries of pain and human suffering, but these messages were pure and simple. He read the words, attempting to make sense of the meanings while incorporating the message into his growing excitement about a different way of thinking and living.

Mason read the introduction of the book by Eckhart Tolle, seeing a man in utter and complete turmoil until the writer experienced an intense and mystifying experience that allowed for a new beginning. Small excerpts of *The Hero's Journey* were absorbed and while many of the historical and mythological characters were foreign and unknown, the style of Campbell's writing was intoxicating. He spent a half hour locked on the front cover, absorbing the words, a hero's journey, wondering if perhaps in some odd and extraordinary way he was a hero on a journey that presented imposing obstacles which, when conquered, allowed for the attainment of the treasure. In Mason's case the prize was not material, in the form of carnal wealth, but spiritual in the desire for personal contentment. He read the first forty pages of the small book on Discovering Zen, which seemed to offer the possibility for self-exploration through focused meditation and a deliberate positive search, with the purpose of revealing a person's true nature.

At times his thoughts would wander. In the past these thoughts were like a wild horse resisting his every attempt at taming, all the while bucking and straining for ultimate control. Fortunately he was beginning to no longer fear the workings of his brain. Through the trauma of the beating and the intensity of the counselling, somehow he had broken the wild and savage nature of the beast. There was now a powerful connection between rider and horse that spoke of respect and cooperation. Inside Mason knew that the relationship would grow stronger as the training moved forward. As a result he could now begin to experiment, allowing his brain to ramble and graze, directing it away from hurtful thoughts while examining the images with the clarity of a painless observation that seemed to shrink the incredible potency down to a harmless occurrence. He became amazed as incredibly painful experiences that had consumed his thinking and overwhelmed his emotional system were now recalled, examined and filed as life events, not descriptions of who he was. The obsessive and pervasive nature of the thoughts was now neutered by the growing command of his brain. He was learning how to lead the finally responsive horse, while hoping his dangerous rodeo days were over.

Also remarkable was the growing and strengthening presence inside. It had been the voice of reason that had begun to grow prior to the assault. Mason was not sure what to call the building energy. It could be his spirit, soul, or being. It could be his life force or energy, consciousness or his true existence. The name did not matter as much as the assuredness that the presence was growing stronger. Now the task was to foster the development. He quickly realized the possibility for growth was phenomenal. Mason shuddered with excitement and some trepidation as he began to wonder who would help keep the process going. The doubts raced into his mind as he fought to dispatch them into oblivion. They retreated with the show of force, but were not defeated, only relegated to the periphery of his mind where the worries lay hidden but not forgotten.

The book, which he left until last, was the Alcoholics Anonymous big blue book. He was not sure why Dave had wanted the nondescript book read, as he saw no need. Yes, he liked to drink and sometimes he blacked out, but he was not in the same company as the people described in the book. He was not homeless or in jail. The denial grew stronger and stronger until he began to believe that he could become a social drinker, managing the alcohol with a newfound strength that was developing inside. Mason fabricated images of his having a cold beer and then declining a second. Of him being the designated driver for a group of fictitious friends, not minding the role at all as he could take or leave alcohol. Of him not drinking for months and then having a couple of glasses of rich red wine at a wonderful supper, and then not drinking again for many more months. He tossed the book on the bed and retreated to the window where he gained strength from the shining sun while letting the denials remain present and unchallenged.

Later that afternoon Mason met again with Dave. He was excited to share his newly discovered insights. The two discussed the reading and the messages that were contained within. Mason would begin to read the Tolle book this evening and was feeling very encouraged by the new journey that lay before him. With a gracious manner Mason began to stand, assuming the interview was over. Dave did not move, but remained sitting in the chair looking at Mason as if the two had unfinished business.

"Aren't we finished? I'm getting a little tired." Mason yawned and stretched his arms in an exaggerated motion.

"We have one more book to discuss," Dave said quietly, but firmly.

"Which one?" There was a long pause as Mason put on a pensive expression, furrowing his brow and pursing his lips as if trying to figure out what the man was talking about. After many moments standing awkwardly in the middle of the room, Mason sat down.

"We have not talked about the Alcoholics Anonymous blue book yet," Dave said in a matter of fact voice.

"Oh, that book. I never got a chance to look at it, but I will later for sure." Mason sat quietly as if dismissing any further discussions. For a long while neither man spoke. Dave sat with quiet locked hands as Mason began to feel embarrassed with his lie, then anxious and finally agitated. Soon the emotions built until he spoke. "I don't know why you want me to read that book. First I do not need to read it as I can get everything I need from the other books. There is something in the other books that is important, but in that book there is nothing for me. I mean, it was first written in 1939. The book is so old, how relevant is it today? Besides, I don't think I need to read about that as I know now I'll be able to control my drinking." Mason stated the comments with a created finality and a raised voice.

"Do you honestly believe that?" Dave spoke in an even tone with no inflection on any of the words. There was no cynicism or confrontation in the man's voice only a desire to know the extent of his denial.

"I've controlled it in the past," Mason said, feeling the anger rising.

"That is true, but you are in a little bit of a different situation this time. It is not that you need to stop drinking. You must stop drinking. All the wonderful discoveries you have made in the past few days will mean nothing if you continue to drink. You will not be able to continue to undertake the journey of discovery if you are drunk and if you continue to drink you will die." The man's tone never changed, presenting the information in a factual way. "I think you better revisit the assumption of controlling the dragon." The choice of the description of alcohol hit him hard. Mason had used the term in the past to describe the strength of the beast and the impossibility of controlling the vast power it wielded over his life. The realization made him more committed to his entrenched denial.

"How would you know what I can control and what I cannot? You don't know me." The anger was rising as his hands opened and closed. The room began to feel warm and still.

"Why are you getting angry?" Dave asked, reverting back to the quiet flatness of a question.

"I have a right to when you call me a liar. I can control myself, you know. Maybe I like to drink and maybe sometimes I get drunk. At times I have gotten drunk a lot. But that was before, not now. I'm now in control of the booze. I was a drunk but never anything else. I was never an.... anything else." Mason was panting hard, sweating.

The two men sat quietly for another long period of time. Once Mason calmed Dave spoke. "I am sorry if you misunderstood my questions. I would never call anyone a liar. The importance is not what I believe or think it is what you believe. We are done for now. I will be coming back tonight and want you to go to an AA meeting we have at the hospital. I don't want your answer now. I want you to think about my request. You can refuse if you want but think about it until tonight, then you can give me your answer. You will simply be a guest and not asked to say anything." Dave got up and with a nod left the room.

Mason sat in the chair, angry and upset. Rather than staying mad, as was the method of dealing with past issues, he began to question his reaction and seek reasons for the anger. At first he blamed Dave for questioning his answers and comments. After a brief time of honestly examining the reasons, the dark curtain of denial began to part. If he truly believed his explanations then it would be easy to make his case and be comfortable with the justification. Mason knew that in the past, when wrong, his weak self-concept often forced the development of an entrenched position to avoid the truth. With a strength and courage that would not be denied the essence demanded the truth. Not a fabrication that was meant for the purpose of destructive deception, but an honest assessment from which personal and spiritual growth could flourish. Mason had often heard that the truth would set a person free. It was time for him to ante up the cost of admittance and accept the power of the absolute truth. The minutes turned to an hour as he strove to find and, more importantly, accept the only answer available. It was the one answer that had been with him since his twenties. It was one detail of his life that he knew to be true and that had been hidden in a deep secret place. He had always known it was there but never accepted its existence, constantly hiding the answer from everyone, especially and most importantly himself. All the incidents of the past years along with the therapy, had rooted the information to the surface where the light of hope could finally penetrate the black exterior of his private shame, exposing the truth. He was an alcoholic.

Mason stated the now revealed disclosure and quickly realized that the words in his head were not enough. In the bathroom mirror he gazed into the clear eyes and with conviction said, "You are an alcoholic." Something seemed wrong until he understood how powerful the denial had become. With a deep breath Mason looked at his entire face and, finally focusing on his eyes, said again slowly, "I am an alcoholic." He repeated it three times, each time with more volume and conviction. Suddenly he became aware of lightness as if a weight had been lifted off his back. It was as if he could breathe easier, move better and think clearer. He was an alcoholic. That was a truth that had been incredibly difficult, almost impossible to accept, but once said it could now be dealt with as a problem. No more minimizing was possible. Denial was out of the question. The information had been released into the realm of his public domain. It could never be recaptured or hidden again. Similar to his dealing with anger, once the light of truth was shone on the statement, the debilitating secret began to lose a great deal of power, while his presence grew noticeably.

In the past Mason had used alcohol to manage his world and quiet the voices and obscure the images. The alcohol was an addiction he used as a way to deal with his personal pain and insecurities. At times the addiction had overwhelmed him, stolen his health and pounded him into the sludge of helplessness where he lay mired. Mason had refused to accept or battle his demons while letting the dragon dictate the terms of his existence. He had never seen the creature with more clarity then he did at that moment. The alcohol dragon's possessiveness, avarice and desire for total control, subtly and powerfully exerted was now on display for him to view, understand and absorb. His denial and delusions had been so great he had never seen the true nature of the villain he had founded, nurtured and let live in his body for so many years. But he knew it now. While he knew that the battle would be extremely difficult Mason would never be able to deny his alcoholism again.

Mason went to the Alcoholics Anonymous meeting that night nervous and not knowing what to expect. When leaving he was no longer anxious, basking in the support of others who understood the battle he would wage for the rest of his life. His first encounter with AA was not unlike tens of thousands who attended meetings different nights of the week. All are welcome and respected with the only real requirement for attendance at a meeting being a desire to stop drinking alcohol.

Two messages came strongly from the hospital meeting. One was the importance of knowing that he was not alone in his battle. As each person took their turn speaking Mason began to feel a sense of camaraderie and kinship with the strangers. There was one very similar message. All admitted being powerless over alcohol and that life had become unmanageable. He certainly accepted this statement and felt power building from acknowledging the truth.

The second message was the theme of loneliness as each spoke of their life with alcohol. One man, currently in a twenty-one day in-hospital program, spoke of how alcohol had driven everyone away and how everything had been lost, leaving nothing. The man was hoping for assistance but did not believe that there was any support in the world. Mason echoed the man's sentiments when it was his turn to speak. He spoke of his search to find a place where he could belong and of the hope to find a person or relationship that would make him whole. The futility of his search was clearly documented to the group.

The final man talked about the search to find fulfillment, but there was a twist of thinking that caught Mason's attention immediately. The man wondered if perhaps the true search for belonging and contentment, which could be used as a valuable support against alcohol, was not to be found in the outside world but could only be discovered within a person's own heart. The man went on to relate the belief that once the internal search was undertaken, perhaps the outside world would not be as uncertain and dangerous. With that the meeting was completed and each member of the group, so intimate and close for an hour, parted and went separate ways.

Dave and Mason went down for a coffee in a basement cafeteria. The two sat quietly until Mason began to speak, listing his observations of the meeting. He asked many questions about the process. At one point he revisited the last man's statement of the internal search, mulling the vision over, almost oblivious to Dave's presence. When Mason looked up the social worker was smiling broadly and he knew that perhaps a direction had been recognized. The social worker would say little other than how successful the meeting was and to read the books that had been left in his room.

Upon returning to his room Mason experienced a sense of anticipation. He was not sure how the next step would be accomplished. He was content to give up control of the process to the power surging within. There definitely was a path available. All he needed was the courage to plant his emotional feet and set off down the new road.

He awoke early the next day, rested. Dressed in his baggy street clothes, which no longer fit due the large weight loss, Mason proceeded to the front doors of the hospital. There he stood for a long while before stepping in front of the automatic door sensor. Both doors opened simultaneously, and with a swish of hydraulics, exposed his still sensitive face to the cool morning air. Mason hesitated many moments while the door remained open. With gingerly, limping steps he passed through the doorway and out into the fresh spring air. It had rained during the night and the water lay in clear pools, filling the imperfections in the pavement that surfaced the front drop-off area of the hospital. There was no moving traffic or people disturbing the early morning quiet. It appeared even the birds were still asleep with the only sound being the light breeze that moved the just budding branches of the trees. Mason walked over to a small sitting park and stood beside a still wet bench. The wind moved his long hair and rustled his ill fitting clothes, finding openings between the buttons and puffing up the shirt like a sail catching wind. The cool air caressed his skin. The chill felt very good after the closed recycled air of the hospital. The only odours apparent were earthy and natural, born of growing and freshness. The overcast conditions fit his mood perfectly, as the dullness seemed to guard and cushion his re-entry to the world. This was remarkably different than the howling maelstrom that had announced his bleeding arrival at the hospital.

Mason walked further in the park until his ankle became sore. While the physiotherapy had helped the legs, it was going to take some time before he would be able to walk any distance. He paused to rest, taking a large breath of the thick heavy air. The resulting coughing spell brought on a pain in his chest and the ultimate expulsion of dark sputum from years of smoking. He spit the black crap onto the ground and paused for a time. This was only the start of the cleansing.

While he could feel the beauty of the cloudy day build his strength, Mason began to realize the great weakness of his body and spirit. From here on the process of living would demand his total focus and commitment. Standing alone in the little park he issued an oath accepting total responsibility for his health and welfare; physically, emotionally and spiritually. He would take full control of his situation. In the past, he had wanted others to make him happy, others to show him the way and others to make the pain and sense of loss go away. Others had failed him every step of the way. Not because they were necessarily evil nor bent on his destruction, but because they had no idea what he needed or how to really love him. He had constantly been looking outward and never inward. Any examination of self had not been a voyage of discovery. It had been a critical condemnation of his person, complete with self-harming judgements full of self-recriminations. He could never find himself as he had buried his presence deep beneath layers of pain and disappointment. Well not anymore. Mason made a pact that he would commit all his energy to courting and eventually loving himself. This would not be accomplished with a narcissistic self-centered approach. He would use an approach that involved building personal strength in all areas of his life. He would grow, replacing the tall tree of discontent with a strong straight sapling of personal commitment and development. The image reminded him of the little meadow behind Grace's motel. The only way possible for the metamorphosis to occur was to begin to love himself. He could do this because for the first time since he was a child Mason began to feel the unconditional strength of complete freedom to pursue a life of contentment.

During his cold breakfast Mason began to read Eckhart Tolle's book, The Power of Now. The book brought him in contact with many concepts that were intriguing. He was introduced to a section on the pain body, which he read with excitement, knowing he would return to the chapter many times in the future. By noon Mason had put the book aside knowing he would finish it later and reread it many times,

Mason ate his lunch slowly, while rereading the introduction to Zen and discovering reality within. The writing exposed him to stillness in the mind and introduced him to meditation. He began to wrap himself in words such as tranquility, joy and self-discovery. Through the brief readings one powerful message appeared constant. The answer to any of life's questions was not, nor ever had been, in the world. The answer had always been inside the self.

By late afternoon Mason was ready to begin reading the big blue AA book that he knew had been waiting patiently on the small table beside his bed. The reading was not as personally uplifting, but he knew it was necessary. He was exposed to individual stories of the battle with booze. The narratives talked about the vicious cycle of alcoholism, the struggles of maintaining sobriety, the tools offered by AA and the commitment necessary to quit drinking. He relived some of his own past episodes and painful memories. The process was difficult, but began to reinforce the necessity of his commitment to sobriety. He was firm in his desire that his last drink of alcohol would be the double black rum on a stormy February night.

Dave showed up at approximately eight o'clock. The social worker was all business as the man pushed the counselling session forward, meticulously seeking clarification on his perspective of the day's activity. Dave was especially interested in the visit to the park and the introspective view about where the important search must be concentrated. Again the man continually wrote down words that Mason had used to describe the insights gained. Soon the discussion turned to the AA big blue book. Mason was open and honest, describing his feelings during the reading. There was absolutely no more discussion or argument possible. He definitely was an alcoholic. As he spoke, the word seemed to issue forth continually, not just emitting from his throat but coming from a place of discovery inside. The more the word was mentioned, the easier it was to say.

By the end of the session Mason was exhausted. The amount of new information he had absorbed was staggering. Throughout the day there had been constant changes occurring. The size and scope of the modifications were not fully realized until Dave made a simple yet extremely complex observation. Just before leaving, the social worker looked at Mason and said, "It appears that you are rebuilding your whole belief system." With that the man left, leaving Mason to ponder the comment.

He lay in the darkness embracing the words and realizing that he was indeed recreating himself. Thoughts and beliefs, mostly destructive, were being shed like the clothing of newlyweds. Mason no longer wanted to see the world with old and tired eyes. He wanted a fresh experience, wondrous in the newness. Strangely, the casting out of the old thought patterns allowed certain characteristics to be reborn, healthy and strong. His love of the outdoors was a gift that had been lost. Now it was found again and after a quick polish began to shimmer, shining with a wide array of opportunities. He would never work a job inside again. That he knew to be a new fact of his existence. The decision almost caused him to laugh out loud, joyous in the clean feeling of granite resolve. Mason experienced a giddy tiredness that made him feel light and floating as he passed into the world of sleep.

His last day at the hospital was quiet and reflective. While the energy still seemed to pulse inside he felt it settle, no longer existing as manic and unsure. It was now anchored and spreading, holding his emotional ship steady while Mason readied for the journey to the next port of call. He shaved with slow purpose. More colour was appearing in his sunken cheeks. Mason was getting used to his facial appearance, accepting the scars. There was a strong light of life intensifying in his bright eyes. He would let his eyes speak to the world. They would carry the message of a promising future. The sparkle caused him to whistle sharply, suddenly remembering a youthful time when he had stood in the back alley of the only true home he had ever had turning the spitting, sloppy sounds into first a peep and then the notes of self-made music. The sound startled him, but soon the one whistled note became two, then three and finally strings of sounds grouped together to create melodies. Warbling and experimenting with his mouth and the airflow brought a sense of connectedness that hooked him directly to his childhood. He knew there were other beautiful experiences, currently resting dormant, waiting to be rediscovered now that the heavy shackles had been lifted and the freedom of expression had been regained.

All the doctors made their final rounds with Dr. Mendelson being the last to visit. The distinguished doctor checked the chart and asked after Mason's health. The small talk between the two men was strained, as the administrator was usually all business. The necessary paperwork had been completed by his physicians and signed off by Mendelson that would offer Mason another three months of long-term disability insurance, giving him additional time to heal before he would need to return to work. He thanked the doctor for the assistance.

Finally the man paused, "I will say what I said when you came out of the coma. Mr. Walls, you are a very lucky man and tough too. You have been given a rare opportunity. I hope you take full advantage. According to Dave, you seem to have risen to the occasion, which is very good. Use the supports Dave can offer on the outside as the challenge to stay on course will be difficult." Mendelson ended with a good luck and left the room. Mason's nurses came in during their appointed rounds wishing him well and saying goodbye. There were other kind words that brought about moist eyes and a constricting of his throat.

Dave came last and the two had a final hospital session, focusing on developing a plan for sobriety on the outside. The men discussed the short and long-term goals that Mason had established over the past few days. Simplicity would be the new theme of his life. He now knew that the answers to contentment existed within, so the goal would be to strengthen every aspect of his person. This was a journey that would be exciting but difficult. Mason realized that patience and the acceptance of small successes would be critical in attaining personal gratification. There was another important revelation that had entered his thoughts in the last few days. The search was not about finding a place in life, it was about the search itself. Just living and experiencing daily life, minute by minute, was now his purpose. This would be the important goal to hang onto when the journey became confused or difficult.

Then it was time to leave. Dave had offered a ride and brought the car around to the front doors as the nurse waited with Mason in silence. The trip to his apartment was quick and quiet. Once they arrived at the building, Dave reminded him of a session that had been booked for a month hence at the free clinic where the social worker did outreach. Mason took the appointment card writing the address and times of the AA meetings on the back. He attempted to thank Dave for all the assistance, but the man would not accept any responsibility for the success Mason had attained, stating clearly that Mason had been the one who had found the answers and established a new direction. When it was finally time to sever the last connection to the hospital Dave gave him one last piece of advice, telling him to stay true to the new beliefs. With those words he exited the car and Dave was gone.

Mason entered his apartment with a slowness that came of apprehension. The air was stale, smelling of old cigarettes and bad memories. The strength that had built inside seemed to shrink under the oppressive weight of painful experiences that were trapped within the walls of the small apartment. The blinds were pulled, allowing a drab darkness even with the light bulb burning in the entrance. Nothing had been touched since he had left for work after the eviction notice had been issued. He stood still with only his eyes moving around the room, almost expecting that any motion would bring on an attack from an unknown source. His heart began to beat quicker, filling his chest with sound and movement. Mason felt the blood enter and pound against his eardrums. His breath became restricted as mindless doubts began to swirl around him like apparitions attempting to steal the goodness now cowering inside. With a concerted effort he shuffled across the room. The garbage and empty bottles noisily attempted to impede his heavy feet as the distance to the far side of the room seemed insurmountable. Finally Mason bumped against the cloth and with an almost desperate motion clutched the curtains in both hands and opened them fully, using a dramatic spreading of his arms. The bright sun hit him fully in the face instantly warming and beckoning his core to come out of hiding. The beauty of natural light illuminated the room and with it the clear destructiveness of his past life. All around was filth and decay, highlighted by empty bottles and full ashtrays. Dirty clothes and dishes littered the room. Pieces of plaster lay in piles where holes had been punched in the walls. It was as if a crazed animal had tried to escape its prison. When the attempt had failed the creature had turned on itself, whirling faster and faster until disappearing in an explosion of futility.

While the scene brought back sordid memories of the blinding rages, Mason forced a slow and steady absorption of the atmosphere that had been created by his depression and alcohol consumption. He never wanted to forget how he had once lived. The life he had lived was a part of him and would be accepted and held close. This was necessary, as he never wanted to forget how low he had ventured. He accepted what he had become, with the goal to rehabilitate his injured soul, hoping to foster a positive climate so full healing could occur. He knew the time for thinking was over. Now it was necessary to accomplish deeds that would show commitment to the plan, which had been building since he had stood naked in the hospital room. With a sense of purpose he looked out the dirty smudged windows for a long time, then turned and left the apartment. The plan was simple. He would re-enter the world and begin to physically and emotionally clean up his life. The goal now would be to establish an existence that would focus on enjoying every moment to the maximum.

With his ankle suddenly feeling strong and his legs full of purpose Mason headed out to do necessary errands. The thought of going to the bank or shopping, once seen as taking time away from drinking, now took on a new enjoyable sense of purpose. Simple pleasures were to be the focus of his existence, while each and every action was to be seen as a new adventure to be savoured and explored. He would turn back in time to a period in his life where peace and harmony was the norm. This would be his new back alley from which to ride forth on a strong and repaired bicycle, ready to feel the wind of joy on his face.

Chapter Eight
ENLIGHTENMENT

The interesting aspect of life is rooted in the unknown. From one moment to the next the interaction with others, the environment or indeed one's self is forever fluid and changing. Every new day brings endless possibilities of interactions that, if embraced, can result in a huge spectrum of experiences. Even difficult, stressful or traumatic situations offer the aware individual an opportunity for expanding personal horizons or to provide deep insights into one's own character. The key to maximizing the growth and knowledge available is to be prepared to meet each new challenge with openness and the courage to examine one's own reactions, either positive or negative. Of the two choices it is probably more critical to examine our negative reactions, always attempting to comprehend the reasons for the poor responses to any situation. This approach demands a kind commitment. The mistake that human beings make is using our emotional or situational mistakes as a truncheon to beat our self-concept senseless. The belief in spare the rod and spoil the spirit is widely used and often explains either a weakening of a person's well-being or a consistent, bitter issuing of blame outwardly towards others. Even in the case where there is some justification of wrong doing, by another, the extent of anger and the amount of negativity generated is often astounding and profoundly tiring. Unfortunately many people live every day in a dysfunctional world of personal bitterness, constantly blaming their unwanted life on everything from the quality of a cup of coffee to the state of the global economy. Complaining becomes the most important aspect of living and even joyous occasions are reduced in value by critical judgements directed at others. If we are correct all the time, then others are wrong all the time. This allows for a safety net of falsehood to cushion weak and frightened people.

Examination of his past coping mechanisms proved difficult, but offered an ongoing source of positive energy and personal fulfillment. At first there were many opportunities for discovery. Old patterns of personal condemnation proved difficult to alter, but once Mason realized the stern denouncement of his personal frailties resulted only in pain, his outlook on these instances changed. The purpose for identifying reactions soon moved away from personal rebuke involving guilty humiliation, to a satisfying awareness involving a strengthening search for the reasons behind the response. This provided daily experiences that built up his character, expanding the growing strength inside. Mason began to relish the opportunity to learn from these daily opportunities.

As he became stronger, Mason began moving towards implementing a living plan that felt right. After cleaning and repairing his apartment, Mason removed all vestiges of his past life, discarding the unhealthy food, ashtrays and liquor bottles. For a month he left an unopened bottle of Scotch and a fresh package of cigarettes on the table as if tempting his old life, challenging it to come forward and do combat. The closest he came to the battle was spending a half an hour looking at the bottle one day. The next day he picked up the whiskey and gave it to the caretaker as a token of appreciation. The cigarettes were eventually tossed in the trash.

After cashing the long-term disability checks Mason consolidated his money, paid the rent, bought an older model, low mileage truck and started a business. During discussions with the caretaker the man complained about cutting the grass and doing yard work around the building. Mason offered to do the work on a contract basis. A deal was struck and he bought a reconditioned heavy duty, rear bagging lawn mower, along with the necessary assortment of rakes, a hoe and a good shovel. Mason had a magnetic sign made for his truck, advertising MJW Yard Services. He used the initials of his name and felt ready to take on any job. The business combined the desire to be outside with his knowledge of growing grass and plants. The caretaker was so impressed, Mason's service was recommended to other building managers throughout the area. An ad in the paper offering a reduction for seniors resulted in a deluge of calls. He worked long hours as the hard physical work felt good, especially when the soreness in his muscles began to dissipate. The overhead of his business was minimal, with the only cost being gasoline and minor repairs of equipment, which he took care of himself learning everything necessary about the lawn mower engine.

Due to the frugal nature of Mason's life he was able to bank most of the earnings. Soon his business grew along with his bank account and it was necessary to expand. He approached a real estate agent whose lawn he cut and asked her to find a place outside of the city with some land for storage and expansion. After looking at several possibilities Mason settled on a forty-acre plot five miles from the city boundary. The house was a run down three-bedroom bungalow that needed some serious remodelling. The condition of the house and the poor quality of the rocky land made the price reasonable. An added bonus was a large wooden utility shed located on the property. When the mortgage was arranged and possession completed he moved to the new home.

Mason had little time for any renovations to the home or land, due to his busy schedule, but he did make time to take care of his mental health. He attended the appointment with Dave who was pleased that he was staying sober and had started a business. Mason attended three AA meetings over a period of three months and connected with a well-established group. While he was not a regular, it was comforting to know support was available if necessary.

Part of each day was set aside for exercise. At first he walked, until his injured ankle was healed. Then Mason began to run. The first attempt lasted two blocks before a coughing fit brought the experiment to a sudden halt. He persevered, increasing the distance each day. Slowly, as his lung capacity expanded and the expulsion of accumulated tar and other pollutants decreased, Mason began to breathe easier. In addition, he did the exercises Lottie had given him, soon expanding his workouts to include daily use of free weights. The combination of outdoor work, exercise, healthy eating and removal of the deadly vices soon gave his misshaped face a robust glow. The right side remaining deformed in structure but the wound from the brass knuckles began to fade. Most of the time he wore a contented smile, which made his appearance less frightening. After discussions with Dr. Scarletti Mason decided to accept his deformed face as further surgery could result in the possibility of complete paralysis. On the positive side his face offered a constant reminder of how lucky he was to be alive.

Mason often tried to take a portion of the weekend off to catch up on chores and play some golf. With the insurance money from the car fire he bought new state of the art golf clubs, a new bag and a push style golf cart. While his swing was rusty and his tempo difficult to find, he played with enthusiasm, enjoying a game that had brought him such joy over many years. Mason played all the courses in the city before settling on a difficult track located a couple miles from his home that offered lush fairways, difficult rough and quick, true greens.

Near the end of the season when almost all the yards were put away and he had posted or delivered most of his flyers offering quality residential snow removal Mason suffered a relapse that lasted two weeks. He woke one morning and struggled to get out of bed, surrounded by an angst that seemed to grip his spirit and squeeze out the positive energy like toothpaste flowing from a tube caught in a tight grip. He could find no reason for the feelings of sadness that turned to hopelessness and brought thoughts of drinking into his head. Somehow the pain had returned and it seemed to affect everything in his life. He began to avoid others, while his usual workout routine suffered and then ended. After a week of anguish, Mason attended a meeting of the AA group. Through listening and talking he left feeling better and the next day forced a return to the workout regime, working harder to sweat out the ill-fated feelings. The exercise helped and with the increase in free time he began to renovate the house. After the two weeks he began to feel regenerated and the thoughts about drinking began to subside to the dark place. The experience reinforced how fragile his sobriety was and how constant diligence was absolutely critical.

Approximately three months after his discharge from the hospital Mason returned to the roadhouse bar at five o'clock one sunny afternoon. He entered the building, moving to the same bar chair where he had sat on the cold February night in a different life. He sat quietly until the bartender noticed the presence.

"What can I get for you?" asked Sid with false sounding civility.

"Just a Pepsi," Mason said as the man turned to get the order.

Sid delivered the drink and then froze. Mason smiled gently. "I wanted to come see you and thank you for saving my life. It's been a while but things have been pretty busy. How are you, Sid?"

"You've changed," Sid said, gesturing to his scarred face.

"Quite a bit. They did a number on me, that's for sure. But they probably saved my life. It's four and a half months this week since you served me the last drink." Mason could see Sid relax as the disclosure of sobriety was announced.

"Glad to see it. You were in serious trouble." It turned out Sid was no stranger to the dragon and could identify a drinker in danger.

The men spent the next two hours talking. The conversation was often interrupted by the necessity for Sid to serve customers or fill orders for waitresses. During the discussions mutual support was offered and accepted. When Mason spoke of the new business, Sid was quick to ask if he ever hired extra help. The man worked as a volunteer assisting young men and women battling alcoholism. Often, in serious situations, the youths had become unemployable due to the risk of drinking, past criminal activity while under the influence or because they simply did not have any job skills. Sid spoke of the program with excitement and commitment, becoming noticeably passionate and verbal, two traits Mason had never seen before in the usually gruff and stoic bartender. The bartender ended by saying the program was looking for employers that could understand the kids' predicament and the nature of the battle. Mason admired the man's dedication to these vulnerable youth, assuring the bartender that if the business developed the way he hoped, there might indeed be work. He got a telephone number and was about to leave when Mason said, "I gotta' ask one question. Why would you work in a bar?"

Sid chuckled. "Well, it helps me to remember what I must never forget. And being close to this poison can offer a chance to help people."

"Does that ever happen?" Mason asked innocently.

"Sometimes." The man shrugged, winked and smiled broadly.

Mason left the bar and walked to the back corner of the parking lot. In the glow of the early evening summer sun the place looked so different from his floating recollections. As he viewed the blackened pavement where his car had burned he shuddered. The irony of the situation left him face to face with the complexities of the universe. He was the one that should have died that night. Almost five months later two of his attackers were dead and one in jail. How had he been given an opportunity for rebirth while his attackers had their existence altered or extinguished? Standing on the blackened spot of the pavement he let the unanswerable questions bound around his mind and soul. In the end he decided that it was just another piece of magic existing in a truly magical place.

Between the end of the yard season and the beginning of the snow season there was a time for reflection. When not exercising or working on his house, Mason ruminated of past interactions with others. He began to realize that many of the messages that important people had given him fit exactly with his present state of being. Grace had told him to believe in himself, which he could finally do, experiencing wondrous success. Margaret had given him a wonderful message about holding onto the beautiful moments in life while not dwelling on the tragic. Victor had shown him the meaning of true friendship, which was both giving and taking freely. Jordan had been saved by an intervention that had offered the lad a chance. Mason had told the boy they were brothers. It was not until these reflective moments that he honestly believed the statement. The feelings of brotherly love, never felt before, coursed through his spirit, bringing on a welling of emotion. All his family had loved him. The final outcome of all the different relationships was unimportant. The only meaningful part to hold on to was the times when unconditional love was offered and accepted. The tragedy and pain mattered little in the face of the beautiful loving moments. Mason wept at the knowledge, holding himself close, while being thankful for the first time in his life.

He thought often of Rebecca, remembering what she had given him. Mason had been driven away from his daughter, but he had proclaimed a father's love before leaving. Once sure of his own rehabilitation he would seek her out and hopefully revitalize the relationship, knowing that he could never make up for the separation but hoping she would forgive him for the absence. He would return to her much stronger and a more committed parent.

The winter went by swiftly propelled by an active, interested mind and spirit, seeking knowledge and experiences with purpose and excitement. He began to spend time at the public library reading and researching topics of interest. Each morning he would rise with a personal challenge to enjoy every moment. Each night he would end his adventure reliving the wonders of the day. Even negative situations and the resultant negative reactions were cherished. They provided a tool for learning more about his true nature. The negative thoughts were massaged until the knots were removed and favourable emotions reigned.

It was an exceptionally snowy winter. Mason revelled in the hard work the blizzards presented, allowing him to make money and enjoy the outdoors. His face remained tanned and became weather-beaten. Gone were the days of winter depression, as he had too many interesting activities to preoccupy the swiftly moving moments. The situation continued forward until Mason again hit a solid obstacle, while approaching his one-year anniversary of sobriety. He awoke in the night, covered in thick sweat and shaking. At first he believed that he was having some form of stroke or a seizure. It took the rest of the night to calm and breathe properly. He made an appointment with a physician the next day and then called Dave, who seemed less concerned, stating that anniversaries could be difficult times. The social worker suggested Mason attend a meeting later in the week. He had not been to one in a long period of time and agreed to go.

Mason was welcomed back to the group with comforting words and much support. Many of the old members remained, while there were some new faces at the meeting. One in particular caught his eye. She was a petite woman with a face looking younger than her grey hair colour. She appeared shy and reserved. He surmised correctly that she was a new member. She said little during her chance to speak, deferring to the next member. Mason did learn her name was Julie. When it was his opportunity to speak Mason was surprised by the intense information he delivered to the group of respectful members. He was also surprised by the length of time it took him to discuss his first year of sobriety. When finished he looked down the table and Julie was staring at him with a slight smile on her lips. Mason instantly felt a constricting in his chest and loins. Since the attack no woman had been shown any interest. He believed that no woman would find him attractive. The practical reality did not result in negative or bitter emotions. As with many new truths in his life, acceptance resulted in a form of liberation that was treasured. Strangely Mason was now in the presence of a woman that was causing a reaction he had not felt in a long, long time. Although his hands were sweating he attempted to remain calm, suddenly feeling nervous. For a moment he even forgot about his face.

They talked briefly after the meeting. It was apparent that she too was damaged by a difficult journey, although she had no obvious exterior scars. Her eyes did not dwell on his deformed face, which made Mason grateful. There seemed to be a natural flow of conversation that came easy, being neither strained nor forced. Julie seemed serious at first, intently listening and watching his movements closely. Mason felt on display while sharing his opinions and answering her pointed questions with honestly and integrity. It was as if the conversation was an examination with her as the adjudicator. At times it felt like the questions were long established and well used. It seemed as though he was being compared to other suitors. The beauty for him was that there was absolutely no pressure to get the test correct. While Mason enjoyed Julie's looks and her deep concentrated questions, he had no illusions as to where the contact would go, as he needed nothing from the woman.

For the first time in his life it was not needy weaknesses that made him want to be with a woman. Julie emitted an energy that was fascinating. Mason could actually feel the sadness, past pain and personal struggles as their kindred spirits connected. Clearly she was a survivor. He sensed this from the cautious and watchful way they interacted. Men had hurt her in the past, and hurt her badly. Surprisingly, she seemed to possess a determination to continue the search for the beauty in life. She still had the courage to believe in the possibility of meeting positive people. In spite of all the pain she had suffered Julie had chosen to cast off the negative while acknowledging and nourishing the goodness. Similarly, somehow the strength of the positive forces in Mason's life had prevailed. The kindred connect made his heart jump as he felt a smile spread across his face.

Julie was staring at him with a look of surprise, mixed with understanding. It seemed one of those strange moments in life when words or explanations are unnecessary. There had been a connection based on the purest of emotions, where nothing is demanded or expected. They went for coffee after the meeting and talked until the café closed. At first it was small talk about their lives. She was trained as a Certified General Accountant, but had left the employment of a small company two years ago when her drinking had reached a peak. The parting had been mutual, before a firing would have occurred. Her two children were grown and now lived many miles away. They still blamed her for the drinking, even though she had been sober for almost eighteen months. Julie spoke of her children with a deep sadness that brought a choking blanket of pain to the small booth. Mason reached out for her arm, willing all the positive energy he could muster into the soft touch of his rough hands. The oppressive cover held for a moment as she looked into his caring eyes and then, combining her strength with his, the clouds parted. They sat quietly in the booth, two hurt and healing spirits connecting in the most honest of ways. The only silent request was that mutual respect, caring and kindness was present at all times. No meanness would be tolerated in the relationship. At that instant, the deepest, purest love Mason would ever know was born.

Mason invited Julie back to the acreage and they sat by the front window in the candlelight, waiting for the sun to come up. At times they talked passionately and intensely about personal beliefs and feelings. Other moments were filled by a comfortable silence that brought them closer together. Just as the sun was looking to rise, she fell asleep against his shoulder. Mason carried her into his bedroom and laid her on the bed, covering her with a warm quilt. Back on the couch he watched the brilliant morning begin and marvelled at how wonderfully unpredictable living could be, with the endless possibilities of each moment.

Julie stayed the night and never left. After honest, frank and humorous discussions it was decided that they would live together. The conversation, centering on the practical demands of cohabitation, moved quickly and efficiently. Without warning, the topic of sex surfaced, bringing an uncomfortable silence to the room. With halting words and obscure vague sentences they attempted to make their thoughts understood. She had been hurt by men, both prior to drinking and during the development of her alcoholism. She would need time and special care. Mason relaxed with a sense of relief. In the end it was decided that they would spend time getting to know each other, with him sleeping on the couch the first week. Then they would re-evaluate the situation.

Julie moved in the next day and both worked hard to establish a home. Mason was very comfortable with the changes proposed as Julie had a flair for decorating. It became obvious that Julie was a very intelligent woman and he quickly began to seek her opinions on business. She had a quick and calculating mind, which was not surprising due to her expertise with numbers. While she continued to work at her secretarial job, Mason began to rely on her assistance in preparing for the busy season. In addition, she began formulating ideas for further growth of the company, including a green house to grow organic vegetables and potted plants. He liked the way she was eager to help out maintaining equipment and although she was small, seemed to have a strong back and a determination to match his committed work ethic.

With strength and purpose Mason began to prepare for the busy spring season. Expansion was necessary, so he contacted Sid, hoping to hire some additional help. The next day the bartender showed up with three young people and together the men interviewed the potential workers. He liked all three immediately, especially Brian, who was a defiant young man with broad shoulders and lots of attitude. Jerry was a sullen fellow wanting only to stay sober and make some money. Carly was an ex-child prostitute who just wanted to be left alone and get her life together. Mason was direct and intense, immediately gaining complete attention of the trio. He explained that he was an alcoholic and had recently attained his first year of sobriety. He made it clear that he understood denial and had been a master of blaming others while justifying his drinking, so any attempt to con him with all the ways that alcoholics usually operate would be a waste of energy, as he would not believe any deceptions. This was a business and Mason demanded only three things, sobriety, hard work and pleasantness with the clients. He would not tolerate poor behaviour with the customers. If the three followed those rules he would give them good wages, benefits and his total support. He would show them understanding, compassion and would fight for them but he would not under any circumstances enable negative behaviour in any way, form or shape. If they did not follow the rules then he would go back to Sid and find others who would. After the three agreed to his conditions he had all sign a contract stating they agreed to work hard, stay sober and respect themselves.

Mason continued to plan for the start of the season. Even in mid-March the calls were beginning, wanting times for power raking and aerating lawns. In addition, the company was receiving more referrals from apartment caretakers. Soon he began to feel overwhelmed with the organizational aspects and the paperwork demanded by the government. At supper that evening he made a proposal to Julie. Mason offered her fifty percent of the business if she would coordinate the office end of the operation. This would free him up to run the crews and ensure good quality work. She gratefully agreed then left the table. He could hear her crying in the bedroom, but chose to leave her alone with her emotions. Later, she made him tea and they talked late into the evening.

Two days later, after the papers were signed they went out for supper at a local expensive restaurant. Mason's deformed face often received shocked looks from others. Defiantly, Julie clutched his arm tight, fixing an intent gaze back at the stares until the rude people looked away. She was telling the world that he was her man and she was proud. Her gesture of commitment brought a bubbling of good feelings that resulted in a wonderful evening. Later that night they made gentle love for the first time. He marvelled at her beauty, while her actions showed a complete acceptance for his scarred and damaged body. The lovemaking completely solidified their relationship.

The yard season flew by with a speed that surprised both. Due to the increase in business the profits soared. Brian turned out to be a wonderful employee, turning the anger and attitude into a commitment to hard work. The lad was very good with the customers and was soon given a crew to manage, along with a raise in pay. Carly became Julie's assistant, working hard at the acreage making sure the equipment was ready each morning, taking calls and learning the necessary paperwork for the business to function. In addition, the two women began designing a necessary business plan for an expansion into the area of potting plants and organic vegetables, which culminated in the erection of the first greenhouse by the end of August. Jerry lasted two months until arrested one night for driving a stolen car, impaired. Because of past offences the young man ended up receiving six months in jail. Sid seemed to have an endless supply of young workers fighting to retake control of their lives. Both Julie and Mason were committed to providing these young damaged souls employment opportunities, so as the company expanded so did the number of employees. Julie ran the business area with efficiency, caring for the young people like a protective mother, but with a firm no nonsense policy.

By the end of October when most of the crew were laid off for the winter, the business was in a remarkable position. Most of the profit had remained in the company, resulting in a very strong financial situation. Brian, Carly and some other employees were kept on working in the greenhouses, as another had been added late in the year due to demands for the vegetables. Some stayed on to work in the snow removal component of the company. The outlook for the business was quite optimistic, as a strong position in the community had been established. The local paper ran a story of the company and the way it helped young people find employment. A picture was taken for the article.

As the bulk of the fall work was finished, the equipment put away and preparations completed in anticipation of the snow, Mason discussed taking a two-week road trip. Julie listened patiently as he haltingly attempted to explain the rationale for the journey. She interrupted him after a few minutes into the explanation, stating she understood and would help him get ready. Mason was relieved, as he could not verbalize the thoughts, but knew the trip was an absolute necessity. There were old places to visit and old feelings to set free.

Once on the highway Mason sought to understand the purpose for the trip and what needed to be accomplished. He had decided that some of the painful relationships and emotions that still surfaced from time to time needed to be exorcised or, if not removed, then accepted. The only way for success was to reconnect with places and people from his past. After many miles he decided to start at the beginning and headed for the back alley.

The stop at his birth city was both remarkable and foreign. So much had changed since his father had been killed. The black bridge had been demolished and a new concrete structure now spanned the river. He walked across the white bridge and was surprised to find that the structure was as high as he could remember, however, the water seemed blacker. The shivers returned as Mason leaned over the concrete railing. He went by his grandparents' home, but had difficulty finding the property, as the entire yard and house had been changed. The backyard was a stretch of grass surrounded by a chain link fence. The garden had been ploughed under and the back workshop had been knocked down. The outside of the home had been redone with vinyl siding and the back porch, where he had spent so much time as a boy, had been removed, replaced by a wooden deck, sporting patio furniture and a gas barbeque. Even the step where he had sat covered in blood was gone. Mason made a trip to the cemetery and laid flowers on the grave of his grandmother and grandfather. In the end they had been buried together, which provided him comfort. Mason walked the back alley and felt a warm connection with the past, even though the fences were no longer white and the alley had been paved. His old house appeared much different with new trees and a remodelled backyard. His old school was still there looking unchanged. Mason thought about entering, but wondered if he would run into Schmidt and be sent to detention. The thought made him laugh, as he realized the intense power of childhood memories. Finally, on his way out of town he visited the old cemetery and stood by Walter Glear's headstone remembering a stormy day that helped forge his character. The visit with Walter made him feel good and he left the city, both refreshed and satisfied that the first step of the trip had been accomplished.

Mason then drove south and returned to the place where so many bad memories lay twisting in the pit of his stomach. However, the scene was so different. In the front yard were children playing and laughing. The house was brightly painted with colourful curtains. The ugly recollections and the current bright appearance offered a strange contrast. In the end there was acceptance that the lingering bad thoughts were not connected to a physical location but inhabited an internal place within his memories. Mason visited Diane, his mother's old friend. The elderly woman came to the door suspiciously but when he introduced himself she brought him into her living room and made him a cup of tea. The room smelt of stale cannabis and accumulated clutter. Apparently Diane still indulged in the long established habit, but her mind was incredibly sharp given age and marijuana consumption. The old woman told him that his mother had gone into a home about five years ago and had died three years later, lost in the fog of Alzheimer's. His sister, Violet, had moved back to the city to be close to her mother and Diane had her address that was a few years old. Mason thanked the old lady after getting the name of the cemetery where his mother was buried. The afternoon was spent at his parents' gravesite as they were side by side. He delivered a large bouquet of flowers. Anyone observing the man would have been surprised at the length of time he stood talking, seemingly to no one. Mason left drained but content. He had finally said all the words that needed to be released.

He went to the address given by Diane and met Karen, who welcomed him like a family member. Karen was Violet's mate and was very pleased to finally meet Mason. The two talked for an hour before his sister arrived home from work. Violet was stunned to see Mason and broke down crying. He held her tight and was very surprised to experience the warm feeling of being close to family again. This was unexpected and remarkable. He stayed for supper and then returned the next day. Both told their stories, which not surprisingly involved addictions. His was alcohol, hers drugs. Violet had been addicted for many years and had fought the world with misplaced anger. It had finally resulted in a jail term, where she had been forced straight and found Jesus Christ. Later, after release, she had met Karen and the two were married six months previous. Violet had no children as a botched illegal abortion many years ago had destroyed her reproductive system. The resulting bleeding had almost taken her life.

The second day they went to the cemetery to visit their parents. His sister spoke of the return to the city that she had hated. Violet told of how their mother had initially remained bitter, blaming her husband, children and the world for an unsatisfied life. The angry moods had changed when Alzheimer's had begun to take the mind. Then it seemed that Alice started to remember positive times, when the family was strong and happy. Mother and daughter had sat for hours reminiscing about long ago tales of fun and excitement. At times Violet wondered if some of the memories were from their mother's own childhood. She decided to embrace all the stories told, as the resultant good feelings were appreciated. Then one day Alice stopped talking. It was as if her mind had decided enough and wanted no more communication. About two weeks later she stopped eating, became bedridden and soon died peacefully while asleep. They both cried as Violet told the story and afterwards hugged each other, offering unconditional support. The day was cold as brother and sister stood at the gravesite of their parents. Silently, and with quiet words, together they spoke of many things. For that afternoon and in that quiet and sleeping place, they grieved for all they had lost. After all the words had been said and a multitude of tears shed they held hands and were a family again.

Mason left the next day after a talkative breakfast and lots of laughter. He hugged both women and brought tears to Karen's eyes when he told her how lucky he was to have such a wonderful sister-in-law. He left this city with a full heart, having shed the remnants of bitterness. He felt good and somehow whole again, free of a sickness that had attempted to consume his spirit. At seventeen Mason had left this city, in the dead of night, full of anger, pain and sick of heart. Over thirty-five years later he left again on a brilliantly sunny day, his heart brimming with joy.

The next stop was to visit Grace. Mason went to her sister's address and found out that Grace had died two years earlier of colon cancer. The woman cried while relating the extreme bravery and courage her sister had shown fighting the despicable disease. The dignity of her passing gave the sister a wealth of strength from which to celebrate Grace and the lives that she had touched. Mason related his own contact, omitting certain parts, and told the sister how Grace had saved him and nursed him back to health. He would never forget the kindness. His words were greatly appreciated, bringing tears and a positive connection between the living and the dead that was wonderful.

Stopping by to see Victor he found the plant closed and boarded up. He located Marvin, Victor's lawyer cousin, in the telephone book. The man was much older now but still remembered him. They spent three hours together. Marvin related that Victor had died about ten years ago of a heart attack after going home with two oversized twin sisters. Both agreed it was a very appropriate ending and would have pleased Victor greatly. Marvin still had a flair for telling stories and they spent the rest of the afternoon roaring with laughter.

Mason attempted to find Jordan, however, the aunt had moved and no one on the block had any information. No name was found in the city telephone book. He travelled on believing that somewhere

Jordan was content with living, a man older and healed, helping others who had experienced similar pain.

A long drive was in order as Mason wished to return to the site of the Living Joy commune. The length of the journey allowed him to absorb all the wonderful feelings that he had experienced. He had decided to unconditionally accept all the moments, finally gaining strength from both the happy and sad events that had shaped his life. Both ends of the spectrum seemed to affirm his humanity and he now firmly believed that any emotion experienced needed acceptance to receive the benefit. This would allow the celebration of all the moments of his life. Driving down the highway Mason began to finally appreciate the beauty of the human creature, in spite of all the weaknesses.

All Mason found at the commune site were empty spots where the barn and house had been. He wandered around the property remembering the time spent in this strange place. As he was getting into the truck he noticed a cat cleaning itself on a mound of dirt, left behind after the demolition of the barn. He paused for a moment as the cat continued to clean its paws. There had been torment and death in this place but the cats had survived. No matter how difficult and tortured humans made their existence, life would remain and be renewed as the cycle continued. He sat in his truck and on a whim began to sing one of the songs he had roared into the cathedral ceiling of the barn. The words came easily as Mason sang the first verse of The Weight, a classic sixties tune written by The Band. By the time the truck slowly left the commune he was belting out the chorus, singing joyously to the cat, "Take a load off Fanny, take a load for free. Take a load off Fanny and you put the load right on me."

The next destination involved a long drive and an afternoon stop. Fortunately warm air had been pulled north by the jet stream so, upon entering the parking lot of the large hotel, Mason was able to remove his jacket and roll up the sleeves of his shirt. He scanned the tree line, but could not find the landmark he was looking for. The large tree was no longer visible. He estimated the probable location of the small clearing and set out into the bush. The hiking was difficult, as the underbrush appeared thicker in places, but he soon found the clearing. Mason stood catching his breath, examining the changes. The hanging tree had been hit by lightning, splitting it down the middle and felling it to the left, crushing all in its path. By the state of decay the destruction must have occurred many years ago. He viewed the scene with wonder, amazed at how the incredible strength of the tree had been dwarfed by the immensity of the lightning's incredible energy. Standing in amazement it took awhile before he was drawn to the other tree growing in the clearing. The small sapling was now a large tree, stretching upward in an attempt to regain the position left vacated by its creator. All he could think about was the revolving wholeness of life. He stayed for the afternoon walking around the clearing, touching the rough beauty of the old and dead or caressing the smoothness of the new and living. By the end of the afternoon, as the sun began to weaken and the air chilled, he walked through to the golf course. He stood absorbing the sight that had greeted him many years ago. While leaning against a tree he saw a white object land out in the fairway. Very soon an older man pushing a golf cart and walking with purpose appeared, heading for the ball. The man noticed him, waved and hurried on, hoping to finish the round before the dwindling fall sun disappeared.

With failing light Mason drove to another cemetery to have a conversation with Bert and Grace, finding them side-by-side just as he knew Grace had always wanted. He could imagine them together somewhere with Grace talking incessantly and Bert smiling at the sound of her lilting voice. He thanked Grace personally for all she had unselfishly given him at a time when he was so vulnerable. He vowed to pass the gift she had given him on to others. Dusk was settling as he made the way slowly out of the graveyard, taking his time, enjoying the quiet and having no fear of the dead.

Mason returned to the truck and headed for the last destination. He would drive straight through, knowing sleep would not come on this night. He arrived early at the last stop, checked into a hotel and caught a few hours of sleep before heading off to complete his journey. With his mind stilled he began to feel the excitement. He pulled into the far end of the car dealership and began to appear interested in a large extended cab truck with all the accessories. It was not long before a salesman hustled out to do business. He recognized Gerry Harcourt before the salesman recognized him. The man was stunned by his appearance, at first unable to talk. Then, realizing the potential for personal trouble, the salesman moved him behind the expensive truck and, with a voice of fear, asked what Mason wanted. Mason took a moment to settle the man, stating his only purpose was to find out where his daughter was living. Gerry related that she was currently in residence at a small university five hours east. The man spoke affectionately about Rebecca, stating she was a fine young woman who worked summers at the dealership and was liked by all. This apparently was not the case with Samuel Jr. who was a chip off his grandfather's block, being controlling and ruthless, but without Sam Sr.'s smoothness at manipulation. Gerry said people were surprised at how similar the two men were in looks and nature. Mason said nothing and remained committed to the pact struck many years ago.

He returned to the hotel, had a refreshing sleep and made the easy drive the following day. It was simple to locate the university and there was only one female residence on campus. Mason checked in at security and asked for Rebecca to be paged. She was in class and not available, so he sat in the small foyer and waited. He stayed calm for the next two hours simply watching the many young, excited students enter and exit the residence. The exuberance of youth gave him many positive moments during the hours he waited. Soon he noticed a dark haired beauty enter the building and talk to the security guard, who directed her to where Mason sat. His whole person tingled as a multitude of emotions screamed through his body. The impact was so strong that all he could do was rise and stand uncomfortably waiting for Rebecca's response. She walked across the room with an assertiveness that choked him with joy and then stopped abruptly, beginning to shake slightly. Finally, with tears streaming down her cheeks, she said the one word that brought them together in a crushing embrace. With relief and love in her voice she said, "Daddy."

They sat close on the couch in the small public room, holding hands, sharing rapid conversation, oblivious to the many questioning looks delivered by the constant coming and going of tenants and guests. The initial speed of the conversation was surprising as if the past seven years needed to be made up in minutes. The great urgency lasted until both tired and then began to laugh at the same time. She had his laugh, which made him feel like he was about to blow up, spreading endless molecules of joy to the outer reaches of the universe. On wobbly legs they went to his truck and drove to a local coffee shop where they had an afternoon lunch. She was now twenty-two and Mason wanted to know everything about her. Most of the conversation was full of sharing and excitement. There were periods of extreme awkwardness when Rebecca became overwhelmed with the fact that she had not heard from him in such a long time. When speaking of his absence, emotions fuelled by anger, disappointment and rejection would surface, causing her to talk with brutal honesty. Mason allowed her to speak openly, never trying to justify or blame, wanting the pain exposed, urging it from the buried spot where it had been festering. After the emotions were released Rebecca would regret the words. He would have none of any apologies, encouraging her to speak freely. In an open truthful manner, they powered through the many years until in a quiet moment they realized that they were in the present.

Dropping Rebecca off at the woman's residence Mason produced a box from behind the seat. Inside were copies of all the letters and cards he had sent her over the years. He had anticipated that she would not have received any of the correspondence. Her reaction told him he was correct. After mailing the originals to her home, he had always mailed a copy to his own mailing address. In this way he had kept a record of the correspondence he had sent over the years. Before he had left home he had sorted all the mail by the date located on the postal stamp and bundled them together. Mason could not return to the past and deliver his messages, but he could allow his daughter to experience the thoughts and feelings he had so desperately wanted her to know. Rebecca burst into tears. Father and daughter hugged and cried as the bond that had been strained but never broken was renewed.

Mason visited with Rebecca for five days. During that time they were inseparable. He attended classes with her, when she absolutely needed to go. They went on long walks, where the destination was irrelevant. He met her university friends. Rebecca seemed to want to introduce him to everyone on campus, saying Dad or Daddy many times in the day as if using a foreign phrase and suddenly realizing it was so fun to say. The word was one of the most beautiful sounds Mason had ever heard and he never got tired of the resulting feeling. She had a wickedly good sense of humour with often one word or a quick look causing both to break into peals of laughter that would rob them of their senses.

Mason met her boyfriend Jeremy, and treated the young man with respect and inclusion, encouraging thoughts and opinions in a non-judgemental and gentle way. Rebecca watched the two interact with joy, as the kindness shown was far different than Jeremy had received during the two visits to meet her mother. Victoria and Samuel only came up twice in conversations. Mason was pleased to see that Rebecca was able to identify some of the weaknesses but was not quick to judge, accepting that her mother and brother, for all their faults, were still her family. He loved that she was so accepting and compassionate at such a young age, qualities that had taken him many years and many very tough miles to learn.

During the stay they had late nights and early mornings. He visited her room in residence on the last day before leaving. All the mail had been opened and the cards on display. He moved about the small room, reading all and remembering when he had sent each one. Mason was touched with the way Rebecca treasured the correspondence. The letters seemed to confirm for her that she had been in his thoughts while they had been apart. Before he left they exchanged addresses and discussed the future. He warned her that both her mother and grandfather would react strongly and harshly if they found out he had made contact. She was firm in the fact that she would not sneak around hiding her dad from anyone. They had been reunited and nothing would separate them again. He liked her spunk and told her how much he respected and loved her. No longer was the past important, only the present and future mattered.

It was the middle of the night when Mason pulled into the acreage. He was extremely tired but almost weightless, as if light from the late fall stars could shine through his body, illuminating every part of his being with warmth. Julie met him at the front door of the brightly lit house. She could feel the positive energy emitting from him as she hugged him close. He allowed the energy to pass to her willingly and unselfishly. She started to speak, then stopped and began to turn out the many lights. Mason stood riveted to the floor until she returned to him in the darkness. With a candle in hand she led him to their bed. No words were exchanged, as none were needed. Silently they climbed into bed and, with a deliberate slowness, spent the rest of the night pleasuring each other with an energy that was far beyond physical.

When Mason returned from the journey he was fifty-four years old. He marked that year as the beginning of his road to enlightenment. He now saw his life as a road because he did not believe the journey would ever end. The word enlightenment kept coming up in his readings. It was new to Mason, however, ancient in the language of the world. At first he struggled to understand the simple, yet complex nature of the relationships necessary for understanding the word's meaning. He finally began to realize that all his attempts to intellectualize the meaning would prove frustrating. This spiritual word referred to the release into the real nature of existence. After much hardship he had discovered that the true way to find contentment was not to look outward, but to search inward. Thus began his commitment to find his own true nature and connect with the immeasurable natural force, so all encompassing that no name could describe it. In the vast scope of all there was he was the tiniest of measure. By allowing his true spirit to connect with everything a great power of contentment could be achieved. The only sense of belonging that was really important was the connection with self, as that belonging could never be disrupted, destroyed or stolen. With that knowledge happiness and contentment flowed within and permeated every relationship and human contact.

Mason began to meditate on a daily basis, releasing his spirit into nothingness and receiving everything. By strengthening his body and spirit, his mind soon grudgingly fell into place. There still were many times his thoughts tried to control his world, succeeding for short periods of time until consciousness returned and the thoughts tamed. He began to treasure these moments, believing the identification of the negative thoughts and the process of managing them was an ongoing step down the pathway to enlightenment.

The next chapter of years slid by with silky smoothness as Mason became committed to personal enlightenment. He joined a local choir, singing bass. In addition, he enrolled in an introductory course of reading music and took keyboard lessons, learning to play simple songs for Julie late at night. He and Julie took riding lessons, soon purchasing two horses that they rode about the property, which had expanded when they bought the adjacent section of rolling grazing land. On a warm day after work they would ride off to one of the secluded corners and eat their picnic supper on a blanket, enjoying the simple peace of the sweet summer air while the horses grazed on the fresh grasses. Interesting university courses were taken in the off-season with a desire to one day receive a degree. Mason and Julie became engaged in any form of the arts, which was interesting and well done, attending events ranging from rock concerts to poetry readings. They would make road trips to attend performances.

The company continued to expand and was hugely profitable. Brian and Carly were indispensable, ultimately becoming both partners in life and in the company. Their business relationship was very positive and timely, as the younger couple took the business in new directions. As the young people proved their worth he and Julie began to relinquish more control, finding it important to feel the grass rather than cut it. They built a modest home on the other side of the property with high ceilings and large windows, as both, having experienced enough darkness in their lives, desired only to feel the warmth of the sun, while being exposed to the power of the light.

Mason and Julie visited with Rebecca and Jeremy twice a year. Soon his daughter was engaged and later he walked her down the aisle. Although there was coldness from the Sandersons, neither he nor Rebecca cared, choosing to celebrate the joyous occasion fully. Regular visits occurred after the birth of their first boy child. He showered unconditional attention on the lad and marvelled at the growth with each subsequent visit. Julie also reconciled with her children, making the family larger. Mason accepted her children as his own.

When he turned sixty Julie had a huge birthday party, which was very well attended. Community members, past employees, current employees and local business associates joined his family to celebrate. Mason was grateful, but found being the focus of attention difficult. He was relieved when most of the visitors were gone and he could spend the remainder of the evening with the people he cared for most. Julie purchased a new set of golf clubs as Mason had been talking about taking the game up again. It felt good to swing a club and he vowed that this golf season would be busy.

Mason's fall birthday marked a milestone of sorts. Negotiations with Julie, Brian and Carly, led to him semi-retiring from the company. He only attended important meetings and was available for consultation if necessary. This left all the day-to-day operations to Brian and Robert, a new partner who had been with the company for many years. Mason had started the business with one truck, one mower and one friendly caretaker, building it into a multi-million dollar company, diversifying into many areas. At every turn he was quick to acknowledge the importance of Julie in the success.

It was not long after the birthday celebration that Mason proposed to Julie. In all the years together neither had ever spoken of marriage, so the proposal came as a complete surprise. For a moment Julie looked unsure and then the past was wiped away, and she accepted. After a short ceremony in early January, attended by only family and very close friends, the two left for a three-month world cruise. After all the difficulties Mason had endured with winter in his drinking days, he finally escaped the cold and snow. They returned in April full of stories and tales of adventure. For both, suddenly the world did not seem so big.

The next seven months was a time of unbelievable weather. The spring brought warm gentle, soaking rains, followed by a hotter than usual summer. The landscape exploded with green as the grass grew fast and plentiful. Spring gave way to summer with the night rains and hot days. There would be days of very hot weather that were enjoyed as everyone became bronzed by the sun. The weather was perfect for growing crops. All the farmers were very optimistic, but as usual quite anxious, until the bumper crop was in the bins. There was a surprising lack of prairie wind that summer, which made golfing wonderful. Mason rejoined the golf course close to his home and played everyday. He walked each round, even in the hottest of days, going early in the morning. Julie would often come with him for the walk, chatting and picking wildflowers to put into a vase on the dining room table.

The glorious summer turned to a mild fall with the most brilliant display of colour he had every seen. Mason and Julie walked the golf course or rode the horses around the land, marvelling at the beauty of the season. All was right with the world as a deep and satisfying peace seemed to settle.

Near the end of October Mason stopped at the golf course and learned it would close on the following Wednesday. He decided to play the final day of the season. Julie said she would accompany him for the last round.

That night before bed, for some reason, he dug out the wooden box his mother had given him when he was eleven years old. She had told him to keep his prized possessions and secret dreams in the case. Mason had used it to store his life reminders, carrying it with him all these years. Slowly he went through the items, absorbing each. There was an old picture of his first house with his father on the front step smiling. There was an old black and white picture of his mother, young, beautiful and hopeful. He looked at the little boy in the newspaper picture standing in front of a broken bike, grinning with his arm in a sling. There was a picture of his grandparent's home, with his grandparents and Uncle Auggie laughing under the apple tree. There were numerous first place ribbons from long ago track meets. He stared hard at the grade eight school diploma that his mother had desperately fought for, hoping her son would experience success. There was the faded picture of the young teenager sitting covered in blood, staring with a lost look. Attached were the newspaper articles, but he did not read them, as he knew what they said. The letter from Violet was old and worn from many readings. There was the feather from his hippie hat and a copy of Fanny Hill with a picture of a clothed Sara tucked inside. The photograph of Tuckel and the young girl frozen in the action of death brought an eerie feeling. The newspaper clipping of the motel with the hanging tree in the background also brought about mixed reactions. There was a picture of him winning the city golf championship and a broken golfer from the top of a trophy. There was the family picture he had taken out of the shattered frame from Victoria's living room. The portrait was beautiful, holding the darkest of secrets. There were school pictures of Rebecca, from kindergarten until he was forced to go. There was wrinkled artwork done by his daughter to show her love. There was Margaret's teapot reminding him of the message she so desperately wanted him to understand. There was the picture of the assault, bearing his former appearance from his former existence that was now accepted and treasured. There was the newspaper picture of Sid, Julie and the young people. He was obscure in the back sporting a serious look. Mason took a moment with the last item. It was an eight by ten picture of Rebecca in her wedding dress arm in arm with a smiling Julie. He sat for a long time realizing the significance of all his experiences. As he put away the memories he remembered an old Jimmy Buffet song. "Some of its magic, some of its tragic but I had a good life all the way."

Mason arose the Wednesday morning feeling strange. There was a pulling in his chest and a slight throbbing in his jaw. He told Julie of the pains, accusing her of punching his mouth in the night. She was concerned, but he laughed off the ailments as old age. The day had dawned rainy and cold. The unusually warm ground had suddenly met with a band of cold air that had moved into the area overnight. The rain had ceased, but a heavy fog covered the land. At first Mason was not sure if the course would even be open, but was intent on playing as there would be no other opportunity this year. Julie was not coming as an old friend had called and was dropping by for a visit. She was concerned with his health, suggesting that he go visit the doctor. Mason was determined to play golf and told her he would go after the round, if he was still feeling poorly.

Dressed in light but warm layers Mason headed for the golf course. The fog was very dense in places, yet seemed to lift slightly as he got closer. There were a few random cars in the parking lot, covered in water where the moisture from the fog had condensed directly onto the metal. Mason was amazed at the utter stillness of the scene as he placed the golf bag on the pushcart. He stretched his left arm hoping to work out the growing pain. The sound of the crunching gravel appeared very loud and deadened in the quiet confines of the fog blanket.

There was a sign on the inside of the small pro shop door instructing golfers to play and settle up later. Mason made his way to the first tee, did his warm up and teed up the golf ball. Taking a deep breath he cleared his mind and swung with a smooth, fluid swing learned over many years of golfing. The ball was caught in the middle of the club and exploded off the tee, ripping through the heavy air and finally disappearing into the fog hanging over the fairway. He started the last round with a comfortable feeling of optimism.

Mason walked to the ball that was in the middle of the fairway and even though the fog was heavy, he could see the green as if looking down a tunnel. The trees on the edges were appearing and disappearing shapes offering little real substance. He chose the appropriate iron and crisped a shot. The ball disappeared into the close sky. He waited quiet moments and then it landed next to the pin. Mason laughed out loud as he proceeded to the green and banged in a solid putt to make a birdie and go one under par for the round. He made par on the second hole and moved to the third tee where he saw a figure sitting on the bench. The size looked like a child, until he got closer and an old man stood up. The man was dressed in an expensive black rain suit and wearing a logo-less black cap. Mason was old but this man was ancient, wizened in the face and sporting a stooped posture to the slight frame. The man was friendly, smiling and possessing a deep jovial voice, which was strange coming from the small body. The man did not ask to join Mason, he simply teed up the ball and hit a rocket down the fairway. Given the man's apparent frailness, Mason was shocked by the beauty of the swing and the resulting power. Brief introductions occurred as the two golfers made their way down the mowed and soggy grass path. The man's name was Bob, but everyone called him Gabe, a nickname given by the man's father. As they proceeded the fog seemed to deepen. When Mason questioned if they would be able to continue, Gabe laughed, stating that the fog would be no problem.

The pain in Mason's left arm was getting stronger and he continued to stretch before each swing. The discomfort was not affecting his shots, which were reminiscent of long ago days when playing his best golf. Through the next six holes the two men talked and played golf. It was as if he had known the man for years, sharing personal thoughts and past stories. Gabe was a good listener, asking questions that were powerful, usually resulting in the conversation going in a different and very interesting direction. There was a curious sense that somehow Mason was learning from the talk, but he was not sure what or how. The time went by at a mellow rate of speed he had never encountered. The two men played spectacular golf, matching each other shot for shot. Mason could not remember sinking so many long putts. It was as if he instinctively knew the line necessary and how much the ball would break. His body would respond, striking the ball with the perfect weight, resulting in beautiful curling putts that fell in the centre of the hole.

By the time the twosome reached the tenth tee box he had recorded the best nine holes of his life. The pain in his arm, which had increased in severity on the fourth hole, had disappeared. Mason felt strong and alert, aware of each rustle in the trees or sound in the thick sky. He hit his tee shot first and then watched as Gabe hit one almost on the same line. Reaching the golf balls Mason discovered his driver had been left back by the bench on the tee box. The man stated it was necessary for him to continue but was sure that Mason would catch up. Walking quickly back Mason retrieved the driver and returned to his ball. Before hitting the second shot he paused for a moment, acutely aware of the solitude. Mason played the next five holes quickly and at three under par. He could feel a growing tiredness as he attempted to catch up to Gabe. Although he knew the man was directly in front, there was absolutely no sign or sound.

Mason finally accepted there was no catching the man. Slowing he began to savour every shot, making three more birdies. Coming to the eighteenth hole Mason began to absorb the surrounding nothingness.

The fog sank into the ground and the ground reached into the fog blurring the lines of his reality. It was the strangest weather Mason had ever seen, but he accepted the unique conditions, finding his body connecting to the grass while his arms seemed to blend into the golf clubs. Only the ball seemed to move as Mason crushed another drive down the middle of the fairway, quickly losing sight of the white object but clearly seeing the flight image and somehow knowing the final location. The last hole was a par five and he knew the prudent move was to lay up, but Mason took out the three metal and blasted a shot where he believed the green to be. The tiredness was weighing on him now, pushing him onward and pulling him back at the same time. Mason willed his body to relax, becoming like a slender reed, not resisting, simply moving in a swirling wind. The fog was dense now, making further shots impossible. He soon found the ball miraculously on the green twenty feet below the hole. He pulled the pin and with a beautiful stroke hit the ball into the centre of the cup for an eagle. It was the best round of golf Mason had ever played. With a very tired body he stood for a moment celebrating with the most important person in his life. He eventually left the green and soon returned to the pro shop, panting with exhaustion, but free of any pain. The area in front of the building and beside the practice green was deserted. The sign remained on the door. Mason stood for a moment trying to catch his breath and regain his strength.

"You appear bushed," a voice said from behind. Mason turned and was greeted by a large man with brilliant blue eyes and a comely face under a few days growth of a salt and pepper coloured beard. "I was just coming back to the pro shop. My name is PJ, short for Pete Jones. Pleased to meet you."

Mason stood leaning on the golf cart, nodding his head in recognition, not wanting to be rude but too weary to speak. The man seemed to understand Mason's exhaustion, moving in to support his weight. There was immense strength in the man as he willingly allowed the assistance. They walked together over to the clubhouse, entering the door and moving to a glassed in porch containing large chairs that overlooked the first tee. Although they were now inside, the open windows allowed the foggy air to somehow pass through the screens and into the room.

Regaining some strength Mason asked why he had never seen the employee before. The man let out a musical laugh. "I'm usually playing but at the end of the season I'm always available to help out. Besides, I like meeting real golfers and this is the time when they play. They're the best kind of people." Pete said with a wink. He liked PJ right off and told the man so. They talked golf for a while longer and then a soothing silence settled over the men as the fog continued to drift through the openings.

"You didn't say your name," PJ said, in a soft tone.

"My name is Mason Joseph Walls," Mason stated proudly.

"Welcome Mason. Middle name same as your grandfather?" said the large man with a cock of the head and a purse of the lips.

"How did you know?"

"Just a guess."

The unusual fog thickened and danced in the pale light that seemed to emit from different sources and angles. The diffuse glow appeared to make objects shine with clarity. Every ripple in the bark of the tree trunks was significant and perceived, while the whole tree was experienced and embraced. Small and large merged into one. Everything in view was captured with all the senses in a glance. It was not only in one direction as it spun in a panorama of overwhelming sensation. Yet the message was of nurturing patience, like the caring commitment and kindness of a new mother. The sensation delivered innocence, soaked with contentment.

"Weird," Mason muttered, focusing on a large squirrel that leapt from one branch to another and then disappeared into the mist. In that briefest of moments he knew its joy, its freedom.

"Wondrous, isn't it?" The velvet voice whispered. "It is a glorious twilight."

"Do I have to leave soon?" Mason questioned.

"When you are ready and the fog lifts. That will make the ride home easier. For now enjoy the peace."

Mason relaxed as his shoulders melted into the softness of the comfortable chair. He sighed and felt an endless stream of air escape his lungs. Although they were behind glass the mist engulfing the pro shop seemed to move in unison with his breath. He could see the outline of forms moving slowly down the cart path.

"There were other golfers out today? I thought I was alone after Gabe left me."

"You were never alone. Even when there were no others you always had yourself." PJ allowed the words to hang in the air like a hummingbird. "The only task we have is to love and cherish that which we are. In the end all we really have is our own spirit and through unconditional love for that spirit we find the glorious magic offered."

"I started to appreciate it over the last few years. It was a tough learn."

"Enlightenment is never easy. Fortunately the learning goes on forever." PJ murmured quietly, as if speaking to himself.

The words lingered and a strange knowledge seemed to spread through Mason's entire being offering hope and joy. A mystical contentment triggered a lingering calmness like the moment before melting into a deep and satisfying sleep.

"Feel better?"

"Yes." Mason paused, "Yes, I believe I do." The gentle sweeping of the overhead fan accompanied the growing smile on his face as the glowing sensation wrapped him in layer after layer of cool warmth.

"At last I think I understand," Mason whispered. In a flash all he was and all he ever hoped to be overwhelmed his soul with wonder. Mason saw everything he had ever given to others, his grandson, Rebecca, the beauty of Julie's face with her healed spirit and finally the glory of the universe. The truth of the absolute message Mason had constantly sought caught him and spun him faster and faster until he was fully absorbed while remaining distinctly separate. In that instant there was total serenity in finally knowing the most important truth of all. Mason had always truly belonged and would forever.

CPSIA information can be obtained at www.ICGtesting.com
Printed in the USA
LVOW08s0930031113

359642LV00005B/24/P